THE PATRIOT'S CHOICE

To Live in Fear and War, or Courage and Peace

BY

OTIS CARNEY

HOW OUR TRUE SELVES CAN CREATE A NEW AMERICA

Bookman llc
Publishing & Marketing

Martinsville, Indiana
www.BookmanMarketing.com

ISBN: 1-59453-284-2

Books by Otis Carney

LOVE AT FIRST FLIGHT (with Charles Spalding)
WHEN THE BOUGH BREAKS
YESTERDAY'S HERO
GOOD FRIDAY 1963
THE PAPER BULLET
NEW LEASE ON LIFE
WELCOME BACK, BILLY RAWLS
CHIHUAHUA 1916
THE FENCE JUMPER
EDDIE BULWER'S GROUND
THROW THE RASCALS OUT
FRONTIERS
ISLAND GIRL
HOG HEAVEN
VICTORY OF SURRENDER
APACHE TEARS
WARS R'US

ABOUT THE AUTHOR

Otis Carney is the author of seventeen books, including the best sellers WHEN THE BOUGH BREAKS and NEW LEASE ON LIFE.. In film and TV he has created series and screenplays for major studios and networks, for such actors as Jack Webb of <u>Dragnet</u>, Marlon Brando and John Wayne. The winner of Freedom Foundation and Western Heritage awards, he does occasional journalism and has written for presidential candidates.

According to the <u>New York Times,</u> his landmark campaign film *Choice* was "unique...a forerunner that enduringly altered political discourse in the U.S."

A graduate of Princeton and a Marine captain, he flew for 22 months in the Pacific during World War II. Mr. Carney and Teddy, his wife of 57 years, have three sons, seven grandchildren and are cattle ranchers in Wyoming and Arizona.

ACKNOWLEDGEMENTS

In a political book, which this is, I suspect it's a no-no to scramble in tales of love, war, American dreams, the human spirit and even showbusiness. But I confess to trying to do just that. What emerges, I'm afraid, is a *mélange cum* memoir with bits of each sprinkled throughout. I never could have pulled the facts of it together without the generous help of friends and experts.

So thanks begin with Charley Bartlett, a Pulitzer-prize winning Washington correspondent with whom I grew up. I also thank Gore Vidal, Lewis Lapham, Noam Chomsky, England's Robert Fisk, John LeCarre and many others whose insights have broadened my view of the world.

For the deeper spiritual and psychological aspects, I thank two good friends, Franciscan priest and prophet Richard Rohr, and David Hawkins, M.D. PhD, a pioneer in consciousness.

For their belief in the book, and skilled editing, I thank my gracious agent, Kathleen Anderson and her talented assistant book doctor, Jessica Lott.

Taking it closer to home, thanks to Hannah

Carney, one of my granddaughters, and as always, for hanging in with my words all these years, my wife Teddy.

Bless 'em all. If there's a story here, they helped make it.

Otis Carney

"To be nobody but yourself in a world that's doing its best to make you into everybody else means to fight the hardest battle any human can ever fight, and keep on fighting."

e.e. cummings

"You are the maker of the dream."

Mark Twain

TO TEDDY

Who always knew the way, and led me along by the hand and the heart

Mark Twain, The Chronicle of Young Satan:

"Statesmen will invent cheap lies, putting blame upon the nation that is attacked, and every man will be glad of those conscience-soothing falsities, and will diligently study them, and refuse to examine any refutations of them; and thus he will by and by convince himself that the war is just, and will thank God for the better sleep he enjoys after this process of grotesque self-deception."

Foreword

WHY WAR?

I don't know about you, but ever since 9/ll my sleep hasn't been better.

I'm not afraid of a terrorist striking me. Out in the mesquite of Arizona where I live, our closest town, Bonita, has a population of possibly 20, mainly ranch folks scattered up a lot of dirt roads. This is a big "see further, see less" country, endless sweeps of high desert and a barrier of wild, hulking mountains. Hardly a target of choice.

Nor am I afraid of war---I already gave it four years in the supposed Good War, World War ll.

So going to sleep isn't my problem. It's waking up to the reality of Now when the fear comes in. Making the patriot's choice. Was the Iraq war just or was it unjust?

More disheartening, could it have been only the beginning of a new cycle of violence, to be perpetrated by the country I love, endless wars for allegedly endless peace?

It's in this battleground that I'm fighting against Twain's "grotesque self-deception," and trying not to live in its "conscience soothing falsities." Not to allow myself to succumb to the fear and the lies anymore, and---God give me strength---with my limited, aging equipment, to do what I can to help others not to succumb to them either.

On the morning of March 27, 2003, our latest D-Day has finally come. We're attacking Iraq. When I go down to the corrals on the ranch, Roberto, a Mexican cowboy who works for us, has nails clenched in his lips. He's shoeing a horse.

Now he's the finest type of old Mexico vaquero. A born gentleman with a fierce pride in his work. He can build you an adobe, repair the bulldozer, track lions, do anything that ranching in the desert requires of a man. Yet this morning, when he stands up stiffly and takes the nails out of his mouth, he looks tired and drawn.

In Spanish, I ask him about it. He smiles sadly. *Mi culpa*, my fault. He and his wife have stayed up half the night watching TV. They have to watch. It's like staring at an awful car wreck, gas tanks exploding, burned, bloody bodies being hauled away. Roberto shakes his head and murmurs, *"Pero, Senor, la guerra. Por que?"*

The war, why?

He and his wife aren't sure where the war is. Over at the ranch house, I break out my atlas and show them the scatter of Middle East nations, all the color of sand, and their boundaries blood red. But they can't process it. They're just scared.

Will the war come here, too? Enemies thundering in to kill us in our peaceful desert? I say no, no, no. It's not that kind of war. I want to say, All the bombs bursting, the scream of jets off the carriers, the switching to grave-faced commentators from across the world---this is just the latest TV spectacular.

It's like the SuperBowl that they watch, football players hurling touchdown passes and in the next moment, Patriot missiles and smart bombs. And the dead? Not people, human bodies, just numbers on the scoreboard. And the fascination that keeps you glued to it, instead of running for an hour or two, this war goes on around the clock. When will we kill Saddam? Osama bin Laden? Where will the terrorists strike us next? Do we have to attack North Korea now? Iran? Libya? Fear has gripped our hearts.

There are a lot of Robertos out there now. Of course we're afraid, rightfully so. Terrified by repeated threats, our minds twisted by the propaganda of war. Small wonder that we feel confused and helpless, hopeless.

Our President tells us that if we're true patriots, we have no choice but to fight a fifty year war so that we can wipe out Evil. He doesn't tell us that even Christ two thousand years ago never taught that evil can be conquered, and least of all by war. We're still on square one. How do we ever get beyond it?

The answer, I think, is already becoming evident. More and more Americans and people around the world are slowly being enlightened. Fifteen million people worldwide, marching in protest against the second Iraq war. Their hearts and minds are opening to an entirely new possibility.

We don't have to live in fear and war. We can choose, each of us, to live in courage and peace.

I was 20 years old when I signed up for World War II. Except for a minority of Quakers and conscientious objectors, hardly any of us questioned the validity of warfare. We felt that we were righteous patriots serving justice and truth.

In the old shooting war against Japan, we all wanted to be heroes. We couldn't wait to go. Still at college, we were terrified that the war would end before we had our chance to get into it. But after two years in the Pacific slaughters, all we wanted was to get it over with and get home.

In the Cold War that followed, I was a propaganda writer. I still cringe at the words I wrote, selling the myth that as Americans, our patriotic duty was to destroy the Evil of Then, "materialistic, Godless communists." In the 61 years after the war, I went from propagandist, to guilty bystander, eventually to protestor against all the later wars, right up to Iraq I and II.

And the Evil of Now? Evil Empire. Axis of Evil. War on Terror.

Today, technology has hurtled every one of us and our planet to the brink of Armageddon. We are all unprotectable now. Clearly, our survival depends on a new look at our meaning in life and our vital inter-being with all of humanity.

According to Albert Einstein, "No problem can ever be solved out of the same level of consciousness that created it." If humanity's gravest problem is war, then to reach a world beyond war demands that we lift ourselves to a higher level of consciousness. Nothing else has ever managed to end man's inhumanity to man. Human sacrifice, slavery, divine right of kings, inequality of women---all these aberrations were considered to be inherent laws of life, not to be challenged or changed. Yet when enough men and women rose to a higher level of consciousness, they struck down the ancient bondages.

Our liberation from the curse of war will happen in much the same way.

But when and if it happens will depend on you and me. All of us. The choice we make between our two most powerful emotions: fear and courage.

If you're like me, it will be a long rocky trip without much of a map. But on the chance that my wrong turns could save you some of your own, why don't we just hit the road together, and maybe between us---*quien sabe, Roberto?*--- we might even find our dream at the end.

One day, God willing, one by one, our inner peace will bring peace to the world.

PART ONE

PEACE BE WITH YOU, ENEMY MINE

I surely loved war.

Pretty hard not to. We were more or less raised on it, as were the generations before us. Our noble old USA has been in a lot of fights over the years, and our kids and grandkids are still getting their own dose of it, right up to tonight's TV news.

It's a world of hurt out there.

It doesn't much matter whether it's actual killing in some bad part of our town, or half way around the earth from us. People are having at each other. And so in truth are all of us. The way things are, just to get by anymore, we almost have no choice. Fights in our marriages, fights with our kids, our peers. It seems that in our jobs, our businesses or our sports, we're having to do this mock killing. Somebody has to win, somebody has to lose. And the loser better not be you or me.

1

When I was a boy, I thought war meant shooting people, and after enough had bit the dust, you captured their flag and declared victory.

We had a grand arsenal to do it with. For real-life war games, we usually played on bikes, swooping past each other with cap guns popping, water pistols dousing and home-made machine guns stinging the enemy with rubber bands. If the weather was too bad to play outside, we did our wars with lead soldiers, of which we had uncounted regiments. When their rifles got too bent or their heads came off, we heated up the lead and molded our own replacement troops, painting them splendidly in the uniforms of the day. We could choose any war we wanted, everything from jousting with our knights to the gallant boys in Blue and Gray being scythed down at Gettysburg. We had scarlet-coated British colonials fighting seedy-looking Boers, we had Spahis, Chasseurs Alpins and the horrible fuzzy-wuzzies of Omduran. A favorite annihilation was noble Custer being pincushioned by the savage Sioux.

But back then in the 1920's, the war we loved best was still echoing in our ears. The Big One, the war to end wars. Our fathers had fought in it. They brought home their tales, saucy French jokes and gas masks fogged with disillusion. We didn't catch that part of it, though. Instead, we dug trenches in our sandbox and had our swaggering doughboys rise up to swarm over the hated Huns.

Then, on a night in 1931 when I was nine years old, my father, Roy, came into the darkened bedroom where my brother Bill and I were sleeping. "Bad news, boys," he said gravely. "Just heard it on the radio. The Japs are marching into Manchuria. They're going to get us into a war."

His words sounded like something I might hear in a movie, and they terrified me. I didn't know what a "Jap" was. If there were any on the north side of Chicago where we lived, I'd never seen one. As for Manchuria, which Roy said was someplace near China, it was too far away to have any meaning for me.

Then he told us briefly about the League of Nations, what a great dream it was, but now the Japanese were killing it for good by pulling out. He shook his head and blew a hissing little breath through his teeth. I'd seen him do this so often during the Depression years.

After he'd left us, Bill and I lay staring at the shadows crossing the ceiling, headlight beams of a last few automobiles out on Sheridan Road.

When Bill finally went off to sleep, I couldn't. I got up out of bed and sat shivering at the window, looking down into the courtyard of the apartment. The "Japs," I knew, would come sneaking in here, no lights, nobody would see them. They'd scale their way up the big window ledges, apartment by apartment, until they reached ours on the third floor. Then what?

Though I was deathly afraid, I longed for them to come. We were playing war all the time, weren't we? Now I had to see for myself what a real one would be like. I knew my father dreaded war, but on the other hand, he had so many books and films about it, he must have loved it, too.

Was it good or bad, and which part of it did I want?

I fell asleep at the window, wondering if I even had a choice.

About then, another aspect of life was beginning to dawn on me. We were raised as Catholics. My mother, Marie, the eldest of 13 children in the Murphy clan was particularly devout. My father, Roy, was perhaps less so, but he gave generously to the church, even if he sighed and dozed through most of the sermons. So my path, early on, was made clear. Mother sent me to a nearby Cenacle convent where Sister Margaret Mary instructed me ever so gently in all the rotes and rites. I memorized the Catechism and when I didn't miss a word of it, she'd drop a marshmallow into my cocoa cup.

Finally, the big day arrived when I would actually receive the Host. I was overjoyed, cleansed, freed. After the priest put the wafer on my tongue, I whirled, and when I reached Sister in one of the rear pews, she was smiling. "Oh, you angel," she said. "Do you realize, you were skipping all the way down the aisle?"

"I have no sins," I said.

As my reward that day, I got two marshmallows in my cocoa.

So sinlessness and love were out there all right, but how the devil to put them together with the war part of me? Thank God I didn't have to make the choice. Not yet anyway.

In November, 1943, I found myself down on New Caledonia, an island in the South Pacific.

We were fighting the same old Japanese "enemy" from my boyhood. On some bullhorn in the fleet, Admiral Halsey is bellowing: "Kill Japs. Kill Japs. Kill more Japs!"

But there aren't any here on New Cal. What a lovely island it is, romantic as Michener's Bali Hai and safe as a church. I'm a Marine 2nd Lt. in a transport squadron, flying ammo and supplies a thousand miles to Guadalcanal and then hauling wounded back out. Up at the Canal we might see the occasional Japanese prisoner, but mostly their survivors have moved further north up the Solomons to fight us again at Bougainville.

Now, this particular afternoon on New Cal, we're between flights, so a pilot friend and I have taken our squadron's single deep sea rod and are out trolling the reef for tuna. It's a short-lived trip. A monsoon sweeps down on us. We scurry to shore, stuff our yellow life raft into our jeep and try to flee back to our airfield.

The first jungle river we hit is running a torrent of mud, uprooted palm trees smashing down the primitive bridge. All escape routes blocked. Finally in the darkness of driving rain, we locate a thatch-roofed *relais* or inn. An old woman in a nightgown and holding a lantern peers suspiciously around the door. In my fractured French, I ask her for shelter. She's cranky at being awakened by two soggy foreigners, but at length, she leads us through the rude hutch and puts us into a big double bed.

We've barely gone to sleep before the lantern is shining in our eyes. Beside the old woman is, of all things, an actual Japanese. He's wearing an island cotton shirt and dirty pants. His eyes dart around at us, and then, following the old woman's gesture, he climbs right smack into our bed.

We're astounded. What the hell is this guy doing here? With thousands of U.S. troops running all over the island, any Japanese would be shot on sight.

So what is he? A spy, dumped off by some submarine? A saboteur of aircraft or other material? Is the cranky old French woman a Vichy supporter in cahoots with him?

No way to know. He doesn't let on to speaking English or French and our Japanese is limited, so we do the only thing we can. We put him into the bed all right, but we make it sandwich style. We bracket him between us, and not knowing whether he's packing a knife and can slit our throats, we pull up the covers and go to sleep.

He's gone in the dawn, nothing ever explained.

So now, back in the incessant terrorism alarms and our newest Iraq war, I keep thinking about that enemy in our bed. Certainly he was "Evil" and we were "Good," but we just accepted him into our bed.

That's what this book is about.

I didn't know it then back in 1943, but it seems to me now that each of us, every human being, is really two people in the same bed. More accurately, in the same head.

One of us has been trying to make war all his life. He loves it. It's him. But the other one of us hates it. That's also him. He's been trying to kick the war habit all his life so he can live in peace.

So who is the real me? The Warrior or the Peacenik?

We're the same person.

We're each our own enemy. We have a false self that lives *down* in those ego-trapped *negative* emotions of making war. And we have a true self that lives *up* in the liberating *positive* emotions of making peace.

Now obviously, one size does not fit all. We're each wildly different. So what is it in our individual backgrounds that makes one person pro war and another anti-war? If we're the sum of our DNA and our choices in life, why is it that some people tend toward positive attitudes and others toward negative ones? We can be fearful and angry in one moment about, say, our job or money, and the next moment be courageously committed *against* war. Or we can live in the high emotions of love, joy and peace, and yet be passionately committed *for* war.

The truth seems to be that none of us live permanently in all the negative energies or in all the positive ones. We're stuck with alternating current, programmed by our unique set of genes and our life experiences.

We're complex creatures, but we do have the free will to override our programming. Thanks to the miracle of consciousness, our hearts know what we don't know we know, and it's our spirit that guides us to our choice.

Scientists in neuro cardiology have now proven that over 60% of the cells in the heart are neuro cells exactly like those in the brain. Heart and brain are wired together. The infant's heart goes into perfect phase coherence with the mother's heart. If you were loved as an infant, when you were within 3 feet of someone sending forth love, your brain waves went into coherence with the waves of the person sending you love.

This is why when you're in touch with your heart, you are automatically in touch with others. The scientists believe that our greatest challenge now is to allow the heart to teach us to think in a new way.

Now that's a radical concept to grasp, this heart/brain link as the mystical power of our spirit. It runs counter to all the information we're drenched with, all the hard facts.

You and I read the newspapers, watch the news on TV. Conscientiously, we ingest the opinions of the experts, bright men and women, dedicated intellectuals, the majority of them are secular. Fantasies of the spirit don't readily pop up on their computer screens. We collate their opinions, shuffle them around and finally have to decide which one rings most true for us. Which seems to have the best solution for the crisis of the moment.

We reason it out. That's how we've been trained: study the givens, measure the facts, *intellectualize* our findings and reach our conclusion.

That's fine as far as it goes, but it doesn't go far enough.

Because the spirit part of our two me's, hoping to be one, is operating out of an entirely different level of consciousness. It's not at all intellectual. It speaks from our hearts. It is *feeling*. It is *experiental*. What our *emotions* tell us.

Our emotions not only dominate our behavior but they can also entrain us into <u>living</u>

10

in those emotions.

Test this yourself. We've all known people in love, so take the case of a lover. Have you ever tried to talk him or her out of the relationship? Spout all your facts and intellectual reasons why this love match will never work, and all you get back is a deaf ear. You're talking to someone who's possessed.

Why? Because that lover has been entrained by the most powerful cluster of positive emotions, love, joy and peace. That lover is acting not out of his head but out of his heart.

Now, turn over the coin. Take the case of a hater, the warrior, or the realist. Someone who believes war is the only answer. Have you ever tried to talk him or her out of it? Spout all your intellectual peace facts and spiritual propositions, and all you get back is a deaf ear. Again, another someone who's possessed.

Why? Because that warrior-realist has been entrained by an equally powerful cluster of emotions, but these are *negative*, not positive: guilt, shame, fear, anger and pride. That person is acting not out of his head but out of his heart.

My premise is this: for all our argumentation, pro or con, for all our "facts" versus their "facts" about whether we shall have war or peace, we are

<u>not getting at the root of the problem.</u>

You can argue with yourself about whether you want war or peace. You can argue with others about it. Quote the experts on both sides, throw out your facts, your pragmatism versus their facts and their equally strong reasons. You can wrangle it out until you're both blue in the face. Neither of you has convinced the other. Neither mind has been changed one iota.

The decision for war or peace, death or life, can only be made in your heart.

I saw it for years in the Cold War. When I finally turned against it and stopped propagandizing for it, I was told repeatedly that the war would never end. Communism would never surrender. I see it now when I answer callers on talk radio shows. They insist we must fight or die. They are entrained into fear.

Only the heart can tell us who we really are and what we want.

The patriot's choice is spiritual. You choose truth over lie. Peace over war.

But at this very moment, the way the world is, how can we choose peace? The odds are too much against us. The dream of peace shatters in the craters of our smart-bombed wars.

Look around at what's happening.

Afghanistan rubbled, more dangerous than before we "liberated" it, warlords again in control and verging on civil war. Iraq, smoldering with hatred for us, burning our flag and shooting down American soldiers, day after day. And attacking us here at home? The next 9/11? When will it strike us again? Where? What does the next siren mean, the next terror alert?

Today, a young woman stopped me in a grocery store and said, "What can I do? What can any of us do? I just feel so completely powerless."

In that one statement, she and millions of Americans have made the fatal admission of their surrender. Knowing not where else to turn, they have bought into the propaganda messages. We the people have been taught to feel powerless, taught to think that we're helpless. And tragically, too many of us swallowed it.

The Bush administration has deliberately crafted their propaganda to strike us in our lowest, most vulnerable *negative* emotions. Whether we're aware of it or not---and probably many of us aren't---ever since 9/11, the incessant propaganda of terror and war has plunged us into *living* in the base emotions of apathy, doubt, shame, guilt, fear, anger.

Because propaganda has entrained us into these emotions, any *positive* emotions---our courage, our personal power, our hope---all of these have been stifled. Thus we have been ground down into living in abject powerlessness and despair.

The purpose of the Bush propaganda is to create in us a dependency relationship. We the people have to be dependent upon the administration. Trapped in our fragile ego self, we don't dare take responsibility for our own destiny. We want someone in charge, a keeper, a defender to tell us what to do.

Yet when we live in our individual spirit self, we have no need to be dependent on any one or any thing. Guided by our intuition and our hearts, we go it alone. We let go and let God. That's our courage.

If opinion polls are to be believed, more than half of all Americans supported Bush's rush to war in Iraq. The media swept a great, drenching, chilling tidal wave of fear over our lives, families, our liberty. Furthermore, they taught us repeatedly that this fear must now extend beyond Iraq. If any Axis of Evil nation ever threatens us in the future, Bush and his warmakers---by their decision alone, not the people's decision---have given themselves the right to preventively attack that nation and destroy it.

Now, why have a majority of Americans swallowed such an arrogant, drastic change in our foreign policy? Particularly when it defies our centuries-old tradition of integrity, justice and freedom for all?

The reason is, we have responded to the propaganda. It has inflamed our deepest primordial fears---an enemy is stalking us in our cave---we're powerless against him, what do we do?

George Orwell warned about this dependency relationship in 1930s England. "Big Brother, in order to control the population, knew that it was necessary for people to always believe they were in a stage of siege, that the enemy was getting closer and closer and that the war would take a very long time."

Hermann Goering practiced this propaganda technique in Nazi Germany, 1941: "The people can always be brought to do the bidding of the leaders. That is easy. All you do is tell them they are being attacked, and denounce the pacifists for lack of patriotism."

So they are being denounced today in America.

The political endgame is not only obvious but already in play. In the climate of fear, lies and war---and the strong possibility of some new, convenient war sometime before elections, the plan is that Bush will be easily re-elected in 2004.

But empire-building is a dicey thing, as many great nations have sadly learned. In my view, the political plan is already in trouble.

The fatal flaw of this approach is that the administration appeals almost totally to *negative* emotions. Bush's speeches are filled with doom and downers, painting himself as the only one who can defend us. But the American people, in their true selves, have a resoundingly *positive* and optimistic persona and history.

We want UP, not DOWN. We want hope!

FDR's speeches were filled with optimism, courage. "Nothing to fear but fear itself." Shortly after Pearl Harbor, Nazi submarines were sinking American ships within sight of New York. Japanese submarines were lobbing shells into the California coast. But we didn't have daily terror alerts or commentators whipping up our fears. We weren't cringing. We were out to win and knew we would because FDR told us so.

Same with JFK, positive, up, he put us into the picture: "Ask what you can do for your country."

Ronald Reagan's speeches were always filled with hope and humor. In his debate with President Carter, when Carter began complaining about the American malaise, Reagan in his genial manner interrupted and with a grin, said, "There you go again."

When he and I talked about it later, I told him, "That line won you the election."

Reagan laughed. "The crazy thing about it, it just came to me, I ad-libbed it."

As psychiatrist Carl Jung said, "It's not what you *know* that heals people. It's what you *are*."

Perhaps the Democratic candidates contending for the 2004 election should take a page from Jung's book. All the Democratic candidates know about and expound a variety of new fixes for the system, hoping that they'll swing voters to them.

But what we ARE is what counts. Optimism, courage and hope are part of the American psyche, but they need to be appealed to and called forth to action. Voters entrained by Bush's onslaughts of fear can have all the factual or policy reasons why he shouldn't be President thrown at them. But, like the lover or the hater who is emotionally entrained, neither facts nor change in policy will sway them an iota.

Let an opponent stand for courage, reason and compassion---mostly for hope, that things aren't nearly as bad as they're painted, we've overcome greater challenges before and have won victory with honor. We're a can-do people and have built the greatest nation on earth---give the voters that confidence, that hope, and a new day could well be borning in America.

If we're concerned about our world today--- and we pretty much better be--- if we long to heal ourselves and in a greater sense our nation--- Mark Twain said it: "Everybody thinks about changing humanity. Nobody thinks about changing himself"---then we have to start that changing by being nobody but our courageous selves. But how do you or I start that spiritual changing?

Even though the word "fear" is repeated in the Bible 365 times, one mention per day, spiritual changing is more than church or prayers or sermons. Religion is only one of many possible expressions of the human spirit. Fly fishing or sky-diving or dancing---even writing these words---they're all spirit. No, the rocky journey to find our true selves is utterly unique and personal. I can't do it for you, you can't do it for me. It's self-taught, I'm afraid, and usually the hard way.

But the dream of your life has already been written for you in your consciousness. Call it your spirit, your soul, but your consciousness is the incredible computer that runs each one of us.

Now, in the way most of us were raised and educated---and I was no exception---the subject of consciousness never came up. Oh, sure, we knew the word, but virtually nothing about the mystery of it: how the thing worked, in us and on us.

That's why I was so stunned when one unsuspecting day, what did consciousness do but grab me by the back of the neck and make me watch a movie of my future life!

There it was, a full length feature, complete with cast of characters and even the dialogue. Who the devil could think up such a script? Moreover, to lay it on me in a vile place at a terrible time? No, it was just too much. I had to see it to believe it.

And I've been astounded---and blessed---ever after.

TEDDY

Pelelieu Island in the far west Pacific is about the last place in the world you'd go if you wanted to find peace. In fact, when I happened to be there, certainly not by choice, I think I'd forgotten what peace was. Or if I'd recognize it if I ever saw it again.

Even getting to Pelelieu was not half the fun. That summer of 1944, we were all pretty wrung out from the Guam battle in July and August. Now in early September, we were off again into the wild blue yonder, tooling north from our headquarters on Guadalcanal and banging through nasty weather for sixteen hours across the endless far west Pacific.

Pelelieu was a tiny needle in an awfully big haystack. Because the battle was raging there, they didn't have a radio range or homing beacon to guide us in. When I finally glanced up from my chart, what I saw was a speck of coral, three miles wide and five miles long.

It looked like a lobster claw, cut off from its body and left to rot in a green, fetid sea. Its open pincers were trapping a blood-red mangrove swamp, and the shell of its claw was a shattered white spine of coral.

I was to learn its name soon enough. Umurbrogol, the Palauan natives call it. The Marines had another name. Bloody Nose Ridge--"that stinking sonofabitch."

We made a cautious approach. There was a lot of artillery fire below us. Finally, somebody standing on a pile of gas drums, the improvised control tower, flashed a green light at us and we came on in, bouncing down on a coral runway, still scarred with shell holes.

The brass in Washington had assured us we'd have the island secured in five days. End of the fight. In reality, we in our plane would spend three weeks on Peleliu's corpse of flotsam, and it was far from over even then. Japanese diehard soldiers kept coming out of their caves for years thereafter, the last ones only surrendering in 1973.

Here on this rock, in a firestorm lasting forty days and forty nights, 22,000 humans would be wounded or killed. Eleven thousand of them were Japanese, all but 35 dead. Five thousand of ours never came back to their Gold Star mothers. The rest of us limped on home, still wondering why. What had it all been for?

In my own small way, I must have been

trying to answer that question. Why was I stuck in this goddamn war? The days dragged on, with seemingly no hope in them.

By the morning of October 14th, 1944, I was sitting under the belly of our plane on the Pelelieu runway. Just to get away from the boredom and obscenity of it, I was escaping in the only way I knew. Ever since I was a kid, I'd always loved putting down words.

Right then, I had a new fantasy going. I was typing a novel about love, war and just possibly, though I had no idea of it then, my American Dream. I'd lifted the book's title from the Bible: "One Will be Taken, One Will be Left." Hopefully I'd be the left one, not the taken.

When you're 22 years old, still cocky enough to be in love with the adventure of war, you pretty much learn to insulate yourself from any downside. After all, we could have been riflemen up on the ghastly Ridge, instead of having a plane to soar away on to escape the hundred degree heat for a moment or two.

Though I scarcely deserved it, I'd lucked into good duty. I was a Marine Corps 1st Lieutenant by then, flying as co-pilot and navigator for a grand, rugged general, Roy Geiger, who commanded half the Marines in the Pacific. Our main job was to get him in and out of the islands where his people were fighting, and to keep ourselves from getting shot in the meantime.

On Pelelieu that morning, I had a box seat for the war part of my novel. A half mile from me, Geiger's Marines were hurling themselves against Bloody Nose Ridge. For years the Japanese had been building this awful fortress, waiting for us to come. It was a warren of caves and interlocking fields of fire. We'd shelled it, napalmed it, turned it into a stinking smoking moonscape of naked coral. A thousand Marines had already been lost trying to scale one slope of the Ridge no bigger than a football field. As I tried to type what I hoped was my epic, the clicking keys of my battered old Hermes portable made a sound very much like the sniper bullets which, at random, would crack and hiss in our direction.

But the love part of the novel was harder to explain. Why, right at that moment, was I groping to find a name for my heroine? Six years earlier, when I was sixteen, I'd written my first novel and it had plenty of love in it. After visiting Gettysburg and Fort Sumter, I'd fallen in love with the South and the epic tragedy of the Civil War. My heroine had to be a southern girl.

I'd known a few authentic ones when I was a boy hunting quail down in Mississippi. These were soft, languid young things who'd melt against you when you danced and whisper gently in your ear---everything I wanted in love, and a far cry indeed from the starchy Yankee girls in my Chicago dancing school. So I made my heroine into the willowy, magnolia-scented Gwendolyn Guerin, a brown-haired graceful patrician from a Low Country plantation.

But now, that morning at Pelelieu, I was stuck for a heroine again. In my new novel, I was writing pure homesickness. Longingly, I was revisiting my boyhood, the games and girls and dreams we'd had in the Chicago suburb of Lake Forest. But what girl? Who would she be? The exact right name is essential for a novelist. It colors everything you write about the lady.

Into my head popped "Teddy." I'd never known anybody with that name. Oh, maybe a boy when I was a kid, but not a girl.

Yet it seemed to fit what I wanted. I typed Teddy several times, filled out her first scene and then put the page down at my feet. I had a couple of hundred pages written thus far. I was using flimsy Japanese rice paper we'd liberated out of a supply dump during the Guam battle. The pages were original only, no carbons. My typewriter was perched on two gas cans, and I kept my precious pages from blowing away by putting coral rocks on top of them.

Writing was not my only job at that moment. For some bizarre reason, considering that I can barely boil water, I'd appointed myself cook for our plane crew. While I'd been off on my flight of fancy with my new heroine, the radioman, crewchief and my partner pilot, Cecil Matney, were all hungry for breakfast.

Our single meal whenever we could get it was basically dog food, meat and beans in a can. To be able to choke it down, we had to heat it, which we did by taking a metal cartridge box liner, punching holes in it, filling the bottom with sand, and soaking it with aviation gas from the sumps of our plane. But unfortunately, just now, our old stove had melted, so I said to our crewchief, "Over there, Mel. That ought to be an easy place to find us a new liner."

I was pointing at a Japanese coral revetment about a hundred feet from the plane. In the circular enclosure lay the blackened skeleton of a Betty bomber, plus about a ton of every kind of ammunition. Aerial torpedoes, mortar and artillery shells, thousands of rounds of machine gun and rifle ammo. The attacking Marines had dumped it here on their way to the big fight against the Ridge.

Mel started out toward the revetment. About half-way there, he stopped and hollered at me: "Hey, Mr. Carney, this damn thing is smoking. You don't suppose it could go off?"

Well, everything was smoking on Pelelieu. Bullets were whistling everyplace anyway. "Oh, hell, no," I started to say, "it'll never...."

Varoom!

The world exploded. A roar, giant flash of flame, then sickening, popping, chattering ammo catching and blowing. The coral runway was throbbing, earthquaking in the blasts, our plane bouncing up and down on its tires, the undercarriage creaking. Half-naked Marines were shouting, running past us, some hit and bleeding, one man with a jagged sizzling fragment protruding from his shoulder.

We were on ground zero, chunks of metal hissing over us and some crashing down like deadly hail. In terror, I was running around beneath our plane like a marble in a teacup, eight hundred gallons of high octane gas inches above my head. Let one fragment stike---well, I wasn't thinking, couldn't think. Cece Matney was shouting, "Get the plane outa here!"

I followed him, racing up through the darkened cabin and hitting the start switches before we'd even sat down. Mel Kurtz, the crewchief, had warmed the engines up earlier, so in the miracle of it they caught in the first go-around. Mat roared the throttles to the firewall. We jumped the chocks and went on a screaming taxi as far away as we could get from the inferno. And not far enough, considering Pelelieu's tiny land area, half of which was still being held by the enemy.

We leaped out of the plane and took shelter in a coral ditch. By now, the whole dump was blowing, screaming rounds of every kind of shell roaring above us, random, unseen, inglorious stuff of our own making. For two hours we lay in that ditch, up to our bellies in stagnant rain water. For my part of it, I was shaking all over. I'd been shelled before on Bougainville and Guam, but nothing like this. These were mindless enemies, not caring who they blew up.

When it was over and the ambulances were carrying the wounded away, we taxiied back to our parking spot on the strip. My Hermes portable was a black crab squashed into the coral. And my two hundred plus pages of love and war?

In the roaring run-up of our escape, our engines had blown them all over the island.

A few days later, a half-naked, bearded Marine came down from the Ridge. He had a few of my precious pages crumpled in his hand. Scuttlebutt was, he said shyly, some fly boy down here had been writing a book. The riflemen in his platoon had found some of it and had been using it as toilet paper---until they began reading the stuff and figured it might mean something to somebody.

I later re-wrote it from memory. If it was bad at first, it was dreadful done twice. But something more than a book was apparently at work here.

Not quite two years after my love/war American dream blew away, I was back finishing up at Princeton. I'd run off to flight training a couple of months after Pearl Harbor. We didn't want to miss a minute of it, and prayed the war wouldn't end before we'd had our shot at it.

But playing college boy again was an awful drag. After four years of having life or death in our hands, now to return and be treated like industrial school cadets was more than I could stomach. The Nassau Hall authorities wouldn't even let us cut a class to go up to New York and find a job. Further, it was June 21st. I had a long steamy summer ahead at Princeton, just to cram myself full of Chaucerian English and the Lake School of Poets.

I was at the bottom of a pretty dismal barrel. I'd just ended a passionate affair with a girl who was wonderful but when she wrote me almost daily, I could feel the dreaded noose tightening. Wedding bells, the end of my freedom.

Earlier, I'd been able to lose myself in baseball and tennis, but now the seasons were over. With six eye-glazing courses on my back, I was so worn out that my only escape seemed to be coming down with one of those traditional colds. Late that afternoon, I'd worked myself up to fever and chills. I was lying in a fog of Vicks Vapo-rub, staring at the wall of my bedroom at Ivy, the eating club where we lived.

Then in came my roommate. He was tying his tuxedo tie. "Get off your ass," he said. "Stop feeling sorry for yourself." We were going to a party, a debut up in Far Hills. He'd already pulled the time-worn stunt of wiring the hostess and asking if he could bring his houseguest.

Reluctantly, I crawled into my own tux. Another crasher joined us en route. We hit the party as the first guests began to arrive. When the hostess scowled at me, I took refuge in the bar and tried to get a drink. The waiters were sorry, sir, but only champagne was being served. I finally worked one of them into cadging me some Scotch from our host's private stock. With a few sips in me, the only place left to hide seemed to be the dance floor.

I turned and under the stately green and white marquee happened to see a girl. Actually, she was the first female guest there. She had a loveliness about her that caught my attention. She was willowy, long brown hair, and wearing a flowing ball gown of white tulle. A smallish young man had brought her to the party. He seemed to be enjoying her immensely while they danced. Finally, I couldn't stand it.

I tapped him on the shoulder and cut in. I gave her my name. She gave me hers.

"Teddy."

Oh my God! Teddy? I was back to my Teddy heroine in my new novel, blown away at Pelelieu. Teddy what?

"Fly."

"You mean Fry?" I stammered.

She laughed gently. "No, Fly. F-L-Y. Teddy Fly. It's short for Frederika. We have names like that down South."

South? Teddy? No! She was Gwendolyn

Guerin in my *old* novel! Had to be! I wasn't dancing, I was soaring. Minor detail, she wasn't from South Carolina, but Memphis, Tennessee. Didn't matter. And a plantation? Well, actually, they used to have them down in Mississipi, but the only one left now in the family was a dreary place in Arkansas.

By then, I was lost in her. She was fascinated that I wanted to be a writer. We swapped lies about how much T.S. Eliot we had read. I faked it with the one line I could remember from *The Love Song of J. Alfred Prufrock*: "I grow old, I grow old, and I wear the bottoms of my trousers rolled." She wanted to be a writer too, she confessed, and someday longed to live out on the land.

My dream exactly. I'd spent much of my youth out hunting birds in the cornfields of Illinois. Someday I'd get a farm of my own, even a ranch. Land-love, I craved it. As we danced on and on, I was so busy holding my fantasy in my arms that it finally dawned on me that we were hopelessly stuck with each other. This was her first debut party and she didn't know anybody here. She was only 18, three days after her graduation from Foxcroft school in Virginia.

Finally, as good southern girls are taught, she

didn't want to be a burden to me. She'd slip off to the ladies room and give me a chance to find someone else, if I wanted. *Who else,* for God's sake! I had it all in her, didn't I?

The ladies room was on the second floor of the old colonial house where the party was being held. With a little wave at me, my new Teddy went up the long staircase and I waited urgently at the bottom. By then, a few of my college friends had spotted me. Many of them were married by that time and were always ragging me because I couldn't seem to find my own real thing.

I just have, I crowed. This girl is really something, fresh out of school, a true southern beauty. "Look," I said, and pointed up at the top of the stairs.

There my discovery stood, all grace and poise. Smiling, knowing we were watching her, Teddy took the first dainty step, tripped, and came tumbling down the entire staircase in a flailing ball of tulle. After I got the poor thing picked up and brushed off, my old pals winked at me and drifted away. "Nice try, Ote." "Quit robbing the cradle, will you? Get one with a little age on her, who at least knows how to walk."

What they didn't know, nor did I, a year from

that very night, in Memphis, Tennessee, I'd be brushing the rice off her, and in the fifty-seven years since, she's never made another false step.

Now, more than a half century later, I wouldn't dream of writing such a hackneyed plot. But do you know something? I don't think I wrote that old one at all.

It wasn't my ego that did it, not the animal brain in the pain of war. It was the spirit part. The higher self in my consciousness. But how could I tap into it again? How could any of us?

Because we can't get there without it.

Consciousness is our first step in making our eventual patriot's choice. We have to understand the power of the elusive thing.

One day I took a shot at trying to fathom it. All I learned was how much I didn't know about the miracle of it, but had damn well better start finding out.

GOD IN THE MACHINE

Eight years after my Teddy novel had been blown up at Peleliu, I was out at sea off the coast of Florida.

Even though I found myself on an aircraft carrier, the <u>USS Lake Champlain</u>, I was, thank God, still a civilian. However, in these early 1950's, the Cold War was beginning to heat up, and those of us on the home front were doing our best to show our patriotic flag.

My small role in this was to write the three-camera movie, <u>Cinerama Holiday,</u> and serve as the green and harried producer of the American sequences. The balance of the movie was being shot in Europe by Louis deRochemont. Famous for <u>The March of Time </u>and <u>The Fighting Lady</u> that dramatized our recently completed carrier war in the Pacific, Louis was a dedicated navy blue and gold man. By his orders, I was to show off the Navy's role in the Cold War.

The Admirals were delighted to oblige. They gave us not only our very own aircraft carrier, but also the Blue Angels stunt team to swoosh off our hats at appropriate moments. And I also had, at my command, a drone airplane, a Grumman F6F that we'd shoot down in a blaze of glory as the finale of the picture.

To set all this up, I'd been negotiating for months with the Navy. Of course, with the Cold War, the Pentagon was delighted to display our newest war plane. My problem was, I needed so many props for the finale that the admirals soon wished they'd never heard of show business.

The first Cinerama film was a thrilling roller coaster ride, putting the audience into the picture almost to the the last screaming dive. Louis, who hadn't produced the first picture, wanted to go one up now.

To give our audience the thrill of hitting a carrier deck at 130 knots, he insisted that I get the Navy to chop off the nose of a fighter jet and mount our three-eyed monster camera in place of it. I begged him not to; this big blunt thing was going to cripple the plane. He refused to listen. Get the shot at all costs.

So off we went into the wild blue yonder. Aerodynamically abused, the jet kept trying to stall out, and when that ploy didn't work, it refused to put down its landing gear. We almost had to ditch it in the Atlantic before the brave pilot stalled it with such force that he snapped down the gear and came in for a heart-stopping landing.

A day or so earlier, we'd also put another hardy volunteer into the ocean. Pretending he'd ditched, we would now show a helicopter winching him up and saving his life. The Navy taking care of its own. By the time we got the camera running, the poor kid was so frozen he could barely hold onto the rescue sling.

On a bright, sunny morning off of Jacksonville, the day of the finale had arrived. I was standing on the bridge with the skipper of the carrier, arranging by radio the proper positions for our destroyer escort, the thundering fly-by of the Blue Angels, and finally, the drone F6F being guided to its death by its mother plane far above.

But first, it was vital that we rehearse the scene. We had millions of dollars of hardware about to go into the water. No second chances. My cameraman was down on the flight deck manually panning the bulky three-lens Cinerama camera. As the drone plane paralleled the ship, I gave the order and the carrier's 3 and 5 inch guns began to fire. Beautiful, billowy white bursts ranged in a few practice yards behind the drone.

Delighted with the trial run, I crackled down

to the cameraman, the ASC veteran Harry Squires: "Okay with you, Harry?"

"Sheeit!" he crackled back. We had no zoom lens on the camera. "All I'm seeing is a fuckinay little butterfly out there. Get that admiral to bring it in within a hundred yards of the ship or we'll lose the goddamn thing!"

Now it began to get sticky. Of course the Cold War was raging, military budgets were unquestioned, vital to our freedom, but, as the admiral wearily pointed out, "If I bring it in that close, it could go out of control and kamikaze the carrier." Did I know what a kamikaze was? I said, Yes, I'd had the pleasure of some at Okinawa. Didn't I realize I was asking him to risk his carrier and his career?

I must have ducked it some way. He sulked a moment, then sighed on the radio to the mother plane: "Bring the aircraft in to within a hundred yards of the ship, not one inch closer!"

As they say in the war movies, this is it. My heart was in my throat, the cameraman barking at me: "Have 'em hit it directly amidships, right opposite me." I relayed it to the gun crews, the bluejackets twisting their knobs, FIRE!, the bursts popping cotton in the sky, blasting yards behind the plane, getting the range for the moment of the kill.

BLAMMO! Exactly in the right place, the drone blew up, arched into a crippled split-S and exploded in a spectacular geyser.

A thousand sailors on the deck began to cheer, flinging their hats into the air. I raced from the bridge down to the flight deck and threw my arms around the cameraman.

His face was ashen. "Harry," I said, "something wrong?"

"I didn't get it," he groaned.

He'd been so fascinated watching the glorious bursts of freedom he'd forgotten to pan the camera! Days later, when we screened the footage in New York, the Grumman managed to splash into the sea about three inches from the edge of the screen.

When deRochemont saw the shot, he pursed his lips and sighed. "Take your crew down to Annapolis. We'll end the picture with the Navy choir singing a hymn."

Ending war with peace. Well, I suppose that's what consciousness is, yours and mine.

The choice is ours. Do we use consciousness to lift ourselves high enough into positive emotions to make the dream of our lives come true? Or do we allow our baser negative

38

emotions to trap us forever in the darkness?

Whatever we call it---luck, karma, synchronicity or God's will---the dream thought we hold of our lives has immense energy. In some ethereal and barely understood process, positive thoughts and healing emotions seem to rocket us into a higher level of existence. Good things happen to happen because, in effect, we've said yes to them. We've trusted. Given up control.

But to tap into your consciousness by living in your higher emotions is a dicey thing. Where do you start?

One moment you see clearly what your nobler instincts are telling you to do. You're dancing in the blinding white light of grace. And the next moment, it's all dark and gone. Finding and losing and finding again. You think you know how to do it, you're rising up into a happy, pleasant space and then---whammo!---some event "out there", some tug from the past flings you back down onto the floor, back to grubbing around in sad and seamy things.

But we are what we think. The thoughts we hold in our heads trigger emotions. If we think love or joy for the dream, or think hate and anger for doom, our bodies and our very lives will eventually act them out.

Our consciousness is totally naive. In its utter trust, it believes anything we tell it. If we want to make our own dream, as Mark Twain said, it will: "Fine, go to it. I'll make your human container give you just that. You've told me it's what you want.

"But if doom's your thing, to wallow in grief, apathy and self-hate, help yourself. You've told me you want it, and I'm so naive, I not only trust and believe you, but I'll start right now to make your body give you your precious doom."

The great scientists--Jung, Einstein, Bohm, Sheldrake, Pribram and many others---have been convinced that consciousness is the incredible data base of the self. In it are recorded all the thoughts and all the actions of every human since the beginning of time.

As neurosurgeon Karl Pribram explains it: "Based on research that goes back even pre-Einstein, we now conclude that our brains construct objective reality by interpreting frequencies that are ultimately projections from another dimension, a deeper order of existence that is beyond space or time. The brain is a hologram, enfolded in a hologrammic universe."

Consciousness is storing our dialogue in its overlapping holograms. It even stores our thoughts. Psychiatrist Carl Jung first named the phenomenon "the collective consciousness." Recent discoveries in particle physics, nonlinear dynamics and chaos theory support his conclusion. Every atom of everything on earth, including thoughts, is connected to everything else.

Surely there have been times in your life, usually unwittingly, when you've tapped into this.

Make the test yourself. Have you ever been struck by:

---The positive energy of certain people?

---The unexpected happening of certain events?

---The unexplained healing of certain ills?

They're all in the mysterious bundle of consciousness.

Why is it that when you're around someone who obviously lives in the lower emotions, you're apt to feel tired and drained? However, when you're with someone who lives in the higher positive emotions, you're attracted to that person's electricity without knowing why. He or she just makes you feel good and right, even freed for a moment. You have been entrained into that person's powerful attractor field.

Why is it that something happens that you can't explain?

Something drops into your lap. Usually it's for your own good, but it can be bad, too. Often it's a mixture of both. But whatever the mysterious force is, you had absolutely nothing to do with making it strike you just at that moment.

Chances are you were at the end of your rope. Tied in a box, trapped. You couldn't see a way out. Then, when you least expected it, a wild idea pops into your head. Why? What put it there? Why were you *told* to do some crazy thing you'd never done before?

Or why did you happen to make a wrong turn on a certain morning, walk on a different street and bump into somebody who was going to change your life? Something snapped on a Eureka light in your head. In an instant, you suddenly knew what you didn't know you knew. It all seemed planned somehow. But who was doing the planning? Who was giving you this strange rush into undreamed of creativity and freedom?

You can call it Providence as they did in the old days, or fate, or luck or just being in the right place at the right time. If you're religious, you try calling it God's will. You're content to leave it at that, but way down deep, you know you'll never know the why of it.

Something spooky is at work here.

When you rise in consciousness, up into a more powerful attractor field, you attune yourself to this collective power. The mystery of synchronicity is, when you manage to rise up into a more powerful attractor field, similar people or events seem to be attracted to you---they find you.

Like attracts like. Two magnets join. You're now open to new contacts, fresh ideas. Things you never expected begin to happen. Concepts like networking arise from nowhere and become a new technique in human relations. The same for the undreamed of neural network of the Internet, mirroring the interconnectedness of consciousness itself.

The third test you can make deals with sickness and healing. Why is it that one moment you can be lying in bed with a bad cold, and when you wake up the next morning it's gone? Did Contac do it or Vicks Vapo Rub? They might have helped, probably more so if you believed in them, but something else turned off your "sick" and made you get well.

For thousands of years, sages, mystics and saints have been able to tap into the unseen power of healing. They're at the top of the box because they've lived a constant motive of enlightenment. They've dedicated themselves to a practice of living as much as they can in the higher levels of consciousness that most of us barely know. Christ is here, Buddha, Lord Krishna and the Mother Teresas of the world.

But what about the rest of us, just ordinary mortals? Can we make it, too?

Perhaps not so high or so beautifully, but we all have a chance to try.

We have free will. Against seemingly impossible odds, any of us can choose to override our programmed fear and rise to this higher level.

It's a search for truth, to get us beyond war to peace. To be honest and committed to our true selves requires discernment as well. We have to lift ourselves up to strip away the myths of war, and dare to see the horror of it as it really is.

The miracle of consciousness can give us that courage, if we trust it to guide us.

Do that and we've taken one more courageous step toward making our patriot's choice.

THE LURES OF WAR

In my novel <u>Frontiers</u>, by using actual history, I told the tale of an Irish immigrant cavalryman who fought in all America's wars, from the Sioux in 1876 to the Japanese in 1941. When a reviewer read it, she wrote: "Carney appears to hate war and all its horrors, but his love for it is very apparent; he revels in the glory and excitement." I think she has picked up on an ancient truth.

Aristotle wrote what a great pity it was that it took war to call forth the most noble human behaviors---courage, selflessness, sacrifice and often even mercy to the vanquished.

Some of the finest men I've ever known I had the privilege to serve with in the Marine Corps. I saw officers so brave and selfless that they were willing to sacrifice themselves to inspire their men. The welfare of their troops always came first. And so I watched them wear down their bodies in total exhaustion, mourning all the boys that they weren't able to save.

So if this war part is so treasured and powerful in me---as I suspect it is in most of us--- shouldn't we ask what its appeal is and why it can have its tremendous hold on us? Yes, love the nobility of its sacrifice, but mourn it, too, because I think we must, if we ever hope to get beyond war as our only means of settling disputes. Beyond our belief that killing The Other is justified for whatever reason.

Today's technology allows us not just to kill massively but to destroy our planet. Perhaps the greatest challenge of our modern world is to teach ourselves and our young how to wage peace. To reject the lures of war.

PATRIOTISM

Who doesn't want to love his or her country? I thrilled at it. I longed to march in the company of heroes, never dreaming where the march would lead me.

Gettysburg, PA, 1935: I'm 13, my brother, Bill, 15. In the April sun, we walk the green hills of the first battleground we've ever seen. We crawl into the grey rocks of Devil's Den, the snipers nest. We stride up the bloody hill of Pickett's noble charge. In an old frame house that peddles curios, we buy fistfuls of flattened minie balls and grooved horrific rifle slugs, bigger than our thumbs, imagining that they've blown six inch holes in Rebel bellies.

Our father flew a Curtiss Jenny in the First

One, our uncle dropped bombs on Huns in France, in a squadron commanded by a pudgy Italian, Fiorello LaGuardia. My uncle sings his squadron songs: "If he can fight like he can love, oh what a soldier boy he'll be...If he's half as good in a trench as he is in the park on a bench... I know he'll be a hero when he's Over There, because he's such a bear in every Morris chair..."

The lure of patriotism is such a romantic appeal that it's hard to resist. Who doesn't love a marching band and thrill at the flag? I still do. Often it brings tears to my eyes. And yet, the ugly manipulation of our patriotism also makes us ignore the reality of war, the dirt, the stink, the boredom, the crass stupidity and the pain, suffering, violence and death.

We're told nowadays, as perhaps in all our wars, that if you're not a patriot, you're a coward. You're either with us or against us. And so, false patriotism shames us into war. True patriotism gives us the courage to stand up and protest the folly. Our nation was born not by conformists but by courageous revolutionaries who dared to fight against oppressive power, whether our own government's or a foreign one's. Protest the desecration of our flag when it's used to herd us into unjust, immoral wars, and to slaughter fellow humans just for the ego, the profits and political goals of venal leaders.

Out of the patriotic lure of war comes the next myth:

WAR AS A GAME

Television and its hold on our population is the most powerful propaganda tool in history.

The Iraq short-form war was a TV special. Photo ops. Rigged "Victories," exiles recruited by the CIA to cheer when a few good Marines toppled the statue of Saddam. Interpreting it for us were correspondents imbedded in a high rated action-adventure series. We see what our administration wants us to see. Journalists who covered World War II often comment on the intense restrictions placed on war correspondents today.

An 80 year old friend described bridge luncheons during the Iraq war where the ladies leaped from their chairs, cheering over their cucumber sandwiches at our smart bombs homing in on their targets. Football fans, while munching popcorn, cheered a quarterback running down the sidelines one moment, and in the next, switching channels to our missiles screaming across the desert to destroy a military installation. War trivialized into a game. Our defense department crafted euphemisms like "collateral damage" to sanitize the slaughter of civilians. De-sensitizing us from the horrors of death was a carefully planned technique.

As a manipulator of public opinion, fear propaganda is unmatched. Did anyone ever count how many times the phrase "weapons of mass destruction" has been repeated since 9/11? And naturally, the media thrive on it. Fear keeps the people tuned in, ratings rise, advertisers pay higher fees, more appropriations shower down on the military. War as a game is a money-making venture.

WAR AS THE GREATEST ADVENTURE

The excitement in it. Join the Navy, see the world. All we want is a few good men. Get out there, see what the enemy looks like. Leap up out of boredom, how you gonna keep 'em down on the farm after they've seen Paree...?

Princeton University, December 7th, 1941: Legs is a pitcher on our baseball team, a better one than me. He's a lanky red-head, a patriotic

Southerner and a fine guy. Now with Coach, another of our closest college friends, we're in our dormitory room, drinking beer and listening to the radio crackle out the first news from Pearl Harbor. We're stunned, angered, excited. For three years we've been marching around together in Military Science, learning how to field strip French 75's from World War I. Totally boring stuff, but in this moment it's finally become real!

"Don't get too carried away," says Legs. "This whole thing could be a phony, you know."

"Aw, come on," says Coach, the clown. "Those Japs weren't up in Hawaii to go surfing. And Hitler, too, that goofy Katzenjammer Kid will start attacking us tomorrow, you watch."

"Let him!" cries Legs. "We'll come down on all the buggers with both feet, six months maybe they'll go belly up, quit, declare Armistice. And the hell of it is, boys," he takes a long suck of his beer, "we'll still be in training. We'll miss the whole show."

We daydreamed about what it would be like. No more would we need our movie heroes showing us how to die for glory. We were them now, mano a mano with the enemy, sinking our teeth into the real thing! Less than a year later,

Coach is blown off a destroyer near Guadalcanal. He tries to swim free though depth charges exploding in the water. At daybreak, other sailors fish him out. The explosions have crushed him. He dies in their arms.

Legs is a hero, fights at Guam, decorated, becomes a General's aide. On Leyte, protecting his general, he walks a jungle road to search out snipers. One that he hasn't found shoots him through the head.

Bougainville, Solomon Islands, Christmas, 1943: I'm a 2nd Lieutenant in a Marine Corps transport squadron, my brother Bill is a Major, commanding a battalion of armored artillery, training in England for the inevitable D-Day.

On this Christmas Eve, navigating our flight, I'm lost over Bougainville. Our radio rattles with static: shout of an American pilot, blast of wing guns, then a raucous taunt from a Japanese. "Babu Rusu eat shit!" They think Babe Ruth is our god. Marine Corsairs are tangling with a flock of Zeroes over the fortress of Rabaul, a hundred miles west of us. "I flamed that sonofabitch!" an American cries. "Mark him down until he splashes!!"

We wheel south into a sharp bank, roar across the sodden beach and around a jungled point. Below us, people! A file, running in the rain, pot helmets, mustard colored uniforms, long sticks in their hands. Guns? Their faces whip up to us, only a few feet above them. They begin to scatter. The pilot beside me pushes back his baseball cap."Goddamn," he breathes, "those were Japs!"

A few moments later, guns flash in the clouds. Marine artillery at Torokina. We slice in from the sea and rattle down on the steel Marston mat. Something blows, swerves the plane. A shell on the strip? When we park and shut down, we laugh at our jumpiness. All we blew was a tire. And to me, it's the best luck yet. We'll be grounded here until a new tire can be flown up from Guadalcanal. I'll get to see some real war now.

Unbeknownst to me, at that moment, one of our transports is banging through the same storm, south from Bougainville. The pilots are my squadron mates. They're also boyhood friends, grew up together in a small South Dakota town. Because their combat tours are over, for old times sake they've asked to fly this final trip together.

Lost in heavy weather like I'd been, they get off course in zero visibility, then pick up what they think is our radio range on Treasury Island. They don't realize that the Japanese in the Shortland Islands which they're now passing have set up the identical frequency. Following the homing beam in, the two boyhood friends are lured directly over an enemy anti-aircraft battery and blown out of the sky.

BONDING, COMRADESHIP

It's difficult to write about war without glorifying it. Throughout history, the greatest stories ever told have come out of the battlefield. There's a reason for this. War is mankind's peak experience. In the horror of it, in the sharing of its terrible dangers, men and women are forced to rise to an incredible level of nobility. Why else will a green, terrified young Marine fling himself on an enemy grenade? He'll die, he knows he'll die. But his comrades will live.

Like no other emotion, war is the ultimate human bonding. You and your comrade become one. Again and again, veterans will tell you this. You're not fighting for your nation. Not fighting for your branch of service, not for Mom and Dad at home, or for your wife and kids. At thirty thousand feet you're risking your life in a screaming blasting dogfight to protect yourself and your wingman, to save him. He'd do the same for you. That's why you fight. *Don't let your buddy down.* In a stinking rotten foxhole, a machine gun chattering at you and enemy riflemen wriggling towards you in the mud, you and the buddy next to you are all you have. You're his eyes and he's yours. Never again will you know and treasure such intimacy with another human being.

The bonding that occurs in war is perhaps the least recognized and understood lure. It's buried so deep in our archetypal emotions that we're not even aware of what it's calling us to do. And even if we face this primal appeal and admit its hold over us, how can any of us not long to bring out the best in ourselves, our valor and nobility?

GUAM, 1944: Some of our wartime friends are Air Corps pilots, flying B-29's on raids to Japan. We swap war stories with them, trade time in our different airplanes. Their airstrip is just below ours. Now this morning I'm in an outdoor shower, naked as a baby, my partner pilot beside me soaping up. Then a roar. Over us, not twenty feet above us, a crippled B-29. Two engines out on one wing, black props windmilling helplessly. With a thundering tearing it plunges in, yards from us. Av gas explodes, and more. This 29 is loaded with firebombs that would have burned out some city in Japan. They're crackling, searing holes in the twisted metal. Is one of our friends in this inferno? The other pilot and I, still naked, run toward it, shielding our faces from the terrible heat. I'm close enough to see a waist gunner kid in his blister screaming at us, burning alive.

GOOD V. EVIL

What about the "evil" of our enemies? There's a helluva strong war lure in that. We are Good, so we are ordained to destroy them who are Evil.

The hitch is that in our lust for vengeance, putting the evil face on our enemy just might make us look in the mirror to see that our own face has become as evil as his. In the miserable mayhem of war, both sides descend into the same pit of man's inhumanity to man.

Bougainville, Christmas Eve, 1943: I'm in a mess tent near the airstrip, maybe thirty of us there, wooden benches, powdered eggs and dehydrated potatoes slopped on our tin plates. Outside, endless dark rain pattering the giant jungle trees. Then a strange whooping sound, far off. Is it coming closer?

Suddenly, the jungle comes alive, roars of artillery, nobody knows whose. Rattle of machine guns. Screams: "They're infiltrating! They're over here!" More blasting reports, hundred foot tall jungle trees hit by shells and crashing down. A groan: "You trigger happy assholes! Knock it off, you're shooting at Marines!"

Dark shapes running past us in the night, tripping, splatting cursing in the mud. We're in slit trenches again, shivering, stagnant water up to our bellies. The man next to me is doubled over with dysentery, can't hold it. I have my service .38 out, flailing it at mosquitoes. I'm coughing, whining clouds of them. A flash close by in the jungle. Shoot at it? Shoot who? I can't see. Machine guns, BAR's chatter their rounds through the trees above me, slicing down more branches. I scrunch deeper into the trench and press my face against the wet mud of the protecting side. It goes on for hours. Infiltration, false alarm? Nobody knows, just more screaming roaring in the night.

About three a.m., somebody must have sorted it out. The jungle goes quiet. We slog back into our tent. The fighter boys have only an hour left before they go up again over Rabaul. Drain the Three Feathers, last swig. The poker cards are floating in the flooded tent. I hear a sound at the entrance, a bare-legged man in a poncho moves past me. He's a soldier, rain dripping off his Army helmet liner. Bearded, his face yellowed with atabrine, his eyes dart around us. He giggles, "Got somethin', you guys." He lifts the poncho and takes out a wooden match box. It's wrapped in rubber bands which he peels off. "Gimme twenty bucks, hunh?" Somebody shines a flashlight. In the box are five Japanese teeth, the gold in them glinting. "Dug 'em out with a bayonet."

The next morning, we get our new tire and start loading wounded Marines for the flight back to Guadalcanal. The crewchief and a Navy corpsman strap in a half dozen litter cases. They're ashen-faced, plasma bottles dangling above them. Then there's commotion at the hatch of the plane. Three Marines are wrestling down a massive, screaming Fijian. He's a scout from the famous Fiji Patrol that's been operating behind the Japanese lines. The Patrol use knives, not guns; they kill one by one. Bones in his ear lobes, this brave man has gone mad. We all fight him down onto a litter, use our belts to tie him even tighter. He's writhing and moaning so wildly the corpsman can barely jab morphine into his arm.

Just as I'm starting back to the flight deck, a Marine officer shouts from the rear hatch. He's shoving ahead of him three tiny figures in ill-fitting U.S. dungarees. Their black heads are shaved, their eyes sullen, terrified. I can't believe it. Japanese girls! Their ages are unreadable but they've got to be still in their teens. "Nip comfort women," says the officer. "Intelligence wants 'em down at the Canal."

As he straps them into the bucket seats, one of the wounded Marines lifts up from his litter. "Fuckin' whores, slice 'em from you know what right up to the neck, toss 'em in the drink. That's what I'd do."

COURAGE

The last compelling lure of war is that it gives us a chance to show our courage. Raw guts. Were we supposed to take the insult of Pearl Harbor or 9/11 lying down? No way! It's a noble act too, to sacrifice your life for someone else. But there is the morning after, for those still around to see it. World War II men are now dying at the rate of 1000 a day. Almost invariably---and I've talked to hundreds of combat veterans---their lips tighten and they ask: what had it all been for?

Pelelieu Island, October 12, 1944: It's proving to be a slaughterhouse.

This particular morning, I walk with General Geiger toward Bloody Nose Ridge. We're close enough that sniper fire is hissing past us. Geiger, like me, is unarmed. As we near a wrecked Japanese fortification, a Marine Master Sergeant motions at us to get down. He's Geiger's longtime bodyguard, a hard-faced Texan with a pair of Colt .45 frontier type revolvers in his hands. He nods at the wrecked building, Sniper in there. Take cover, General.

Geiger has told me once: "I've been in so much combat, I figure I've used up all my chances." Instead of taking cover, he turns his back and takes a leak. The Texan and other Marines blast out the sniper. We move on a hundred yards or so, pausing by a group of dug-in Marines. A mortar position. As Geiger watches, they chuff off several rounds, bursting on the lower slopes of the Ridge. A Colonel, an old-time China Marine comrade of Geiger's strides towards us.

A flat, greenish crack. Somebody shouts, others running, ducking. The Colonel is down, writhing in pain. A Japanese knee mortar shell has exploded among us, the fragments striking him in the kidneys. He dies that night.

I follow Geiger up onto the slope of the ridge. Above us, only hundreds of yards away, I stare at the dark eye holes of caves. We know the enemy is in there, know they watch us. Geiger strides over to a long coral ditch where dozens of Marine riflemen are crouching. I'm stunned. These are kids...sixteen, seventeen, I don't know how old, but they're all that's left now of the proud First Marine Division. Replacements for the veterans who have died at Guadalcanal, Cape Gloucester and now this. Their camoflauged helmets seem bigger than they are. Heavy with bandoliers of ammunition and grenades, some of the riflemen are tense, white-faced, first time they're being shot at. But others are tough kids, Hell's Kitchen types, Italians, Irish, Poles, maybe New York, Boston, Philly, Chicago.

Geiger kneels beside them. They're down protected by the coral trench, but he's on top, wearing khakis, his two stars and wings. The

Japanese above us have to see him. I want to curse his folly---and then love him for it.

Showing the flag, giving courage to these kids of his. He goes from man to man. He has no small talk. It's not his way. Just a gruff pat on the shoulder, a thumbs up. The kids smile, some try to salute but he waves them off. Then he turns and looks at the platoon commanders who are spread out along the trench. They wear no insignia that the Japanese can target on. Just ragged, coral dusted dungarees.

A Captain nods at Geiger. Then he scrambles out of the trench and blows a whistle. Other whistles sound all along the line. The Marine kids go, half bent over, running up the slope of the Ridge. They scatter, take cover among blasted coral rocks. Some are firing at shapes we can't see. Demolition charges are hurled into the caves. They run higher into chattering fire increasing every minute.

The Ridge top is hundreds of feet above them. The objective—Get there, hold it. They're far from us now, tiny black specks clawing their way up through the coral. There are no cries, no human sound above the roar of war. I see one speck sit down. Others crowd around him. Whitish blast of a shell. They're gone, black objects scattered in the coral. None get up. The long line curls and works higher on the left side of the Ridge. Now many are falling, but more go on, more are nearing the top.

When they reach it---and they reach it day after day---it's over a hundred degrees up there. Searing sun, no shade, no water. Ammo low, too much shot up on the slope. Nobody reinforces them. Not enough left. By the time the sun flames away and the Ridge falls in shadow, they can't hold. Have to fight their way back down, carrying, if they can, the corpses of their buddies.

For a worthless, strategically unnecessary hunk of coral, five miles long by three miles wide, 9,172 kids like these will be wounded or dead, and with them, 11,000 Japanese, fighting almost to the last man.

At the time, I was caught up in the last powerful lure of war: the romance of it that Michener captured so well in *Tales of the South Pacific*. How could I not be ripe for it, aged 22 to 24? So, whatever it was, the ego of my animal brain, thriving on the danger, or my pride, telling me I could tough it out and win---or maybe it was even the wildly beautiful peace that I'd sometimes find swimming on some exquisite beach, I just wanted to stay out there. I didn't want to go home.

Our combat tours in the South Pacific were 14 months. Shortly after Pelelieu, my time was up. On the other hand, flying for Geiger was unbelievably good duty. We had no squadron responsibilities, no chickenshit, as we used to say. When the General didn't need us, we had a plane of our own to roam the Pacific and we went soaring off to islands that weren't even on the map.

We went to places like Rennell island south of Guadalcanal that had only been touched once by the war. The natives hadn't even known the war was going on until a Japanese submarine had surfaced there and robbed them of their melons. When we landed in the atoll's lagoon in Geiger's PBY, these strapping Polynesians came out to greet us in war canoes. They were beating their paddles on the gunwales and chanting hymns, loading us aboard, grinning their red betel-nut stained teeth and hugging us.

We were back to Captain Cook's time. From a missionary's Bible a century ago, they had learned and passed down scattered phrases in Biblical English. Because we'd brought them some delicacies like Spam and Vienna sausage, they sat with us on the palmy beach and in gratitude forced upon us trade goods of beautiful pearl-inlaid hand-carved war clubs.

They also, genially, offered us their bare-breasted young ladies. The idea was, bring some white blood into their pure island strain. So the PBY's radioman and gunner took them up on it. The maidens gently placed their fists in the boys' hands and led them to their thatch huts. As for me, the poor little things, their shoulders covered with the sores of yaws, were a case for our doctor we'd brought along, and he did treat them. I contented myself lounging on the beach, making deals for the war clubs.

When we got back to Guadalcanal that night, Geiger was furious that we'd swiped his PBY for such a joy ride. Then he grunted, "Gas it up. You're going to take me down there tomorrow."

Unfortunately, a first lieutenant doesn't make deals with a gruff warhorse like him, but when I learned in December that he was going stateside to report to Admiral King in Washington, I asked if I could possibly get my own thirty days at home? But only on one condition: that he wouldn't let them beach me back there, but instead send me out again to his plane. He jerked his thumb at his adjutant and growled, "Write up orders for the kid."

The distance I covered was more than geography, and it seemed incredible. It had taken us, at 140 knots, three days to fly Geiger and his staff up to Pearl Harbor. Then it was overnight on a NATS DC-4 to San Francisco. I hit Union Square on Christmas Eve, 1944. There must have been a thousand servicemen thronging the streets, and most of them, it seemed, were packed into the little United Airlines office on one corner.

Because there was no military ride available, United was my only hope. Somehow I managed to pry my way up to the counter and got a pretty female agent. I must have given her some horrific war stories or looked the part of a hollow eyed shell-shocked vet because she took pity on me. One seat on a UAL DC-3, leaving for Chicago at midnight.

The flight was incredibly beautiful, snow blanketing the country and a full moon, too. After so long in the heat of the islands, I'd forgotten what snow looked like. I wanted to put on hockey skates again and play in the wonderful cold stuff. The two pilots were old-timers, overage for the service. They let me sit up front with them and we swapped lies about several famous United pilots who were flying with us in our South Pacific Combat Air Transport command.

Early in the morning, we slid down onto the snowy runway of Chicago's Midway. There was no megalopolis of O'Hare then. Just a few semi-empty hangars with the look of a country airport.

From there I hitched a cab. I was freezing cold with only a flight jacket over my Marine greens. I barely made the Chicago and Northwestern train, one of the few heading north on Christmas day. Dumping down on the familiar Lake Forest station platform, I put a nickel in the pay phone. Mother answered. "I'm home," I said.

She screamed with surprise, delight; I thought she was going to faint, and when Roy raced up to get me in our old red Cadillac, he hugged me and just shook his head. "You've got horseshoes, Otis, pulling this one off."

But coming back was a rude shock. It was all downhill from there, and it hurt. I would never know the boyhood world again. I was sunburned, jumpy-tense, lost a lot of weight from malaria. In my old room, with clean sheets, flush toilets and my favorite old foods Mother and the cook would spoil me with, I felt as if I were living in a trance. This wasn't the real world. Where were the rain-leaking tents, muddy jungles, K-rations, dehydrated gorp slopped on tin plates. Where was the quivering tin of our planes and the monster storms we'd had to fly through? Where were the corpses rotting in the swamps of Guam or shredded on the coral rocks of Pelelieu?

Here, home again, nobody knew what we'd seen. How could they? And more painful, they didn't seem to care. For them, life was going on exactly as usual. Dinners at the country club. Still going out in the corn fields, shooting a pheasant. No debut parties for the Christmas season, but some hasty, angry booze fights among the few lucky ones of us who'd made it home. At one of these, I met a girl and we clanged together like a pair of cymbals. All I wanted was to take out my rage at the change back here and raise holy hell in my few free days that were left.

What I hadn't realized was that in my race to kisses, I was burning up all the family's gas ration coupons. Roy let me know in no uncertain terms, using his World War I aviator's phrase, "You're grounded. And don't upset your Mother any more."

So bleakly, it ended. I was on another NATS DC-4, heading back to our soggy, lizardy tent on

Guadalcanal. About half way there, we lost two engines and had to scream down into Samoa. An omen? I wondered.

Geiger's final operation of Okinawa was over, and we were going to fly him and his staff twenty long hours back to Hawaii. After seventeen months with him, I knew that this would probably be our last flight together.

We had just brought him a new R4D (DC-3) from Pearl Harbor, and with it a bottle of fine Scotch from Admiral Nimitz. After 10th Army General Simon Bolivar Buckner had been killed by Japanese artillery, Geiger had taken overall command and finished the last battles of awful Okinawa. Nimitz's bottle of Scotch was congratulations to him as the first Marine ever to command an Army.

We carried it up the hill to Geiger's Quonset headquarters and he shared it with us. He was grinning sardonically. "Well, boys," he said, "this is a first all right for the Corps and for me. But don't get your hearts set on it. Give the Army bastards in Washington a week or so and they'll send out one of their own to replace me."

They did just that, General Joe Stillwell of China fame.

What we didn't tell Geiger that night was that

we'd been having a problem with his new plane. On the way out, I'd noticed that we were burning ten or fifteen more gallons of gas per hour than we should have been. This loss can be critical on the long overwater hauls we were going to make. Now, I'm a mechanical cretin, and at once, I leaped to an obvious solution.

On our old plane that didn't suck out gas, the vent tubes to get rid of the fumes from the cabin tanks were flush with the skin of the fuselage. But on the new one, the vent tubes protruded six inches. Easy, I told the crew chief. They're creating a suction, draining out our gas. Whack 'em off with a hacksaw, which he did.

A miserable night closed over Okinawa. Cold rain, wind, no visibility. But neither weather nor any enemy had ever stopped Geiger. As the fifth Marine aviator, he'd flown Wright Brothers type pusher airplanes, commanded a bombing squadron in France in World War I. Thereafter, he'd flown all over the world, China, the Banana Wars in Central America. In the early terrible days at Guadalcanal, he commanded all aircraft and his "Cactus Air Force" virtually saved the island. In his mid-fifties then, he even made his own dive bombing missions to inspire his young pilots who were fighting against impossible odds.

And finally, much be-medaled by then, he commanded the bloody assaults of ground Marines at Bougainville, Guam, Pelelieu and Okinawa.

But that night, as he and his staff climbed up the rainy hatch into our plane, Geiger, now 60, was no longer the vigorous leader I'd known. The strain of too many wars, the pain of too many lost kids had worn him out. He grunted down into the airline seats we had in the cabin; his staff officers followed suit.

We made an unpleasant take-off. Turbulence, ink black sky, white lashes of rain. His aide who was first pilot was at the controls. We banged up to 8,000 feet, our normal cruising altitude. And we stunk of gasoline. Normally, we'd always get some gas vapors on takeoff, and kept our side windows cracked open about an inch.

But now, even with our windows wide open, we were a flying Texaco station. Finally we had the crew chief, my co-conspirator in the hacked-off vent lines, pull up the floorboards in the cockpit.

The entire belly of the plane was sloshing in av gas, three or four inches deep over all the wires and control cables. We shut off radios and anything electrical. Then I got the job of padding back to the General and warning him that we were a flying bomb, and would he kindly put out his cigar. In horror, I remembered my friend, Big Ernie, two years before, blown up by the exact same gas fumes.

They were all smoking, Geiger reading a newspaper. I hurried among the staff officers, passing out lifejackets. Some cigarettes went out the porthole windows; I could see the alarm in everybody's faces. These poor colonels and generals were ground officers, trusting their lives to us kids.

When I handed Geiger his jacket, he glanced at it and tossed it on the deck of the plane. That had the immediate effect of dousing everybody's panic. Then he went back to reading his paper, and somehow we mushed soggily back to Okinawa, the secret of our close call caused by a brainless kid never revealed.

Back finally at Pearl, I saw the new stateside war that I'd been trying to hide from for nearly two years in the islands. The bureaucracy couldn't reach us out there, but here now it was all spit and polish, a giant engine of power, fleets, squadrons, a bureaucratic roar. In the old Terry and the Pirates days back in the Solomons, we'd borrow different types of airplanes from friends in other squadrons. Swap time, swap flights, have endless adventures.

Not here, not anymore. Uniforms squared away. Your military role was this or that, you didn't stray. By the numbers, everybody. I bridled. We'd earned something better, hadn't we? Freedom from regimentation. After several weeks of bureaucratic chickenshit, I went over to Geiger's office at Fleet Marine Force. Standing at attention in front of his desk, my captain's cap in hand, I asked him if he'd send me home.

Behind him, I could see the map tables and charts his staff officers were working on. The coming invasion of Japan. It was no secret. Just when, and how many deaths.

Geiger came around his desk, sat on the edge and snubbed out his cigar. "Why do you want to go home? For what?"

There was no point reminding him I'd already put in my 14 month combat tour plus 8 months more on this round. He had men with him who'd been out there since the first terrible days on Guadalcanal in 1942. So I just stammered, Well, going back and finishing college, getting on with some kind of career, now the war was winding down.

He put his hand on my shoulder. "How about

staying in the Marine Corps? It's a good life. We're going to be around a long time, and I think you'd do well at it. I might even help you if I could."

I was deeply moved, and uncomfortable with it, too, because the world of peace I was envisioning certainly had no clear shape to it. All it had was freedom from orders and fear and regimented death. Yet this had been Geiger's life, and in his stubborn courage he'd thrived on it. When I started to repeat again that I just wanted out and home, he cut me short and barked an order to his adjutant, "Cut stateside orders for Carney, get him out of here tonight."

When we shook hands and said goodbye, Geiger was smiling. Only a few hours later did I realize what he'd done. Maybe it was his way of saying thanks, because he'd booked me on the Pan American Clipper to San Francisco, a rare luxury reserved only for officers of flag rank.

So on my last flight over the Pacific, the end of my war, I slept in a berth and had breakfast served by a stewardess. And I gulped it. Because I'd been so tired, I only awakened when the Clipper was making a curving approach over fog banks and the Golden State Bridge, rubbed gleaming in the sun of dawn.

Done? Was this the end of the adventure? I thought so for several days in which I wolfed down the splendors of the California coast. By a morning in early August, I'd run all the way down to the beach at LaJolla, and was lying in the sand with a girl I'd picked up the night before.

Until she propped up on her elbows and said, "What's that kid shouting about?"

A newsboy was running down the beach, waving papers in his hand. Over the roar of the surf, I heard his shout, then saw the black banner headline: "Atom Bomb!"

The girl and I looked at each other. We didn't even know what an atom was. By that night, anti-aircraft batteries were blasting salutes over San Diego Harbor, the sky blazing with a bursting roaring that was the world rejoicing. We had just won the last great war, and because we were the most powerful now, our reward for victory, our homage to the dead we'd left behind was that we'd never permit war again.

We had won this. Now all that remained was to seize it, revel in it!

A year later, having just finished Princeton, I was living with six other hopeful job seekers, all sleeping on cots in a squash court at the Princeton Club in New York. I happened to stroll through the reading room and saw a headline. "General Geiger, Marine, Dead at 61."

We had no way to know that we were about to be propagandized again. From that day on, militarism would become our way of life. War and peace living side by side.

PROPAGANDA: LEARNING TO SELL WAR

In 1947, in the first legitimate job I've ever had, I'm trying to make it as a green reporter on the Minneapolis <u>Star.</u>

My deskmate, an old news veteran, thrusts me a teletype just off the wire from Washington. It's labeled Department of Defense. "Russian Bomber Sighted Over Alaska." My deskmate smiles. "Wake up, kid, don't you get it?"

"Get what?"

"They've got a fight over military appropriations coming up in Congress. There's opposition so they've got to scare the dummies into giving them more dough. Next week, count on it, they'll probably surface a Russian sub off California."

I think: you cynical bastard, you sit out four years of war behind your desk and now you're the expert. "Aw, come on," I say, "our government doesn't work that way."

I was reacting like any veteran, back from World War II, star spangles in our eyes, full of pride in our nation and hope for the future. It was all love and kids and career. I'd never been a political person. The last thing I wanted to think about was more war, least of all to suspect that our government was manipulating my patriotism with fear.

I wasn't alert enough to question why our old War and Navy Departments had suddenly been melded into something called Department of Defense. It never occurred to me that war propaganda had now become language. While we dozed in our peace dreams, our managers in Washington had already hatched their Grand Area scheme. Under the guise of making the world safe for democracy, it was actually to make our corporations safe to sell and profit by our ever-more bounteous gross national product.

In Oliver Stone's movie JFK, there's a scene where a Mr. X sits down on a park bench and gives Kevin Costner full details on who pulled off the plot to kill the President.

The real Mr. X is a man named Fletcher Prouty. He's now a veteran defense analyst. He'd taught at Yale and served in the government. But several days after V-J day in 1945, Prouty was an Air Corps colonel flying a transport into Okinawa. He happened to stroll down to the docks and saw lines of tanks, trucks, artillery being loaded aboard Navy vessels. He assumed the stuff was being returned to the States, but the Navy dockmaster shook his head. It was being shipped to Korea and Indo-China, which was not even being called Vietnam at the time. Prouty was astounded. Why to those places? We weren't fighting there. The war was over, wasn't it? He got no answer. The Navy dockmaster didn't know either, and was just following orders.

Washington was already setting up our "defense" of Korea and Indo-China. Had the public known, somebody might have tried to stop it. But in 1945, the foreign policy elites knew they couldn't sell their Grand Area scheme by tipping their mitt. They didn't dare expose the truth that by protecting American corporate markets worldwide, we'd inevitably be hurling ourselves into future wars. The nation was basking in peace. It wouldn't stand for more war. How about Defense, though? Didn't that connote security and guarantee us comfort in our lives?   Nobody could argue if we were "defending" against enemies attacking us.

Dwight Eisenhower knew what was happening when in his final speech as President, he warned the nation about the incredible power of the military-industrial complex. We were launching the Cold War to bring our "freedom" (e.g. a free market in which we could sell our goods) to peoples we regarded as backward, 3rd World, and so we divided humanity into Us vs Them. To get the public to buy it, use the propaganda of war. We had to paint the Russians, the Soviets, the commies as massive evil empire threats to our lives, liberties and pursuits of happiness. To scare hell out of American citizens was the surest way to get Congress to pass gargantuan defense appropriations.

Minneapolis, 1948: My tough old city editor sends me out to interview the first dreaded communist I've ever met. Gerhard Eisler, an East German provocateur and, I assumed, obviously spying, for some occult reason, in safe old Minneapolis. "I don't want that sonofabitch saying we don't have a free press!" the city editor rasps. "Give him four paragraphs." I find the bespectacled little guy in a crummy hotel. He doesn't seem all that evil, in fact insipid, but he does have a motor mouth, spewing out the party line. How in hell, I think, can anybody believe that crap? I give him two paragraphs.

Chicago, Ill. 1951: a fellow reporter and I quit the dreary newsroom. Leap into TV, form a production company with $15,000. High burn rate, in three years we're broke. Well, what about going back into the Marine Corps? We're into Korea now, evil really closing in. Before an answer comes back from the Corps, a college friend hits me up to join CIA. Secret bios and clandestine phone calls. By now, I'm writing TV commercials for a major advertising agency, more money than I could ever be worth and hating every minute of it. Sitting in endless meetings deciding whether our client's refrigerator should open in my commercial with a "whoosh" or a "whaash."

Old Corps and college friends are getting shot at in Korea, and I'm doing this idiocy? I bag CIA and the ad game and go back to freelancing. A priest tells me about a Czech girl, actually a countess, who made a perilous escape through the Iron Curtain. I interview her, poor thing is so scared and tongue-tied I have to hide my tape recorder under the sofa. But with war everywhere, her story fires me up. It runs in three installments, <u>Chicago Tribune Syndicate.</u>

An acquaintance from Minneapolis calls and asks me to write a one reeler anti-commie picture. He's a high level corporate executive, and I wonder why he's mixed up with something called Radio Free Europe. Only later I find out that CIA is shilling for public support to beam freedom's message behind the Iron Curtain, and is picking up the check for most of it.

I jump at it, title the film The Bell. (I can't remember now if it was our Liberty Bell or some bullet-pranged one our GI's had liberated from the Russians when they were stealing East Germany.) I write in a part for General Lucius Clay, hero of the Berlin Airlift and all the nastiness going on over there. Henry Fonda does the narration, and when President Eisenhower hears about it, he wants to be in it too.

Los Angeles, CA, 1952: Maybe The Bell has rung the cash register at Radio Free Europe, because now they call again, want a second one-reeler. Pull out the stops on this one, get a stand up actor, an appealing American figure not only to do the voice over but appear in person. Sell it.

By now I know a few actors, in fact I'm working for Jack Webb, Sergeant Friday of Dragnet. But Jack, an orphan, grew up in a police station. Too coppish. What about Peter Lawford who'd married JFK's sister, Pat Kennedy. Cheery Peter, too Britishy, also a Demo. He wouldn't be right for this mainly Republican show. Who, though?

Clipping in the paper. My God, Nancy Davis has just married actor Ronald Reagan! I'd grown up with Nancy in Chicago, same Latin schools, roller-skated the Gold Coast together, waltzed primly at dancing school. A great girl. I call her and within an hour, I'm out at their house in Pacific Palisades. Ronnie strides in, gives me that genial handshake. Hell, yes, he'll be honored to do the picture. He's been fighting commies in the film industry.

So I put in some jack-booted commissars, really evil guys. Our exile hero has heard Radio Free Europe. Its message of freedom gives him the guts to run through the Iron Curtain and come down on our side. The Big Truth, I call it.

We win a Freedom Foundation Award. When I tell Ronnie, he grins and says, "Your words did it."

What they did was to bring the Reagans and ourselves together in our common determination to defeat the Evil Empire.

And what I didn't know---didn't even suspect---was that all of us, in the geopolitics of the moment, were being used to help change the American Republic into our own worldwide Empire of the corporate warfare state.

I had no way to foresee then that the New

World Order we were creating would, in later years, send us rushing off to far away lands, ostensibly to make them safe for democracy, but in actuality to make safer, more orderly markets for our corporations.

Is that why we have to be the world's cop?

England, Germany, Italy, France and Japan all have powerful name-brand transnational corporations operating worldwide. The difference is, they do not have 250 military bases spanning all the continents, or a Department of Defense owning more foreign real estate than the land area of Kentucky. They do not have fleets in every ocean, a meddlesome CIA, or a foreign policy staffing our alliances.

Recently, two young men came out to our Arizona ranch to hunt. They were U.S. captains, West Pointers, combat veterans, one in the Air Force, another in Army infantry. These seasoned junior officers are the vital future of our military. But both had just resigned their commissions. When I asked why, they said, "We chose the military as a career. Our understanding was that our mission was to defend the United States. But that's not true anymore. We're being used to defend the American economy overseas. That's not what we signed on for. We gave them back our bars and opted out."

Long before them, I remember General Geiger chewing his cigar and fondly reminiscing about the worldwide exploits of his former commander.

This legendary hero of the Marine Corps, General Smedley D. Butler was a two-time Medal of Honor winner. From the Boxer Rebellion of 1900 on up, he'd fought in much of the world. In the 1930's, he said in a speech:

"I spent most of my career being a high-class muscleman for Big Business, for Wall Street and the bankers...in short, I was a racketeer, a gangster for capitalism. I helped make Mexico safe for American oil interests in 1914...made Haiti and Cuba a decent place for the National City Bank boys to collect revenues in. The best Al Capone had was three districts. I operated on three continents."

For telling the truth, General Butler was placed under house arrest and virtually drummed out of the Marine Corps. He'd dared to question, even then, our economic imperialism.

So who were the people driving it? I got a glimpse of it in New York, 1981.

Ronald Reagan has just been elected President. I'm at a fancy cocktail party in a Park

Avenue apartment. All bigshots in the room except for me. One, a prominent international financier, sidles up. "I hear you've been an old friend of Reagan's. What kind of President do you think he'll make?"

"Well," I answer, "in my experience with him, he's always been likeable and articulate. Strong in his beliefs. What you see is pretty much what you get. He's a decent guy, but whether he has the ability to run the nation and the world, I just don't know."

The financier smiles. "Exactly what we want. A patriotic figurehead up there, wave the flag. We'll take care of the rest."

"We?" I thought.

Who is we?

I was still under the delusion that our Republic was a true democracy where each one of us had an equal voice in deciding our policies. Only in the gradual shift from Republic to Empire did we learn that it was no longer true.

Noam Chomsky, the MIT professor whom the New York Times once called "the most important intellectual alive," wrote that "the decisions that guide the destiny of the United States are primarily made by the business community and other allied elites." This political or ruling class, Chomsky estimates, is probably 20% of our population. The other 80%, journalist Walter Lippman called "spectators of the action. The bewildered herd."

"The doctrinal system," Chomsky continues, "serves to divert the masses and reinforce the basic social values: passivity, submissiveness to authority, the overriding virtue of greed and personal gain, lack of concern for others, fear of real or imagined enemies, etc. The goal is to keep the bewildered herd bewildered. It's unnecessary for them to trouble themselves with what's happening in the world. In fact, it's undesirable--- if they see too much reality, they may set themselves to change it."

John Jay, a signer of the Constitution, said, "The people who own the country ought to run it."

They did then and they still are, but the difference is, the power of the elites and their corporations over the minds, the politics and the economy of the U.S. has become so massive that it's almost insurmountable. And, by its own choice, unassailable.

Why the secret of the controlling elite doesn't get out, Harper's editor, Michael Lind, contends, is that every time a politician from the left or the right proposes to "speak for the many," the nation's "better newspapers (Washington Post, New York Times, Wall Street Journal)" react in "wrath and denial, claiming demagoguery." Yes, the pundits admit, economic and social inequality have been growing in the United States with alarming results, but the ruling and possessing class cannot be blamed because, well, there is no ruling possessing class.

"The American oligarchy," he concludes, "spares no pains in promoting the belief that it does not exist, but the success of its disappearing act depends on equally strenuous efforts on the part of an American public anxious to believe in egalitarian fictions and unwilling to see what is hidden in plain sight."

Now let's be clear about one thing. Despite corporate influence on our foreign and domestic politics, business itself is not a demon nor are the men and women who carry it out.

In an age that demands a conspiracy behind every great action, the corporate warfare state is no such animal. It's not a John Birch Society goblin of greedy CEO's meeting at the Yale Club and plotting how to take over America and the world. Corporate executives are some of the brightest, shrewdest people in the nation. They know what they're doing and it's to serve their bottom line. That's what they were hired for. Many of them have reached far beyond their corporate realms to establish foundations and visionary programs that benefit all Americans.

The majority of politicians I've known are also dedicated people. To serve the country, they've given up precious time with their families. They lose out on job opportunities at home. They work very hard, and it's not just for the ego-stroking, the influence or the power in it. These men and women honestly want to make a better country, but they're trapped in a brutal money-system. Some representatives actually call their big donors "clients." Mondays and Fridays in Congress are often devoted to fund-raising for re-election. If the peoples' representatives don't go along with the owner's wishes, they go home.

How did all this happen, this great accretion of power that became the corporate warfare state? And how, eventually, was it able to launch a foreign policy that became a war on the world, we the people doing the paying and dying for the prospering of the few?

Our American thrust toward Empire actually began in 1845. We went in, defeated Mexico and snatched what's now California and the

Southwest. The Mexicans were a brave but comic opera army---imperialism always works better when you've got a weaker opponent. Henry David Thoreau, the lanky idealist of Walden Pond was so shocked that he wrote an essay about it, "On Civil Disobedience." He was the first conscientious objector to war, and was jailed for it. Thoreau was echoing George Washington who warned our weak and tottering nation to "avoid foreign entanglements." After all, most Americans had fled the royal wars of imperial Europe, the endless intrigues. We had no stomach ever again to hurl ourselves into bloodbaths beyond our blessed shores.

So we founded a Republic whose ideal was to defend us at home and prosper us. From the Civil War's end and onward, we flowered in invention, growth, culture and amazing accomplishments. But by the 1890's, not only had we conquered our last frontier but our country had succeeded so well that Teddy Roosevelt was inspired to say: "America's ability to produce manufactured goods will soon outstrip her capacity to consume them. The only thing we can depend on is sea power. If we have it, we have the world."

In short, we'd outgrown ourselves. The world

needed us and our products. Henry James called T.R. "the very embodiment of noise." And the British Ambassador, reporting to Whitehall: "We must never forget that the President is seven years old." But when the battleship Maine blew up in Havana under suspicious circumstances, Teddy and William Randolph Hearst got their "splendid little war." Lost in the flag-waving of the moment was the reason why, as thundered out on the Senate floor by Albert Beveridge of Indiana, "God has made us the master organizers of the world. We are the adepts who must administer government to savage and senile peoples. God has marked the American people his chosen nation to finally lead in the regeneration of the world."

Three years ago, defending our use of cruise missiles against Iraq, Secretary of State Madeline Albright said: "If we have to use force, it is because we are America. We are the indispensable nation. We stand tall. We see further into the future."

Years later, when we hurled ourselves into the Banana Wars of Central America, we used the excuse that we were trying to bring those poor people freedom, democracy and good government. Now, how is this foreign policy of worldwide aggression sold to the people?

When President George W. Bush announced our attack on Afghanistan, he put a beatific face on it. "We're a peaceful nation. The most free nation in the world. A nation built on fundamental values that rejects hate, rejects violence, rejects murderers and rejects evil."

We Americans are one of the most churched nations in the world, God fearing, generous, the biggest donors to charities. Whether hurricane, earthquake or flood, our aid rushes in first. It's more than our technology, our ingenuity, our courage. It's the openness of our American heart, our willingness to share with all peoples the freedoms we've won the hard way and rightly hold sacred. We want to live at peace, but we haven't had much of it.

"In the United States' 200 plus year history," writes John Stockwell, "we have fought 15 wars." A former station chief in Angola, the Congo and up-country Vietnam, Stockwell holds the CIA's second most coveted decoration---which he handed back when he became the highest CIA officer to resign in protest.

"We have put our military into other countries to force them to bend to our will about 200 times, or about once a year. As justification, the U.S. leaders have always cited national interests or the protection of U.S. lives or property (at the expense of the local people's lives and property.)" Invariably, we called it 'national defense.'

"Was it in our defense," asks Colman McCarthy, former <u>Washington Post </u>columnist and now director of the Center for Teaching Peace, "that in the last ten years Washington has sent troops to kill people or threaten to kill people in Lebanon, Grenada, Libya, Panama, the Persian Gulf, Somalia, Haiti, Sudan, Yugoslavia and Afghanistan twice? A familiar pattern has been followed, glamorize (our wars), demonize, victimize, rationalize."

Just in the period since World War II, the United States has also warred with: China, Korea, Guatemala, Indonesia, Cuba, the Belgian Congo, Peru, Laos, Vietnam, Cambodia, El Salvador, Nicaragua, and Iraq.

Now, why has this happened?

Could it be what the financier told me in discussing Reagan? "Leave the rest to us." The "us," unfortunately, is a skein of elite combines in politics, media, corporations, and defense industries who need these wars to further or protect their own special interests.

As for the wars making us safer at home, again agent John Stockwell, testifying to

Congress: "The Church Committee in 1975 revealed that (up to then) CIA had run 3000 major covert operations and over 10,000 minor operations---all illegal, and all designed to disrupt, destabilize or modify the activities of other countries.

"Coming to grips with these US/CIA activities is very difficult, but adding them up as best we can, we come up with a figure of six million people killed---and this is a minimum figure. (Civilian 'collateral damage') Included are one million killed in the Korean War, two million killed in the Vietnam War, 800,000 killed in Indonesia, one million killed in Cambodia, twenty thousand killed in Angola---the operation I was part of---and twenty-two thousand killed in Nicaragua. These people would not have died if U.S. tax dollars had not been spent by the CIA to inflame tensions, finance covert political and military activity, and destabilize societies."

The way many of them were killed, Stockwell continues, was gruesome beyond belief. Latin American death squads, trained by us at our School of the Americas at Ft. Benning, Georgia, have repeatedly performed unspeakable atrocities, wiping out whole villages of Indians down even to the last child.

The School of the Americas provided military manuals for the Latin American trainees, teaching them torture and assassination techniques. Against documented evidence, Congress voted down a bill to terminate the School.

The *contras* in Nicaragua, also trained and armed by the U.S., made a practice of coming into small towns and selecting a family for punishment. The children were dragged outside to watch as *contras* castrated their father, raped their mother and cut off her breasts. At one point in the "war," Ronald Reagan said proudly, "I am a *contra*."

Under Somoza, whom the U.S. supported for years, Nicaragua was a miserable, brutal dictatorship. When the Sandinistas took over and were democratically elected, Washington reacted in horror. The beards, the wild propaganda, the combat dungarees---it was Castro all over again, a possible Soviet base within hours from our border. Ignored in the hysteria was the fact that in the 20th century, the U.S. had been to war three times in Nicaragua, fighting to protect what we regarded as our economic turf, which now a revolutionary rabble was threatening to take away. However erratically, the Sandinistas were giving land back to the people, giving them medical care, dramatically raising their literacy levels and providing amnesty to Somoza's assasination squads.

It wasn't enough. The threat was perceived as being too great. The U.S. spent $1 billion dollars to transform Nicaragua from a struggling but then hopeful nation into the most ravaged, poorest country in our hemisphere.

"CIA destabilizations," Stockwell writes, "kill people who never were our enemies---that's not the problem---but to leave behind for each one of the dead perhaps five loved ones who are now traumatically conditioned to violence and hostility against the United States. This ensures that the world will continue to be a violent place, justifying our endless production of arms to 'defend' ourselves in a violent world."

But back in the '60's in palm-lined Beverly Hills, California, I think I can safely say that none of us, Ronnie Reagan included, saw this dreadful future we were embarking on, and, regretfully, we were unable to realize that we were being used by it.

The most important thing we couldn't foresee was that we were there for the birthing of what's been called The Reagan Revolution. In what we did in those years, embattled conservatives all, we began laying the foundations for the corporate warfare state, from Reagan to George Bush I and finally to George W. Bush II. We gave him the power of attack indiscriminately.

But back then, in those early days of struggle, perhaps because I'd just been through a war and loved and trusted my nation so much, I never considered for a moment that my emotions were being manipulated. I wanted to serve the cause, and the war propaganda that swept over all of us then, as it does now, is so effective because it seems so reasonable. It has to have just enough elements of truth in it to make you believe it.

The Soviet Union was a brutal, suffering place. The Russians were dangerous. They had nuclear weapons and immense armed forces. But they had also lost 22 million of their people in World War II. Despite their threats about burying us, they were a wasted nation leading more from bluff than strength. Their bellicose propaganda was intended to scare us and cover the truth that they were terrified of another war, and lived in fear that we would wreak one upon them. Justifiably so, because our containment policy had encircled them in a ring of steel.

Americans went along with the Cold War for two important reasons: our politicians needed it, and we needed it in the pocketbook. The B-1 bomber, for example, was jiggered through Congress by the simple expedient of having at least one of its myriad parts manufactured in each congressional district of the nation. In turn, we bought into the Cold War myth, in part because it created jobs, a horn of plenty. Thus we accepted the crushing debt and reduced freedoms of a warfare state. Bomb shelters at first, then school kids being drilled to hide under their desks lest the Big One hit. And finally, pock-marking our land with forts, airbases and missile sites.

While the Cold War was raging, I was invited to London for a seminar of U.S. military and industrial leaders. I was supposed to give a brief talk, asking the question: was the Cold War really necessary, and how could we get beyond it? I never got off the bench, too many other speakers. The conference room sparkled with generals, cabinet secretaries and CEO's of some of our largest corporations. The Pentagon had prepared a costly doomsday book, showing in living color the arsenal of dreadful Soviet weaponry. Terror was being sold here.

Shortly thereafter, a friend who was CEO of a major corporation began doing business with the Soviet Union. When word leaked out about it, war-supporters in the U.S. retaliated against him. He received a thick file of angry letters. Distributors refused to carry his company's products. Garbage was heaped in front of his factories. There were even threats on his life because he had dared to say the Soviets were businessmen like ourselves, and we had better start trusting them and healing our differences.

When the Cold War finally ended, a Russian general said sardonically: "We have taken your enemy from you. What will you Americans do now to run your country?"

I didn't know any of that then. Having swallowed the manipulated patriotism of the Cold War, I kept on trying to fight it in words, wake people up. I wrote a full length documentary feature for Paramount, <u>Russia and the West</u>, based on Ambassador George Kennan's book. The producer jiggered it around into violent anti-commie propaganda---Kennan's book was reasonable, anything but this. The studio never released the film, fearing the theaters would be stink-bombed by commie agitators.

I did a novel, <u>Good Friday 1963,</u> a plea that citizens get in and start exercising responsibility, put pressure on the government so that we could end the interminable fear and violence of the

Cold War. The book struck a chord, went through several editions. I did speaking tours. Everybody seemed to want to know what they could do to get the country back on track. Then JFK was killed and all of us went into shock.

Where now?

EVIL EMPIRE: SELLING FEAR

The last time I saw Jack Kennedy alive was on the beach at Santa Monica. He was out there that early summer of 1960, attending the Democratic convention that would choose him as their presidential candidate.

We were in swimming trunks, both of us, lying on the hot sand. I don't remember if I shot a few waves. Jack didn't. Most of the time we were spinning yarns about the Pacific war.

We had some very close friends in common and also some family interchange, Irish clans sticking together. Jean, my late sister, had roomed with Jack's sister, Jean Kennedy Smith at a convent in Connecticut. Jean Kennedy would visit her at our house in Lake Forest, and our Jean would go back to Hyannis with the Kennedys. I'd gone out a few times with Jack's sisters, Eunice Shriver and Pat Lawford.

At one party in Chicago, Eunice stood on a chair, shouting out Kennedy politics at a bunch of quite stuffy Midwest Republicans. Right after dinner, Eunice, who loved games, had her guests play a sort of blind man's bluff. She blindfolded all of them, and while they were whirling around on her orders, she took their hats and coats and dumped them out into vestibule of the apartment. After ringing the bell for the elevator, she locked the apartment door; the bewildered Republicans never knew what hit them.

Sarge Shriver was running the giant Merchandise Mart, owned by his father-in-law, Joe Kennedy. When I bumped into Sarge out in L.A. for the 1960 convention, he said, "Dammit, Otis, this is your last chance to change sides and join us." Could be he was trying to get even with me. A few years before, my doubles partner and I had beaten Sarge and his for the championship at Onwentsia Club in Lake Forest.

Of Jack's closest friends, my childhood pal journalist Charley Bartlett had introduced Jack and Jackie to each other, remained intimate with the entire family and of course was out there with them, assisting Jack at the 1960 convention.

The other, Chuck Spalding, I'd grown up with in Lake Forest and co-authored a book, <u>Love at First Flight</u> when we were both in flight training. Shortly after Jack's PT 109 had been blown up, Chuck and I sat on the flight deck of his carrier at Guadalcanal. He told me then how worried he was that Jack would never recover from his injuries.

Like all Americans, we were stunned and grief-stricken when Jack was shot down so needlessly.

Then, a few days later in the turmoil of our loss, I happened to stumble into one of those defining moments I never saw coming.

The CIA, under orders from the Kennedy administration, has just destroyed the Diem government in Vietnam. Because of my Good Friday 1963 novel, a French intelligence agent comes to see me.

This blonde, blue eyed woman was an ex-communist. Re-canted by then, she had helped author the NATO manual on psycho-political warfare. She'd also been with President Diem and Counselor Nhu the night before they were murdered, a by-product of the botched CIA coup.

To my amazement, she tells me the U.S. has now created a vacuum of power that we can only fill by plunging American troops into a massive land war in Asia. "How do I know?" she says. "Because exactly the same thing happened to us in France. You are involving yourselves in an unwinnable civil war. You will be financing Vietnamese general after general. They are all corrupt, unable to defeat the communists. We learned that. Our war was settled not on the battlefield but by riots in France. Yours will end in riots on the streets of America."

I'm stunned. I call in friends to listen to her. At this point in 1963, the U.S. has only a few thousand military observers in Vietnam, but the French agent is talking in terms of armies. Obviously, we're being duped into a war nobody wants. The public has to be warned.

We think we can do it. Maybe a dozen of us are listening to her in the living room of our house in Beverly Hills. Some are journalists, a few ex-government with good Washington contacts. Ronnie and Nancy Reagan are there too. As a TV spokesman for General Electric, Ronnie has considerable visibility. Certainly between us we can muster up press coverage on such a shocking revelation. Immediately we begin calling our friends in the media. Their answer is always the same: Our story doesn't jibe with Washington's story.

For weeks, using the gory TV symbol of the protesting Buddhist monks immolating themselves in flames, the Administration has been launching massive war propaganda, dramatizing why we have to become involved in

Vietnam. But we, now a handful in a Beverly Hills living room who have learned the truth, are threatening to spike that lie.

But we can't get a single line in a newspaper or a sound byte even on local TV. I'm so enraged that I write a novel, <u>The Paper Bullet</u>, dramatizing how the American people have been patriotically manipulated to rush into war. By the time the book comes out, we have thousands of troops in Vietnam, launching the major land war disaster the French agent has predicted.

The rest is history. We plunged into an unwinnable civil war on the other side of the world because we had been propagandized to believe that Asia would go communist. The only effect was that our communist enemies became capitalists on the war riches we'd left behind. Diplomatic recognition came next, a booming market in which to sell our products.

The U.S. lost no freedoms to evil empires. The loss was good kids who knew not why they were there. Forty-seven thousand Americans with their names on the black marble wall in Washington. Probably two million unnamed Vietnamese. When it finally did end, a Marine General stood on the roof of our embassy in Saigon and watched the last of our defeated troops being evacuated by chopper. He asked sadly, "What has it all been for?"

When my novel finally leaks out, a state secret would have got more publicity. Reviewers don't want to believe that such pervasive war propaganda exists, let alone has the power to plunge us into actions deleterious to our nation. My agent and publishers beg me to get off the soapbox. Forget the Cold War, go back to boy-girl stories, or better yet Westerns, where the guy in the white hat always wins.

When you reach the point where war propaganda becomes repugnant to you---a voice contrary to your spirit---and each of us has to come to it in our own way---when you get into resisting it, your view of the world begins to change. You begin to see that the ancient cry of kill or be killed is being used as a controlling tool. You begin to see that sharpening your own discernment is essential: that recognizing the myths of propaganda is the only way to go free.

Though I had my doubts about what I was doing in supporting the Cold War, I wasn't yet in touch enough with my true self to break away.

Furthermore, many of the leaders on both sides of the war-peace issue were my friends.

Palmy old Beverly Hills and Bel Air were a

seething volcano of politics. Teddy and I found ourselves dropped into a polarized society that we'd never known before. It was structured as rigidly as protocol at a Byzantine court. Hard right wing conservatives on one level and left wing liberals on the other. Then on another level were the suspicious, tight-fisted old Angeleno families, their names on the L.A. streets. Not admitted at court were the movie and TV people, sometimes "passing," sometimes not, but anxious to. And finally the steely-eyed mostly self-made tycoons of law and business, many of whom were later to form Ronnie Reagan's cabinet.

Unlike conservative Lake Forest where you kept money and status in the closet, out here whatever you were or had made of yourself you wore as proudly as a carnival barker with his electric coat.

For Cinerama Holiday's glittering premiere on Sunset Boulevard, I'd planned to take my director and his wife along with Teddy and me in our car.

Then they saw it, a working person's Ford sedan with too many miles on its old tires. The director blanched as white as his tuxedo shirt, ran back into his apartment and summoned a limo. It was not stretched enough to include us. Off they went in gleaming black splendor, Teddy and I

Fording it mendicantly, barely able to get a car parker to touch it.

In fact, later at a flossy wedding in Bel Air, our battered Ford drew us the honor of being sent by a parker to the service entrance.

In the glamorous excitement of it, Teddy and I refused to play by the show and tells of stratification. All our friends of whatever political stripe were fascinating. Fun to be around. We'd have radical Dan Ellsberg, not yet of the Pentagon Papers, mixed in with Angelenos, industrialists and movie types.

For one party, Jack Webb, who never wore anything but a sweater, went out and bought an elegant blue jacket. It had a huge gold crown on the pocket. Our son John, a little kid trotting around and saying good night in his bathrobe, fingered the emblem. "Mister Webb," he piped, "isn't that the Seagram's Gold Crown?" Jack went crimson. Next day at the studio, he asked me earnestly: "Tell me the truth. How did I do with those society friends of yours?"

Sadly, my old false self also had me awfully pumped up with Cold War fervor. One night, at an actress friend's house, she seated me beside a prototype movie star, a famously beautiful woman married to one of the real power players in the industry. I should have stuck with her, for she was too dreamy to care about politics. But instead, after dinner, over coffee and brandy, I began trying to persuade her producer husband that of course Hitler had been a monster, what he did to the Jews.

On the other hand, what about the Soviet monster, Stalin? His purges, his concentration camps had exterminated millions more people, including Jews, than Hitler ever had. Why couldn't the powerful movie maker put some of this tragic truth into a film?

"Because we're Jews!" he raged.

That should have done it, but not long thereafter, at the same actress friend's house, I began arguing with an innocent-seeming woman who was married to a Time reporter. Prior to their recent arrival in L.A. she had been supporting and sending donations to Martin Luther King. To me then, as to much of the press, the very idea of civil rights verged on giving comfort to the enemy. I was so arrogantly closed-minded I began blathering about pinko stuff, possible commie ties. Broke up the party. As she was leaving, she whirled to me and cried, "You're the most despicable man I've ever known."

But I could hear nothing but my own flag-waving arrogance. At another dinner, in the Kennedy-rage times at the 1960 convention, again I happened to be seated beside a new actress beauty. The movie oracle Hedda Hopper had just written a column warning Jack Kennedy to disassociate himself from his rat pack friends, Frank Sinatra, Sammy Davis, Jr., Dean Martin et al. Their reputations were bound to hurt him, she said. So what did my stunning dinner partner think?

She whirled to me, eyes blazing. "You sonofabitch, I'm going to crack you across the mouth! Don't you ever say anything like that about Jack!"

I was bowled over by her fury. I stammered, well, it wasn't me saying it, it was Hedda. No matter. Finally I got mad. "Look," I cried, "this is a free country. The Kennedys are great, I know a lot of them. But they're not royalty. Aren't I entitled to an opinion?"

By then, our argument was shattering the party. People were jumping up from our table to get away. My hostess was in tears. The actress' husband, a well-known actor, was stalking around growling, "Show me that sonofabitch who insulted my wife!"

In a highly emotional election campaign, Barry Goldwater seemed to be our patriotic American white hope, to defeat seamy Lyndon B. Johnson, who was only dragging us deeper into the quagmire of Vietnam. I hurled myself into flacking for Goldwater.

Beverly Hills, CA, October 1964. The Republican National Committee hires me to do a TV special for Goldwater's campaign. I title it CHOICE, the theme: there are two Americas out there, folks, LBJ's seamy and corrupt, Goldwater's clean and honest. I persuade John Wayne to do an ending for the film, and bring in Raymond Massey as a homespun Abe Lincoln in Illinois narrator.

All downhill from there, into the dirty swamp of national politics. Clandestine meetings, memos from Washington slid into our pockets as if they contain secrets of the A-bomb. We hope to do a sequence of LBJ's cronies Bobby Baker and Billy Sol Estes. Though they've both been testifying to Congress and are covered by thousands of feet of news footage, when we approach film libraries, not one foot of their testimony is available. The Administration has pulled it. We have to do the sequence with stills, all we can get.

We also use repeatedly the propaganda trick of symbol. It was in the press that LBJ would often drive around his ranch and throw his beer cans out the window. So we recreated it with our own black Cadillac and the empties bouncing arrogantly beside the road.

We don't talk on phones, which might be bugged, our identities revealed. Then the real bomb goes off. One night, agents of the Democratic National Committee, a la Watergate, break into our secret studio and steal one of the prints. When it reaches Washington, a thunderclap of outrage. Herblock is doing daily lurid cartoons in the Washington Post, exposing the perpetrators of this plot to vilify our President, columns filled with accusations of Republicans stooping to pornography. I'm hiding in a foxhole in my Beverly Hills house. If my right-wing conspirator name ever surfaces, it's going to be curtains for any tenuous film career I might have.

Duke Wayne comes down with the same dose of panic. He's on the phone, threatening me with legal action if I don't get him off the picture. I say, "But Duke, I read you the script. You approved it." No matter. Barry Goldwater's advisors pull the picture. It's never shown.

In a press conference the day after the election, reporters are given the one and only public glimpse of <u>Choice</u>. The <u>New York Herald Tribune</u> writes: "This was the finest campaign material Goldwater had. It was exactly what he'd been saying throughout the campaign. It should never have been cancelled."

Years later, the <u>New York Sunday Times</u> does a full page of text and scenes from the film, saying: "<u>Choice</u> changed political dialogue in America forever."

I thought that was my swansong in politics, but not quite yet.

A week after Goldwater has ditched <u>Choice</u>, Duke Wayne calls me, apologetic, sorry about that. Now, he wants me to write his own TV special, give him a chance to show how the commies are stealing the world. He's scrawled some notes on a legal pad, I bust my butt to make a screenplay out of them in less than a week. Duke has me go over and see an unemployed politician named Dick Nixon. Actually, I know him slightly because as a Navy air base officer, he used to sign our flight manifests when we landed at Guadalcanal. Anyhow, Nixon is delighted to get involved and agrees to do a tag ending on the film.

Wayne, "The Duke" is a guy you can't help but like. Real patriot, rough and tumble, too many times we've stayed up half the night, hearing him bellow out history and politics over more drinks than I need. Sometimes Pilar, his wife, gives up on him and goes home. We pack him off in the wee hours in a taxi.

Now we're into the last day of filming our TV special. We have to do it at Duke's house because he's wan and frail from a cancer operation and can't take studio lights. We've hung a wall map over his fireplace, showing the nations the communists have stolen from us colored in red. Wayne taps them on cue and rasps out his attack on our failed foreign policy.

But in the middle of a take, I notice that Italy and France have suddenly blossomed out just as red as their communist neighbors. "On Mr. Wayne's orders," says the art director.

"Duke," I plead, "you can't do that. Italy and France aren't communist!"

He whirls. "Well, goddammit, if they're not, they're gonna be any day now! Leave it colored red!"

When Duke goes off to take a breather and smoke a cigar (which he's forbidden to do with his lung cancer), I sneak in the art director and

113

have him spray paint Italy and France back to Freedom's Side. Duke never notices the change.

But by then, I was sickened by the fears, lies and just plain crookedness of politics. The money trail alone was repulsive to me. More than once, I'd seen executives of publicly traded national corporations acting as bag men for the campaign, literally carrying in briefcases stuffed with high denomination bills. They were robbing their shareholders by doing this. They were buying votes away from average citizens who still believed that their voices counted and that we had a democracy. This was all a rich man's game, power people who would stoop to anything to win.

Beverly Hills, CA, November 1964: a day after the election that Barry Goldwater has just lost to Lyndon Johnson, Nancy Reagan, sounding tired and distraught, calls and asks if she and Ronnie can come over for dinner.

During the campaign, Ronnie had written his landmark speech, A Time For Choosing. When Goldwater's timid advisers refused to give him air time, Ronnie called Goldwater himself and said, "Barry, have you seen the speech?"

Goldwater hadn't, so he screened it and immediately called back. "Those bastards," he

114

roared to Ronnie, "they're trying to talk me out of the finest thing in this campaign. We're running it!"

Ronnie's speech not only raised the most money of the entire campaign, but launched a future Reagan presidency.

When a drained-looking Ronnie and Nancy get to our house, we go into the study and have a drink. Ronnie drops the bombshell.

That morning, the Republican power group in California has asked him to run for governor. "I told them," he says, "I don't want to savage other candidates. I won't be party to political fights. But if they could clear the way for me..." he shakes his head uncertainly. "All these years I've been making speeches about what we ought to do in this country, get out of the mess we're in. Now they've dropped the ball in my court. Don't I have to pick it up and run with it? What do you think, Otis?"

"Hell yes," I say. "You pretty much have to."

After dinner, Nancy is in our bedroom with Teddy, sitting on our bed with tears rolling down her cheeks. "Ronnie and I have such a wonderful life together. After these last terrible weeks of the campaign, all I can think is: why? Why do we need to wreck what we have and get the garbage

115

of politics dumped all over us?"

Hours later, they go home and I turn to Teddy. "Damn, they're such decent people---a humble, kindly guy like Ronnie---put him into the political jungle, those gorillas will tear him to bits…."

So much for my skill as a forecaster, but by then, frankly, I wanted out of the whole game. Something indeed was changing in me, which was why, when the end finally came, it was like pushing forever against an iron door, and then miraculously having it burst open. I was sick of politics, war propaganda, and worse, being used by it. My spirit, which I was groping to touch, however haltingly and painfully, was begging me to get beyond all this and be myself. Start writing what I truly believed.

In 1976, I did a piece in the <u>Wall Street Journal</u> about land takeovers in Mexico. Not really communists, just a bandit government at work. Ronnie liked it, called and asked me to put some of those thoughts into a campaign speech for him. (His first failed run at the Presidency.) So I wrote him an idealistic appeal that we put our American spirit back into our governing, titling it, unoriginally, <u>God Bless America.</u>

A few days later, I went down to the ranch

mailbox and found a handwritten note from him in Pacific Palisades:

"Dear Otis,

Home to pick up clean laundry and your speech---please, my heart-felt thanks. Maybe I'll just keep it for Sunday mornings on the road when I can't get to church. I'm not joking Otis it's beautiful and will be of great value to me. Again, please accept my gratitude. I'll try to be deserving.

Ron

To my knowledge, he never used a word of the speech.

I'd written a no-no, talking about spirit. Though Ronnie was a church-goer and a believer, for a pragmatic politician, dedicated to doing/winning, the vapory being of our spirit part had to be anathema. Spirit talk smacked of religion, and no politician dared mix it with politics. Indeed, hadn't we pretty much burned out spirit in generations of faithful churching that mixed up God with religion until we thought that the rotes of it were all we needed to find our true selves? Small wonder that so many of our youth abandoned religion entirely, and even the loyal believers were searching more and more for answers they weren't getting from the pulpit.

Ten years later, on the night of November 21, 1986, poor Ronnie is clearly lost in the fog. In confusion, he is publicly fumbling around trying to defend himself to the press for the Iran-Contra scandal. What did he know and when did he know it? His TV audience, including us in an apartment in New York, are even more lost, as if suddenly we're in a place we don't want to be, and don't know how we'd got there.

I truly feel for him. Over the next weeks, the press is on him like a hound pack. There's even talk that he's so depressed now, he'll either be impeached or have to resign. On top of this, surgeons need to operate on his prostate. By Christmas night, I'm moved to drop him a quick note, saying, Look, you've had the world dump in on you. I only want to tell you and Nancy that you're good people, you've done many good things---in short, you're worthy human beings, far beyond this moment of political sound and fury.

A few days later, I'm at the kitchen sink at the ranch, cleaning some quail I've shot. When I pick up the phone, I've got feathers on my hands, and

Ronnie and Nancy both at the other end. Ronnie, in a tired and downcast voice, is saying over and over that <u>he did not know</u> about the Iran-Contra deal. The press, and he named names, was trying to crucify him with it.

When we finally hang up, I want to believe him but the avalanche of accusations thundering over him makes me doubt myself. Who's right, who's wrong? Mostly it saddens me that he'd be so down in the bottom of the barrel that he has to reach out to me to tell his story. I'm not a donor, a party biggie, I can't do anything for him.

All I could think then, and regret, was how far we'd drifted apart. I wasn't even a Republican anymore. I'd shot past liberal and out the far end to radical. Again and again, in my letters to Ronnie and Nancy, I'd tried to encourage them to end the Cold War. End the war propaganda that was keeping the world frozen in fear.

I knew Ronnie was a good man, so kindly that he kept up a voluminous correspondence, hand-writing notes to hundreds of Americans, total strangers whom he felt obliged to help. Often he'd send them donations out of his own pocket. Yet on the other hand, this same man could seem oblivious to the "crimes of patriots" his administration was performing. Why would he not know what a secret arm of his government was doing in his name?

I was appalled by his determination to run up the largest military budget in history and the largest deficit. This from a man who was a dedicated fiscal conservative. Days after his first election as California's governor, I watched him stand up in front of a group of his heaviest backers, tough, California businessmen, self-made millionaires. They growled protest when Ronnie said he was canceling the proposed governor's mansion and other bloated state programs. "I intend to govern," he said, "like I'm in there for one term only. Do what I believe is right and best for the state, not for my re-election."

Why the change? It wasn't his nature to enjoy political in-fighting. Rather, he tried to detach himself, sometimes even dozing through meetings. I saw plenty of corporate defense suppliers circling Ronnie when we'd visit him at the White House. And others, I'm sure, gifted PR men, were playing on his heartstrings to let them go clean the communists out of Nicaragua.

The White House, June, 1988: Ronnie and Nancy are standing with Teddy and me in the South Portico. They've just returned from their first epochal meeting with Gorbachev in Geneva. Ronnie grips me in his robust way, hugs Teddy and I hug Nancy like we're back again at dancing school. A photographer scurries in and takes our picture.

I think of all my letters over the years, begging Ronnie to see through the fraud of the Cold War and end it. So now that they're just back from the heart of darkness, I wonder what their reaction is going to be. I thank them for their courage in making this great leap toward peace.

Ronnie grins. "Listen, it wasn't hard to do. I've got to tell you, Otis, those Russians are wonderful people. Sure, they tried to bug us in the shower and everyplace else, we practically had to walk around naked to talk to each other, but that's just their suspicious way. They're great, we really enjoyed them." Nancy adds, "This window of opportunity Ronnie has opened has to stay open. We've got to keep this thing going, and change the way we think about Russia."

I gasp. Am I hearing right? Russians wonderful people? What happened to the Evil Empire? Korea, Cuban missile crisis, Berlin Airlift. Vietnam, Grenada, Nicaragua? Evil turned suddenly good? The lives of Americans we've flung away, defending against it. I'm un-moored, even sickened.

When Teddy and I walk out on Pennsylvania Avenue, I could only whisper, "What a turn-around! Can you believe it?"

"Thank God," she says. Then even the roar of rush hour traffic seems quieter. We sit down in an outdoor restaurant, no need for words.

Historians might say that Ronnie only initiated *glasnost* because it was good politics at the time. Or that it was economic: we were going broke in the Cold War. Our businessmen needed peaceful access to the markets in Eastern Europe. We were tired of the whole thing. But it took a broad-gauge man to swallow his own words about "evil," make a 180 degree turn away from everything he'd been led to believe, and come down finally on the side of humanity.

We can't trust our government to give us the truth. We can't trust our mainstream media to give us the truth because it is too is dependent on corporate money. Wars are good for business--- somebody always profits---and for the political elite they're splendid diversions, spinning the bewildered herd's mind away from problems at home that our system has failed to solve.

As Shakespeare said in Henry IV: "The best way to govern is to busy their giddy minds with foreign quarrels."

We can only trust our true selves. And living in them is the hardest battle of all our wars because, I truly believe, it's the only way we'll ever reach peace.

EVIL EMPIRE 2, AXIS VERSION

In 1946 when President Truman was about to launch the Cold War, veteran senator Arthur Vandenberg of Michigan warned him: "To get the American people to spend all that money in peacetime, you're going to have to scare hell out of them." In that Cold War, between ourselves and our proxies and the Soviets and theirs, we managed to kill more humans than all those who died in World War I and II combined.

I hadn't the faintest idea then that our seemingly interminable war against communism---like our new war in Iraq and probably all wars---are at their root a spiritual battle in my heart or yours.

Nothing in my upbringing or education had exposed me to the idea that I could make a choice between living in war or living in peace. So instead, I went gallantly along with the system and the party line of being a patriot in the nation I loved, lent it my meager talents and prayed God for victory at the end.

But is it fair and just for any administration to withhold the facts and the grievances caused by our foreign policy that may well have led to the 9/11 tragedy? To refuse any public investigation of them?

"I think we are just tired of being lied to," writes Robert Fisk, a respected British foreign correspondent who lives in Beirut and has interviewed bin Laden. "Tired of being talked down to, of being bombarded with Second World War Jingoism and scare stories and false information and student essays dressed up as 'intelligence.' We are sick of being insulted by little men, Tony Blair and the likes of George Bush and his cabal of neo-conservative henchmen who have plotted for years to change the map of the middle east to their advantage.

"We do not like being lectured and whined at by men whose experience of war is Hollywood and television. Still less do we wish to embark on endless wars with a Texas governor-executioner who dodged the Vietnam draft and who, with his oil buddies, is now sending America's poor to destroy a Muslim nation that has nothing at all to do with the crimes against humanity of 11 September."

My conscience tells me that neither you nor I had any choice in the Iraq war. It was decided for us. There was not an hour of debate in Congress.

Despite all the marching, all the protests, despite mail to our representatives running 100-1 against the war, both the Republicans and Democrats were virtually silent on the issue. Said <u>Newsweek's</u> Howard Fineman, "I'll just never understand how the American people swallowed this without a peep of protest."

They, you and I, swallowed this revolutionary new policy of Empire because we did not know. We weren't supposed to know. Our news media kept it from us.

Major corporations and mega-news chains have engulfed and devoured most of our information sources, merging them increasingly into a single establishment voice. Shills for the administration's wars. General Electric gobbled up NBC, meaning that our number one military contractor could now depict the wars that sold its products. When the popular longtime TV host Phil Donahue expressed anti-war views on his new show, GE's MSNBC promptly fired him.

In 1983, 50 corporations dominated the media in the U.S. By 1990, the 50 media companies had become 23. By 2000, the number was down to 6.

At that point we were too concerned with the stock market bust, evaporation of our 401K's, the arrogant lies of Enron and other corporate

126

dens of thieves. For the average working man and woman, it was: who gets downsized next, how do we pay the mortgage and the grocery bills? We were stalemated, depressed, afraid.

Just before 9/11, a <u>Harper's</u> magazine article characterized President Bush as "a lawn jockey at a Houston country club, waiting to open the doors of the limousines of the rich." But now, in the holocaust of 9/11, he was transformed overnight into an embattled, courageous commander in chief, tall in the saddle: "We go forward to defend freedom and all that is good and just in the world."

This is war. And it begs the question—Are you a patriot or not?

It's not the people's business to know who actually did 9/11. It seemed unpatriotic to ask whether this sophisticated plot was the work of scattered religious fanatics, or would it have taken a nation to organize and implement such a tragedy?

In his <u>Dreaming War</u> (Thunder's Mouth Press/Nation Books), novelist and historian Gore Vidal makes an intriguing case. Why, for instance, would one Mohammed Eikal, noted journalist and sometime foreign minister of Egypt, tell the Manchester <u>Guardian</u> on October

10, 2001: "Bin Laden does not have the capabilities for an operation of 9/11's magnitude. When I hear Bush talking about al Qa'eda as if was Nazi Germany or the Communist party of the Soviet Union, I laugh because I know what is there.

"Bin Laden has been under surveillance for years: every telephone call was monitored and al Qa'eda has been penetrated by American intelligence, Pakistani intelligence, Saudi intelligence, Egyptian intelligence. They could not have kept secret an operation that required such a degree of organization and sophistication."

Why, too, would Eckehardt Werthebach, former president of Germany's domestic intelligence say on December 4, 2001: "9/11 required years of planning. The scale of the attacks indicates they were a product of 'state organized actions.'"

And finally, from a home-grown American skeptic: *The So-Called Evidence is a Farce*," writes Stan Goff. A retired 26 year army veteran, Goff had taught Military Science and Doctrine at West Point. Vidal quotes him: "I have no idea why people aren't asking some very specific questions about the actions of Bush and company on the day of the attacks."

Such questions as: when planes under FAA surveillance deviate from their flight plan, it's a mandatory law that fighters are sent up to find out why. This did not happen. According to Goff, "The planes are all high-jacked between 7:45 and 8:10 AM Eastern Daylight Time. This is an event that is unprecedented. The President is on his way to a Florida elementary school to hear children read. He is not notified. By around 8:15 it should be very apparent that something is terribly wrong. The President is glad-handing teachers. By 8:45 when American Airlines Flight 11 crashes into the World Trade Center, Bush is settling in with children for his photo op at Booker Elementary. Four planes have obviously been highjacked simultaneously, an event never before seen in history and one has just dived into the world's best-known twin towers—and still no one notifies the nominal commander in chief."

The final mystery to Goff is the end of the tragedy. At 9:35, the last fateful plane screams past the White House no-fly zone, makes another turn over the Pentagon, all the while being tracked by radar. The Pentagon is not evacuated and there are no fighters in the sky. "Now the real kicker," Goff says. "A pilot they want us to believe was trained at a Florida puddle-jumper school for Piper Cubs and Cessnas, conducts a well-controlled downward spiral descending the last 7000 feet in two and a half minutes, brings the plane in so low that it clips the electrical wires across the street from the Pentagon, and flies it with pinpoint accuracy into the side of the building at 460 nauts.

"When the theory about learning to fly this well at the puddle-jumper school began to lose ground, it was added that they received further training on a flight simulator. This is like saying you prepared your teenager for her first drive on I-40 at rush hour by buying her a video driving game. There is a story being constructed about these events."

But if it is, or was, that story will remain buried. The President and Vice-President met immediately with Congressional leaders and quashed any present scrutiny about 9/11 lest it jeopardize the war effort. After the Pearl Harbor attack, Congressional investigations were launched within hours, but not this time. The blame was pinned on Osama binLaden, whom we failed to find. He was finally declared immaterial.

On September 14, 2001, the respected *Jane's Defense Weekly* wrote: "In 1998 with U.S.

knowledge, bin Laden created al Qa'eda (The Base), a conglomerate of quasi-independent terrorist cells in countries spread across at least 26 or so countries...Washington turned a blind eye to al Qa'eda."

So many curious facts and loose ends remain unexamined. Who knew, for instance, that the hated Taliban terrorists were not only trained by U.S. Special Forces but some were brought illegally to the U.S. for their training. Yes, they were our allies fighting communists then, but the terror techniques we taught them were not forgotten. Why, too, the day after 9/11, from the very same Boston airport where the terrorist planes took off---why did the U.S. allow a private jet to leave the U.S. with many bin Laden family members aboard? Or why did General Mahmoud Ahmed, director of Pakistan's Inter Services Intelligence agency attend mysterious meetings at the Pentagon? According to the India *Times*, the General was later fired because India "produced evidence to show his links to one of the suicide bombers." The *Times* confirmed that the General had wired "$100,000 to hijacker Mohammed Atta from Pakistan."

No answers. Instead, conquer Afghanistan, then militarize and control the adjoining Stans which, as a dividend, accrete to us their own vast, untapped reserves of oil. The new President installed is a former employee of Union Oil, as is our present U.S. Ambassador to Afghanistan. Union has been negotiating for years, even with the hated Taliban, to build a pipeline across Afghanistan so that the Caspian basin oil can go to us, not Russia.

Regardless of Palestinian grievances, which many feel are the real bone in the Muslim throat, we give unqualified support to Israel, billions in cash and weapons to help them in their seizure of Arab land.

What the New York Times calls the "warriors of the right," Christian fundamentalists, an enormous voting bloc, are now joined with politically powerful Jewish neo-conservatives and most of the corporate controlled media of the United States.

"The men driving Bush," writes Robert Fisk in the London Independent, "are mostly former or still active pro-Israeli lobbyists. For years they have advocated destroying the most powerful Arab nation. Richard Perle, one of Bush's most influential advisers, Douglas Feith, Paul Wolfowitz were all campaigning for the overthrow of Iraq long before Bush was elected--

-if he was 'elected.'

"A 1996 report, *'A Clean Break'* was written not for the U.S. but for the incoming Israeli Likud prime minister, Binyamin Netanyahu and produced by a group headed by, yes, Richard Perle. The destruction of Iraq will of course protect Israel's monopoly of nuclear weapons and allow it to defeat the Palestinians and impose whatever colonial settlement Sharon has in store."

As an additional dividend, "pro-Israel organizations foresee Iraq not only as a new source of oil but of water, too. Why should canals not link the Tigris river to the parched Levant? Although Bush and Blair dare not discuss this with us, a war for Israel is not going to have our boys lining up at the recruiting offices."

Writes Charles Bartlett, a longtime Washington correspondent: "On a Sunday walk 16 days before his 1960 election, Jack Kennedy told me that he had attended a New York city dinner on the previous night at which a group of American Jews had offered to pay the costs of the rest of his campaign if he would leave them in charge of Middle Eastern policy after becoming president. This offer is regularly made to Democratic candidates, I have later learned, but rarely to Republicans. Although Bush has aligned U.S. policy more tightly to Israel than any previous president, I find it impossible to believe that he would be party to such a corrupt and contemptible deal. He has however stiffly supported Sharon's refusal to make any solid moves toward peace."

Since 1973, Bartlett continues, "The U.S. has given Israel $300 billion in direct aid." Normally foreign Aid grants from the U.S. are given to other nations in goods we purchase from American corporations, but we pay Israel in cash. Now because of the Iraq war Israel has made a "shrill request for $4 billion more in special military aid and a $10 billion loan guarantee. The new finance Minister, Netanyahu, has been telephoning leaders all over Washington to plead for the request. The leaders of Congress, totally responsive to the Jewish lobby, have appealed to the President to make the money available."

Instead, the Bush administration pursued Iraq and Hussein.

In the Saddam propagandist films, the producers overdosed us with the same repetition gimmick that we used against communist leaders in the Cold War. How many thousands of frames have we seen showing Saddam at his vilest, always with a raised shotgun or a sword? Repeated day after day: gasses his own people, tortures his own people, attacks defenseless countries, thumbs his nose at UN resolutions, kills babies in incubators, has biological, chemical and very soon, nuclear weapons.

Noam Chomsky writes: "On August 1, 1990 Saddam Hussein was a favored U.S. client. The United States was offering him credit (a billion dollars, it was later revealed), lavishing support on him. The U.S. was his major trading partner. We were the largest market for his oil. We were providing 40% of his food. The Iraqi-American business forum was praising his progress toward democracy. He was just a good guy.

"A day later, he was the incarnation of Genghis Khan and Hitler. What happened was that he conflicted with U.S. interests. He could set up one of the most brutal tyrannies in the world, that was all just fine as long as he was seen as conforming to U.S. interests. When it became clear that he was another one of those radical nationalists who was going to go his own way, not ours, he had to go."

While we were supporting Saddam, Chomsky continues, "he was one of the major monsters."

But to my conscience at least, U.S. foreign policy since World War II has always supported such thugs all over the world. As Franklin D. Roosevelt said about Somoza in Nicaragua, "Yes, he's an S.O.B. but he's our S.O.B." So are they all as long as they go along with the wishes and market protection of our corporations.

In 1954, for example, the democratically elected Arbenz government in Guatemala had no revenues. Its biggest income maker was United Fruit Company. (The first President Bush's oil company, Zapata, later bought United Fruit and allowed the CIA to use the company's airstrips for the attack against Castro's Cuba.)

"So Arbenz put the tiniest of taxes on bananas," writes Gore Vidal, who was in Guatemala at the time, "and Henry Cabot Lodge got up in the Senate and said the Communists had taken over Guatemala and we must act. We sent in the CIA and they overthrew the government. We installed a military dictator, and there's been nothing but bloodshed ever since. Now, that's the way we operate. And that's why we got to be so hated."

How ironic it is that we Americans, who were born out of the idealism of our own revolution, have never, to my knowledge, supported a peoples' revolution for *their* life, liberty and pursuit of happiness in their native lands. Instead, we have become, by the actual record of our attacks, overt and covert, the leading terrorist nation in the world.

As for Saddam *"torturing his own people,"* indeed he did, but does that make him unique and a target for destruction by us?

Amnesty International has documented torture going on all over the world, including by such U.S. allies as Turkey, Egypt, Philippines, Lebanon, Spain, India, Pakistan, Morocco, Russia ("violence against women.")

In China, Amnesty cites, "internet users are at risk of arbitrary detention, torture, execution." And in Kuwait, our ally and staging area for the attack on Iraq, "a brutal repression," writes Noam Chomsky, "and a lot of torture."

What about the terrorists that the U.S. has captured after 9/11? How have they been treated?

Says the Washington *Post*, "approximately 100 suspects have been transferred to U.S. allies including Saudi Arabia and Morocco. Many have been sent to Egypt, where according to our State Department's own human rights report, "suspects are routinely stripped and blindfolded, suspended from ceiling so feet just touching the floor; beaten with fists, whips, metal rods, subjected to electric shocks. In Syria, at least one of our suspects was subjected to torture methods including pulling out fingernails, forcing objects into the rectum, using a chair that bends backwards to asphyxiate the victim or fracture the spine."

Saddam is another Hitler. He poses the same threat to Americans as Hitler did.

The fact is that Hitler had perhaps the finest military machine the world had ever known. He had an ultra-modern navy, deadly fleets of submarines, a state of the art Luftwaffe, Panzer divisions with armor superior to anything the U.S. had, plus an immense Wermacht ground force that proved itself unbeatable as it overran Europe.

And what of Hussein? He commanded a nation the size of California, mostly sand. Had no navy, no air force, and with the exception of his relatively small Republican Guard, most of his squalid soldiers didn't even wear the same uniforms. Their arms were shoddy and at the first shot fired in anger, they mostly threw up their hands and hollered "Kamerad." They did exactly this in the latest Iraq war.

What about his attack on Kuwait? He attacks his neighbors.

The fact is that we enthusiastically supported Saddam's Iraq in its war against Iran. In the '80's, Donald Rumsfeld was negotiating a pipeline contract with him for our Bechtel Corporation. This is the same Bechtel that has now received the first multimillion dollar contract to rebuild Iraq. The first President Bush awarded Saddam a medal for his "democratic progress." So what happened?

Through Kuwait, the CIA had been destabilizing Iraq. During the Iran/Iraq war, Kuwait advanced its border further north and seized valuable Iraqi oil reserves. By manipulating oil prices, Kuwait cost Iraq billions of dollars in revenues. Shortly before we launched Gulf War I, Saddam protested to U.S. Ambassador April Glaspie that "Kuwait was waging economic war on Iraq" and turning a deaf ear to the complaints of both Iraq and Saudi Arabia.

In the transcript of this meeting, Ambassador Glaspie answered: "We have many Americans who would like to see the price of oil go above $25 because they come from oil-producing states.

We have no opinion on Arab-Arab conflicts like your border disagreement with Kuwait." Saddam read that to mean, go ahead, straighten out your borders with Kuwait.

As for Kuwait being such a small, defenseless nation attacked by the Saddam tyrant, a wire service story at the time states: "The oil rich ruling family which owns Kuwait has invested 250 billion into the economies of the United States, Britain and other western nations. Not only does Kuwait own stock in almost all of the 70 leading companies on the New York Stock Exchange, but has a multi-million dollar ownership in U.S. oil companies. Kuwait has also invested in the politically-influential Houston oil community which backed Bush 1's bid for the Presidency."

Saddam has weapons of mass destruction and did not disclose them in his 12,000 page report to the UN.

If it's true that he did have such weapons---none have been found to date--- why was it that the mainstream media failed to tell the public how he happened to get them?

"The Berlin daily <u>Togeszeitung,</u>" writes Alexander Cockburn in <u>The Nation</u>, "got a world-class scoop by getting hold of Iraq's 12,000 page document. The UN obeyed the U.S. demand that it censor the report before it was given to members of the Security Council."

What the U.S. did, Cockburn claims, was to "swiftly excise the corporations, mostly U.S., British and German that supplied Iraq with nuclear, chemical, biological and missile technology prior to 1991. Such shipments, encouraged by the relevant governments were illegal under solemn international treaties and laws."

U.S. corporations included "Honeywell, SpectraPhysics, Rockwell, Hewlett Packard, Dupont, Eastman Kodak, Bechtel and others, 24 in all. In addition, the U.S. Departments of Defense, Energy, Commerce and Agriculture were designated as suppliers.

"A big story?" Cockburn asks. "You might think so. But in the U.S. corporate press? Nothing that I can find."

Saddam is a brutal, sadistic tyrant.

"The Incubator Returns," writes Cockburn in The Nation. Saddam's troops, upon entering Kuwait, reportedly pulled newborn infants out of their incubators and flung them on the concrete floor to die. This tale was often used in propaganda for Gulf War I and was resuscitated recently.

The truth? None whatsoever. The scam was crafted by the daughter of the Kuwaiti ambassador to Washington. She ran it over to the famed Hill and Knowlton, the PR firm which represented Kuwait, and hours later you and I saw it on the evening news.

Saddam tortures his own people.

Writes John LeCarre, formerly in British Intelligence and author of many best-selling spy novels. "If Saddam didn't have the oil, he could torture his citizens to his heart's content. Other leaders do it every day. Think Saudi Arabia, Pakistan, Turkey, Syria, Egypt.

"What Bush won't tell us is the truth about why we're going to war. What's at stake is not an Axis of Evil but oil, money and people's lives. Saddam's misfortune is to sit on the second biggest oil field in the world. Bush wants it, and who helps him get it will get a piece of the cake."

"The imminent war was planned years before bin Laden struck, but it was he who made it possible. Without bin Laden, the Bush junta would still be trying to explain such tricky matters as how it came to be elected in the first place:

Enron; its shameless favoring of the already too-rich; its reckless disregard for the world's poor, the ecology and a raft of unilaterally abrogated international treaties. They might also have to be telling us why they support Israel in its continuing disregard for UN resolutions."

The fact is that Israel has broken many more UN resolutions than Saddam. So have other countries, including ourselves. Also unreported to the public was the identity of the corporations hired by our government to clean up the mess in Kuwait after Gulf War I. Enron and the oil giant Halliburton, formerly chaired by Vice-President Cheney.

Who will rebuild Iraq now that we've destroyed it? It's an estimated $100 billion plum and the contracts are already being let to major U.S. corporations. One subsidiary of Cheney's former Halliburton received a $7 billion dollar contract even though many larger, financially sound companies were ignored in the bidding.

General Jay Garner, appointed by Bush to be our military governor in Iraq, and shortly discharged, has long had his own defense corporation, selling war equipment to the Pentagon.

My conscience asks me: is it fair and just that

American taxpayers have to finance the corporate rebuilding of Iraq?

Domestically, is it fair and just to keep Americans in a state of ignorance and fear? The constant terror alerts are a prime example. In the hundreds of them that have been terrifying the public since 9/11, has any actual attack struck the U.S.? The protective agencies will try to claim that their efficiency has thwarted such attacks. Yet, if that's true, have they caught any actual terrorists on our soil? Have such persons been arrested and convicted? A handful in foreign countries but none that I know of threatening us here at home.

After their tragic failure in 9/11, it's only natural that our intelligence agencies will be at work now. Maybe it's even comforting, but for you and me in Boston, Boca Raton or miniscule Bonita, Arizona, what are we supposed to do if we meet up with a real terrorist? Frisk him? Call 911? Terror alerts are one more add-on to the baggage of fear.

Yet still, in all the propaganda and cooked intelligence that created such urgency to destroy Iraq, because America is still America, a few patriots did find their strong loud voices unafraid. "In the space of two short years," cried crusty statesman Robert Byrd of Virginia on the Senate floor, "this reckless and arrogant administration has initiated policies which may reap disastrous consequences for years."

According to economist Paul Krugman in the New York <u>Times</u>, when Bush entered office, "the Congressional Budget Office was projecting a 10 year surplus of $5.6 trillion. Now it projects a 10 year *deficit* of 1.8 trillion. Even though the business community is starting to get scared---the ultra-establishment Committee for Economic Development now warns that 'a fiscal crisis threatens our future standard of living'--- investors still can't believe that the leaders of the United States are acting like the rulers of a banana republic."

Continued Senator Byrd: "I truly must question the judgment of any President who can say that a massive unprovoked attack on a nation which is over 50% children is 'in the highest moral tradition of our country.' This war is not necessary at this time. Pressure appears to be having a good result in Iraq."

"The Bush budget bureau," writes journalist Charles Bartlett, "cites cuts in heating subsidies for the American poor while we pay for ten new power plants in Iraq and promise that electricity will be restored to 75% of its pre-1991 level. The Budget bureau cites the plan to build 3,000 miles of new roads in Iraq while American highway funding is cut severely; 5,000 new public housing units in America while 20,000 are planned in Iraq; rebuilding 21 hospitals and 25,000 schools in Iraq while American hospitals and schools struggle under heavy financial pressures."

On the day the war finally started, Senator Byrd, at 87, fifty years in office and nothing to lose, had the courage to rise up in the Senate and say: "I weep for my country. No more is the image of America one of strong yet benevolent peacemaker. The image of America has changed. Around the globe, our friends mistrust us, our word is disputed, our intentions are questioned.

"The case this Administration tries to make to justify its fixation with war is tainted with charges of falsified documents and circumstantial evidence. We cannot convince the world of the necessity of this war for one simple reason.

"It is a war of choice."

Said Chas Freeman, U.S. Ambassador to Saudi Arabia during the Gulf War: "It's a war by people who know nothing about the Middle East. Perle and Co. are seeking a Middle East dominated by an alliance between the United

States and Israel, backed by overwhelming military force. It outdoes anything in the march of folly catalog. It's the lemmings going over the cliff."

Meanwhile, on the floor of the House, Ohio congressman Dennis J. Kuchinich asked: "Why this war? There is no answer which can separate itself from oil economics, profit requirements of the arms trade or distorted notions of empire building. War with Iraq is wrong. We must advance the cause of peace in this country. We must be prepared to stand up, to speak out, to organize, to march. It is urgent we oppose this war."

But who was listening? It's doubtful that you or I saw such speeches reported on mainline TV.

Nor, with the exception of finding it reprinted in the New York <u>Times</u>, did we ever read the courageous protest of a twenty year U.S. diplomat, John Brady Kiesling. On February 27, 2003, as Political Counselor to the American embassy in Greece, Kiesling sent a letter to Secretary of State Colin Powell: (quoted in part)

"I am writing you to submit my resignation from the Foreign Service of the United States. I do so with a heavy heart. The policies we are now asked to advance are incompatible not only with

American values but also with American interests.

"Our fervent pursuit of war with Iraq is driving us to squander our international legitimacy. We have begun to dismantle the largest and most effective web of international relationships the world has ever known. Our current course will bring instability and danger, not security. We have not seen such systematic distortion of intelligence, such systematic manipulation of American opinion since the war in Vietnam.

"This Administration has chosen to make terrorism a domestic political tool, enlisting a scattered and largely defeated Al Quaeda as its bureaucratic ally. We spread disproportionate terror and confusion in the public mind, arbitrarily linking the unrelated problems of terrorism and Iraq.

"The result, and perhaps the motive, is to justify a vast misallocation of shrinking public wealth to the military and to weaken the safeguards that protect American citizens from the heavy hand of government. September 11 did not do as much damage to the fabric of American society as we seem determined to so do ourselves."

Writes the Carnegie Endowment for International Peace: "The war in Iraq is a textbook case of how a small, organized group---they call themselves a 'cabal'---can determine policy in a large nation, even when the majority of officials and experts originally scorned their views."

What about our new policy of shock and awe? Has it worked? President Bush "forgot" to include aid to wrecked Afghanistan in our new budget. Though some improvements have been made since 9/11, warlords still flourish. Senior Afghan officials are advising their various commanders to "hold onto their weapons for the time being. It's not finished yet." Afghanistan is tottering on the edge of civil war.

In the quick and blazing success of our Iraq invasion, the enemy was deflated and fizzled out like a spent balloon. So what my conscience asks me now: where was Iraq's deadly threat to us?

Why were we in such a hurry? Yes, destroy the tyrant Saddam but he's vanished or dead. Destroy his weapons of mass destruction, yet where are they and were they ever?

To date, 800 American soldiers have been killed in combat or related deaths and uncounted thousands of Iraqi military 'its.' The AP reports as a preliminary figure 3,240 Iraqi civilians killed, those identified by hospitals. Many more families, in fear, buried their dead surreptitiously.

U.S. troops in our occupying army are daily being sniped, bombed or killed, and will continue to be even though the TV cameras have mostly gone home. The public is not allowed to see the morning after of an unnecessary war.

The summary propaganda image used by the administration is that we won a splendid, militarily efficient victory. We have a new oil and power state to privatize and sell to the highest bidder, namely our corporations. As writer Naomi Klein put it in The Nation, "It's Free Trade Supercharged, which seizes new markets on the battlefields of pre-emptive wars."

"In wartime," confided Sir Winston Churchill, "truth is so precious that she should always be attended by a bodyguard of lies."

Fairness and Accuracy in Reporting (FAIR), a media watchdog group, cites some revealing statistics. Of 1,617 on camera sources before and during the Iraq war.

 ---63% current or former government employees.
 ---52% Bush administration officials
 ---64% pro-war

---10% anti-war (man-on-the street soundbites only).

Three percent of all U.S. sources were anti-war. *Zero percent of all sources who were invited to have a sit-down on camera interview were identified as being against the war.*

U.S. media has an integral role in determining what information the populace will receive. The executive suite, not the reporters, decides. And the executive suite itself is taking its orders from its giant corporate advertisers who finance the politicians.

But the good news is, when even some of the elites begin to worry about the trembling tower, there's change in the air.

Writes Paul Krugman, Princeton economist and columnist in the New York <u>Times</u>: "I'll tell you what's outrageous. It's not the fact that people are criticizing the administration; it's the fact that nobody is being held accountable for misleading the nation into war."

I wonder now if that change isn't happening.

What caused this biggest protest in history against the Iraq war?

To me, it came out of the peoples' hearts. No, it didn't stop this war but it will someday. As Dwight Eisenhower put it: "The people want peace so much, one day we're going to have to get out of their way and give it to them."

The Berlin Wall didn't fall, the Soviet Union didn't implode because dictatorial leaders simply decided to step down. The people made that choice, hundreds of thousands of ordinary citizens sitting around kitchen tables or talking to each other out on the streets. The first Russian Revolution took a hundred years of people talking to each other, writing, marching, protesting until their anger swelled into a tidal wave that toppled the Czarist empire. Joining together in one common heart, their emotions finally gave them the courage to just say no to the brutality and violence they'd been suffering for too long.

I hear or read emails of uncounted dedicated, committed American patriots. Mostly, just ordinary people like myself. But to them, the state of our nation is more important than their jobs or kids' soccer games. More important than re-decorating the living room or buying a new dress. More vital than playing the Dow Jones or planning the next Carnival cruise. To them, their new and true patriotism now comes first.

And in the end, it does come back down to conscience of each one of us. The courage to change ourselves.

PART TWO

ADVENTURES IN FINDING AND LOSING

On that rocky road to whatever spirit might be, I kept asking myself, "Despite what the saints tell sinners like me, can anybody really live in the higher, positive emotions most of the time?" I certainly didn't have the formula.

And yet, what about my grandfather, Will, and his sister, my great aunt Nora? I like to believe that they knew how to do it. They were an inspiration to me. In fact, it could be that my dream of living on the land and loving it, however impractically romantic, was a throwback to them.

A friend once told me, "Carney, do you realize that with the exception of whoring, you've spent your life in the oldest and least paid occupations in the history of mankind. The telling of tales and the pasturing of beasts."

As my mother sighed, after I'd had a best-selling novel and a small cattle ranch, "Well, I suppose, dear, we just have to face it." Then she added the old Irish expression. "It's a poor family that can't afford one gentleman."

Will and Nora came from Mayo, the poorest county in Ireland. The lorded English owned practically all the turf there was. Even now, tell an Irishman you're from Mayo, he'll roll his eyes: "Mayo, God help us."

In the tradition of the Irish clan sticking together, they lived with us in our cavernous apartment on Sheridan Road on Chicago's lake shore. Years later, when Teddy and I had three sons of our own, we returned to Will and Nora's humble birthplace. On a lonely moor stands a tiny, cobbled house, whitewashed walls and a thatch roof. The old woman who was living there at the time swept out the dirt floor and invited us in for tea. "Ah, yes," she said, her eyes clouding, "this was Carney's Field. But they've all gone out long ago. God keep them."

At 11 years old, Will came to Chicago in 1866, the year after our Civil War ended. He came alone. His mother and father, still in Ireland, had sent him out to make his way on what was called "The Other Side." He went to work on the Chicago docks as a tally boy, marking lumber for $4 a week. Because County Mayo is so poor, I doubt if Will could have had much education there. When the great fire struck Chicago in 1871, he, Nora, and their younger brothers and sisters who had now joined them, fled to the lakefront. They heaped what few possessions they had into a skiff and Will rowed them out to safety.

After the fire, Chicago needed rebuilding. Will traveled north into the timber of Wisconsin and Upper Michigan. He began to cut the trees and later to dig the coal that his new land required. Though he started out penniless, as Mother used to say, "He never met a stranger."

He managed to put together the funds to finance other pioneer lumbermen of his day, the Hines company in Chicago and Oregon and the Weyerhausers in the Pacific Northwest.

When telephones came in, Will found tall timber for the poles. He sent one of his brothers, Bryan, to Spokane, Washington to start a pole company. A short time later when Bryan died, Will brought over a distant cousin from Ireland and gave him the company. Today, it's the largest of its kind in the nation. Neither Will nor our family ever received a penny out of it.

It's strange how the karma of his generosity still echoes in my own life. In the 1970's, when I was buying cattle for a ranch we then had in

Arizona, the owner turned out to be a man who knew my name well. Early in this century, he'd been a telegrapher at Carneyville, a coal mine Will had established along the Tongue River in Wyoming. When he contracted tuberculosis and could no longer work, Will gave him $10,000, a large sum at the time, and sent him off to recuperate in the dry air of California's Imperial Valley. The once-telegrapher not only began again but became one of the largest produce growers and ranchers in the valley, a millionaire because a man he barely knew, Will Carney, gave him his start.

Long after Will had arrived in Chicago as an immigrant boy, he was approached by another Irishman who claimed to have come over with him on the same boat. Nearly fifty years had passed. Though Will couldn't remember him, the fellow said he was down on his luck and needed help. By that time, Will owned several properties in Chicago, one of them being an empty store building on the south side.

His Irish compatriot asked Will to lease him the building which he'd operate as some kind of store. Will decided to give him the building. The man was overwhelmed and ashamed to accept such a gift. All he had in the world, he told Will, was several thousand acres of worthless, cut-over timber land he'd homesteaded across the lake from Chicago in Michigan. He insisted that he trade Will the land for the store. Will finally accepted, and paid a few dollars in taxes every year.

When I was leaving for Navy flight training in early 1942, my father Roy took me across Lake Michigan on a ferry boat. We stood together out on the worthless land. Oil had been discovered on it. The rigs were already there and pumping. Not a big field, but one that repaid Will's generosity many times over for many years.

By the end of the first World War, he had pioneered towns with his name on them in four states. He employed thousands of people, mostly immigrants like himself. He endowed hospitals and churches, and set up his brothers, sisters and their families into businesses of their own. He supported maiden aunts like Nora, as well as his mothers' sisters.

Though he was a mini-conglomerate of his day, he wore off the rack suits and worked in a cubbyhole office, meticulously recording in a tiny notebook every penny he spent---"cigars, 18 cents, taxi fare, 24 cents"---although he never recorded donations.

When his ailing wife, my grandmother, demanded that he care for her---she was mourning the death of their eldest son, my namesake, Otis---Will shut his office door, turned his back on his career and took her traveling for months. At his death, many businesses in Chicago and other cities he'd touched closed their doors for an hour in his memory.

Will's spirit deeply moved me. I could sense it even at a very young age. His natural instinct was to live in wholeness, combining hard work, love of family and concern for his workers, with material detachment, a letting go of the world. When I was a kid sitting on his knee at breakfast and swiping his bacon, he'd say softly, "Moderation in all things, lad." With him, it was smoking his occasional cigar, having a whiskey or a game of golf out in the green with his friends. Many days, he'd take me by the hand and we'd stroll in silence along the lake shore, watching the sea gulls and the distant bobbing sailboats. He didn't seem to have anything to get or anyplace to be.

His sister, my great aunt Nora, was an incredible story herself. She made her dream. When you motivate yourself to live as much as possible in the higher levels of consciousness, you not only have an excellent chance of creating the life you've imagined, but more important, you can heal yourself on the journey.

Nora did just that. Tall, raw-boned and henna-rinsed, she lived with us in our house from the time I was born through all the years until our own children were raised. As a young girl, she'd come from the soft green land of Ireland to be dumped down into noisy, brawling Chicago. In terror, she'd had to flee the great fire, clinging in a rowboat to what few possessions she had. A few years later, trying to elope with a man her brothers disapproved of, her lover's carriage overturned. Nora was thrown out and suffered internal injuries. She had to have a hysterectomy, surely a perilous operation in the 1880's. She developed angina, crippling her in painful spasms for the rest of her life.

But Nora's dream was to be a painter and a world traveler. Thanks to her pluck and her brother Will's support, she visited places like Zanzibar, Zululand and Tristan de Cunha before most people even knew where they were. When my brother Bill and I were young, Nora fascinated us with her tales of adventure. She'd read us stories by the hour, or she'd dress up in outrageous costumes and delight us with her skits of the tinkers and leprechauns from the Other Side.

In later years, she wintered at the Arizona Biltmore Hotel in Phoenix. She was the first guest to come there, and had a room of her own that was never rented out, filled as it was with her paints and desert landscapes. After 40 years, the Wrigley family who owned the Biltmore gave her a silver loving cup. She was the grande dame of the place, dressing for dinner every night, tall and erect, sweeping down the red-flowered stairway with an ermine cape swirled over her shoulders.

And she was still so frugal that when she tipped the "butter boys," as she called them, a dime at dinner, one of them handed it back and said, "Miss Carney, you need this more than I do."

Always the optimist, she refused to wear black or go to funerals. She wouldn't even read the Irish Sport Page, which was what we called the obituaries. As her incredible years of good health spooled on, she wouldn't let herself dwell on sickness or death. When oldsters at the Biltmore would try to tell her about their latest illness or operation, Nora would smile, make a graceful exit and hurry to the keno games. She loved to gamble. When I'd slip off to the race track, against the wishes of my father, Nora would always sneak me a fiver to bet for her.

She lived in our house for 50 years. At 96, she was still gamely out on our lawn, chipping approach shots to an imaginary green. At 97, she happened to break her foot. Mother took her to the hospital. The young doctor was amazed at the x-rays. "Miss Carney," he said, "these are incredible bones. Would you mind telling me how old you are."

Nora drew herself up. "You're the doctor, lad. You tell me."

What he did tell her was to wear the corrective shoe he'd prescribed. In the first snows of Christmas, Nora flung the ugly things away. She winced into her smartest pumps and pegged around shopping at Marshall Field's.

When she was 98, still with all her faculties and joy of life, she came down for breakfast one morning and told Mother that she'd seen "the bird at the window." Mother, Irish herself, knew what the old country saying meant. The bird was there to take a soul.

"I won't have the Lord seeing me in such a mess," Nora said, and asked Mother to take her to the hairdresser. That night, with a new permanent, henna rinse, and a Biltmore evening gown, she had dinner with my mother and father. Then she went up to her room, lay down with her rosary, and sometime before dawn, she went with the bird.

I still marvel at the majesty and peace of her surrender.

*

The immigrant dream of the Wills and Noras of America was not to last very long. The magnificent isolation we'd known in wilderness land was thundered away by the storms of World War I. Cavalrymen of the frontier, trained in fighting Indians, were soon leading American soldiers across the bloody battlegrounds of France. Black Jack Pershing, who'd been a lieutenant at Wounded Knee, South Dakota in the final massacre of Plains Indians, now found himself commanding the engines of the first modern war: trucks, tanks, poison gas and aircraft.

As a boy, my father Roy would sit by the woodstove in the mine store at Carneyville, Wyoming, and listen in fascination to tales of blanketed Sioux. Only a few years earlier, these men had killed Custer at the Little Bighorn and later fought his 7th Cavalry who were thirsting for revenge, and got it in the shameful shootdown at

Wounded Knee.

What a leap it must have been for Roy to remember this, when, by his mid-twenties, he'd be learning to fly the cranky Curtiss Jenny of World War I. The contraptions of flight were so new that the Army didn't know how to classify them, and finally dumped them into what they called Aviation Section Signal Corps. The only signal those planes would give would be nearly a century of dog fighting, dive bombing, fire bombing, and the final mushroom cloud of the atom. From the painted braves of Custer's Massacre, Roy lived to see men on the moon.

It was a mind-boggling, wrenching transition, but history gave us no choice. In the wiles of European statecraft and the red ink of international finance---money our banks had loaned to the Allies---we found ourselves swept back to the world the immigrants had left behind. Our leaders told us that the U.S. could never again go it alone, despite George Washington's warning that we should never involve ourselves in the bloodbaths of Europe.

We buried much of our immigrant dream in France. When our fathers came home, they rejoiced in the Boom, until, less than a decade later, and not knowing why, they had to begin mourning it in the Bust. And fearing for the future.

Wall Street crashed, along with world economies. The capitalistic free enterprise system so enshrined by the immigrants had failed to create the jobs or deliver the goods of the good life to enough of us. Now, the heirs of the immigrants, my father's generation, were cast adrift on the gray angry sea of the Depression. The immigrants had not been blinded by material possessions. But it was a different story with us, the inheritors. We'd fallen in love with our things. We'd felt that abundance was owed to us. We cherished respectability and acceptance into tight-fisted Yankee society.

Thus, when the Depression threatened to sweep it all away, we had no choice but to clutch our things more desperately, lashing ourselves harder and harder to protect what we had. So often during the Depression, I remember Roy coming home late from the office and sitting at the dinner table, chin in his hand and his face taut. Day after day he was having to bite the bullet, being the hard guy to relatives Will had endowed, closing the coal mines and piece-mealing off the empire Will had built. He used to tell me, "Never put off bad news. Get at it first thing in the morning. It won't go away."

It's human nature to be competitive, and no single trigger touches off an increase of it. But the Depression girded us with a special sort of fear. We felt as if we were in a war that swirled across the dark streets of Chicago. In "working class" neighborhoods where I wasn't supposed to go, I'd see angry men, warming themselves beside flame lit barrels, and trying to sell me an apple. When I'd refuse in fright, they'd say, "Fuck you, richie."

From our school games to our corporate boardrooms, we were honed on the Performance Ethic. Money-getting and money-keeping was to be our goal and meaning in life. We were judged on what we do, what we earn. Our embattled creed had shifted from Christ to Calvin: if it didn't hurt, it wasn't good for you. And lest we forget, we were raised on horror stories: "Three generations, shirtsleeves to shirtsleeves." "The squeaky wheel gets the grease."

In 1937, psychologist Karen Horney identified the forces that were detaching us from the true selves of our spirit: "Aggressiveness grown so pronounced that it could no longer be reconciled with Christian brotherhood; desire for material goods so vigorously stimulated that it can never be satisfied; expectations of untrammeled freedom soaring so high that they cannot be squared with the multitudes of restrictions and responsibilities that confine us all."

Relentlessly, we began to classify ourselves according to what achievements we'd made in competition with our peers. We learned to objectify each other as rivals in our fight through the jungle of the industrial world. In our schools and colleges, shadowed by the Depression, we learned that sports' letters, attractiveness, popularity and leadership were the attributes deemed essential for success. We wanted to be seen as comers so that we could separate ourselves from the pack and be guaranteed our share of the economic pie.

When I was at Princeton in 1941, one of my classmates was so desperate to "make" our eating club, he broke down before us and wept. He was a legacy of old immigrant wealth. Getting into our particular exclusive club was the last chance he felt he had to prove his social worth and value as a human being. But as one of our In-group put it, "Oh, don't take that clod. What's he ever *done?* He's a first-rate second-rate guy." And so, rejected, he sobbed away, a loser in a winner's world.

World War II hurled an even greater challenge at our competitive creed. For our very survival now, we had to let our killer reflexes take over. We did what humans have always done to justify war. The only way we could destroy our enemies was to whip up massive hatred against them.

In almost two years of flying in the Pacific, from Guadalcanal to Okinawa, my own objectifying of the enemy had so benumbed me that when we blew off our two atomic bombs, I had no feeling whatsoever for the burned ash streaks on the Japanese earth. I just thanked God that it was them, not us.

What none of us could foresee was that peace would never happen. The immigrant dream was long gone down. Those of us in the two world war generations now had to become defenders of our way of life.

From 1945 onward, we were asked to live the lie of the warfare state. For the first time in our history, we found ourselves literally scared to death. The atomic weapons we'd loosed on humanity were now poised to be used against us. We and the Russians alike were trapped in a mutual death dance of pathologic horror, lest either side be wiped out by another Pearl Harbor surprise attack.

My showbusiness adventure began with <u>Cinerama Holiday</u>. Despite my failure to shoot down the drone plane properly, the movie went on to become one of the top grosser of its year. But by the end of it I was too worn out even to feel elated.

For fourteen months I'd been herding my crew all over the U.S., filming Apaches in Arizona, a county fair in New Hampshire, jazz musicians on the Streetcar Named Desire in New Orleans and gamblers in Las Vegas.

But before we'd even taken the bows at the premiere, the reality of my future hit me like snake eyes on the crap table.

The movie was done. I was out of a job again. Where now?

It was choosing time again.

CHOOSING THE TRUE SELF

New York, April, 1955: My father, knowing I'm jobless, keeps saying, "Get on somebody's payroll!" Fine. But whose?

Then lightning strikes, blasting me up to one of New York's most exclusive clubs. My host runs one of the largest advertising agencies in the world. He's charming, fatherly and a true visionary. In the years before <u>Cinerama</u>, I've worked in the distant Chicago outpost of his agency. Back then I was a faceless wordsmith, earning more salary than I could ever be worth, all this for churning out TV commercials selling cheese or new refrigerators that open with a gentle whoosh.

But now the great man at the top has discovered me. He's seen <u>Cinerama</u>, and though I insist my work on it was fairly inconsequential, this leader won't be put off. "You've filmed," he says, "on many locations in the U.S. What I'm seeing is a spectacular new television show. It will be an hour in length every week. That's a departure from these ephemeral half hour programs, but we will dare to break fresh ground.

One client alone, our largest, will sponsor it. His desire and mine is to dramatize the greatness of America by telling the most uplifting stories of our past, and filming them on the actual places, the very land on which they happened. Could you create such a thing?" He smiles. "Of course you could!"

By then, I'm rising about three feet out of my chair. "It would be," I said hoarsely, "a landmark."

"Exactly! You have said it. That's the title!"

A waiter stands above us, bowing. "Your drinks, sir?

The great man has a modest white wine. I'm into stingers at the time. I've hardly sipped the first icy jolt before fear has gripped me. Could I do it? Wouldn't I want to? My God, what else did I have going for me right then?

Only this. There seemed to be two me's sitting at the table. One of them was the competitor, brazen young man on the move up, doing at last what my father, my peers and the world were shouting at me that I ought to be, had to be. The old "never enough" scenario that never ceases.

But then, timidly, the other me-voice kicks in. Don't you remember, though? You made a

171

commitment a long while back. You promised it to Teddy as well. Fumbling in this dialogue, I finally say of course I'm flattered, truly excited, but then it squeaks out: my secret vice. I'm really hoping to be a writer. Books.

"A writer?" He smiles, leans back in his chair and his visionary eyes sweep across the majestic city of lofting towers spread out before us. "Of course there's value in writing. There is a satisfaction in putting down good words. I sometimes do it myself. But from here…" his wine glass tracks slowly across the city… "you really do see a far bigger picture. Up here, you have the power, that's the difference. You can follow the tangential lines of force, move the pieces around on the chessboard in a far more meaningful way than you ever could sitting at a typewriter. You have to admit that's true."

In my frowning and fluttering, I was still trying to cope with the tangential lines of force. He must have understood that because he added, comfortingly, "If this dream of mine works out--- and I know you're the man to do it---I'm prepared to make you the vice-president in charge of all television for us. And from there, the presidency of the agency, I would say, could have a real chance of becoming yours."

I thanked him and asked him to give me a day or two to think it over. That night, I rushed back to Teddy in Lake Forest. In my months away on Cinerama, we'd bought a small house. I'd missed our three boys so much that I'd hardly recognized them when I came home. We'd resolved to settle here, and I'd become an unemployed freelance writer. Teddy had even fixed up an office for me in an adjacent loft that had been for servants.

From my desk, I could look out on trees and heavy grass where my Labrador would race off and retrieve the corncob pipes I'd thrown away. But everybody else, I could see from my "writer office" window, was rattling in on the old Chicago Northwestern commuting train. How come I considered myself so special, touched by the gods of muse, that I was above it now?

For me at least, the Competitor Ethic branded on us in the Depression had left enduring scars. Before <u>Cinerama</u>, when I'd decided to leave what Mother called the "legitimate" business of advertising and start working at home freelancing, one of the suburb's matrons was shocked. "At home?" she asked, "Why aren't you on the Train, commuting to the city?"

I mumbled something about my writing

dream, but the woman couldn't process it. Nobody we knew *wrote*. Sympathetically, she said, "This flu that's going around is a terrible bug. You just rest at home a few days, you'll get over it."

I never did. Decades later, when Teddy and I decided to raise our kids out on a cattle ranch, one of their godmothers said in alarm: "It may be fine for a summer vacation, but it's so risky. Suppose they get to *like* the life?"

To the competitors, liking, loving your living, trying to get at the truth of yourself instead of denying your spirit in acceptable work---no, that was the ultimate cop-out. The societal death sentence.

But that night when I came home to Lake Forest and told Teddy about my luncheon in the clouds in New York, the Landmark dream, she was as stunned as I'd been. But the more we talked about it, the more doubts crept in. "Oh, darling," she said, "of course it would be wonderful, you'd probably make a fortune, never worry about money again. We could have a big house in Greenwich like they all do. But that's not us, is it? And truly not you. Even when we were courting in New York, remember how you used to say, We'll get out of this some way.

You've always had a longing to be part of the land, a far simpler community somewhere in the West. Can we really give all of that up?"

We didn't. The next day, on the phone, I tell the great fatherly man no. He understands, but in a compromise, he makes me a consultant. Hollywood is where they make real movies, not <u>Cinerama</u>. He moves us there, cats, Labradors, kids, bag and baggage. We can't afford to buy a house so we rent a dump up Benedict Canyon, not all that far from the Beverly Hills Hotel where the stars go to dine.

Landmark? Sure, I create it, write down a dozen or so great American stories to be filmed on the land where they happened. Our client, the Ford Motor Company loves it. So will their Ford dealers scattered across the land. I scurry around and get Columbia Pictures to say they'll take a chance. They'll film it, they and Ford sharing ownership of the priceless epic.

We're at the threshold of glory. And the door slams. The great TV networks want absolutely nothing to do with an hour show. No one has ever tried one of that length. Walt Disney was flacking some silly hour called <u>Disneyland</u> and he'd already been turned down by 42 agencies and clients. Furthermore, the networks would not put on a foot of film unless they owned it. By then the Supreme Court has decided that the networks, instead of just being a show window, could actually own the product.

Landmark dies. I'm not consulted, out of a job again. All that's left is to burrow myself into the one piece of ground our rented house has. A swimming pool with a tiny poolhouse about the size of the cockpits I used to fly in during the war. Here, perilously, I drown my sorrows in writing a novel, <u>When the Bough Breaks</u>, the Bough being the security we've left behind.

Security, what is that? e.e. cummings said, and I put him on the frontispiece. Then, years later, I use him again in this book: "To be nobody but yourself in a world that's doing its best to make you into everybody else, means to fight the hardest battle any human can ever fight, and keep on fighting."

About a year later, one of the same networks that turned us down hires me to write for them the identical two stories that I'd planned as the opening guns of Landmark. The first show was the killing of Sitting Bull, the second, The Massacre at Wounded Knee. Because the network owned the films, it was now proper and commercial to do hour programs and history. So the bugles blew and the cavalry charged, under the grand banner, <u>The Great Adventure.</u>

By 1958, Teddy and I and our boys were rooted into Beverly Hills, and to pay the freight on the trip, between my novels, I was relentlessly hammering out mind candy for TV.

By now, Hollywood has come down on the Wild West with all four feet and guns blazing. I've just written the opening TV show for Dick Powell's <u>Zane Grey Theater</u>. Powell, the ex-crooner, has for his Four Star Partners David Niven, Charles Boyer and June Allyson. But on this critical first show, because it's the one that gets the ratings, Powell himself has the lead.

I've written him as a lithe, brave cavalry officer whose beautiful wife has just cuckolded him. How brave is he? Does Dick shoot down the dirty dog who's been fooling with his wife while he has been out fighting Apaches? Or, is he tall enough timber simply to forgive and forget her?

We hold the suspense, the twists and turns, it's called, until the very last scene. Here in the lonely desert sunset, to a background of Army wagons, mounted troopers and a few cowed Apaches, Dick and Maggie, his lovely auburn haired wife, have their moment of truth. Dick, grim at having been shamed, kisses Maggie goodbye. He turns, mounts his horse and courageously begins to ride away. Maggie, pleading, runs after him. She clings to his leg on the saddle. On her anguish is the last closeup. Dick pats her head, releases her and rides on alone to the fade out.

I'm up at my house in Benedict Canyon trying to forget the whole thing. A call from the studio. "Otis, you've got to get down here. Trouble."

Now the last person they ever want on a set is the writer, so this is highly unusual. I rush over the hill to Studio City and into the cavernous sound stage. Dick, a genial fellow, is seated in a camp chair having a Scotch. He beckons at me and gives me a plastic cupful. His Cavalry blouse is unbuttoned, he looks concerned, even drawn. "Otis," he says, "that last scene. I just can't do it, fella. We need something else in here."

"Well, why Dick or what?"

There is no why, just a shrug. Doesn't work. So we sit there for five minutes, draining Scotch and empty of ideas. Now this is a cost factor. Surrounding us are all the wagons, horses plopping out manure, Hollywood Indian Apaches sweating in their black wigs, to say nothing of studio crew delighting in letting the payroll clock tick on. Finally Dick says he has to drain out some of the Scotch and heads for the porta-potty.

It's a moment of destiny. The old assistant director takes me by the arm and draws me aside. "Look, kid," he says, "there ain't nothing wrong with the scene. It's just Dick. You got him mounting that horse…"

"Right. He has to exit some way."

"He don't like mounting horses. He's too big in the butt. You're gonna see only butt in that shot, and what's more, Maggie, clinging to him, she gets the final closeup. He's the star, not her."

Well, whaddya know? Dick comes back a moment later and I say, "I've got it. Dick, you don't mount the horse. You stay right on the ground and lead him away. We lose Maggie and you get the final closeup."

He grips my arm and gives me that bandleader smile. "Perfect, Otis. Places, everybody. This is a take."

What does it take to beat the ego?

Movies and TV are about the last place you'd ever want to try to do it. But I still didn't know that. I had to keep running the laugh track to the final fade to black.

At least, though, by that time, I'd begun to realize that there was something else out there that people called spirit. If I could ever come to understand it, God willing, maybe it might even get me out of the box of myth and let me inch my way toward truth.

A SPIRITUAL JOURNEY

When we were filming <u>Cinerama Holiday,</u> we did a sequence in a church in Louisiana, the black congregation joyously booming out the grand old spiritual "Down By The Riverside."

The second line was: "I ain't gonna study war no more, I ain't gonna study war no more."

Soul war, they were talking about, the fight between our ego selves and our spirit ones.

In those years, while I was floundering around groping for the spirit, Teddy was more and more diligently into deep-dish spirituality. She can listen for hours to tapes or wade through industrial-strength theology tomes that glaze my eyes over on page one. She's an intellectual, devouring ideas I simply can't swallow with my limited equipment. I tell her it's because she grew up in the South where beauty was worshipped and a pretty girl wasn't supposed to have a brain. All these years, she's been proving the good ole boys wrong.

When her desire for sanctity began seriously to include me, I felt like the warning when the Teletubby dolls were introduced, "Be very afraid." She was determined to get me out of my spiritual closet. Straight from Calvin: "If it didn't hurt, it wasn't good for me."

Oh-oh, I thought, what now? In the past, I'd usually send her off alone to her retreats, seminars and holy gatherings that our sons call "Catholic Camps." But this time was going to be very different. She was going to take me 10,000 miles around the world to an ashram in southern India.

When I protested, she reminded me of all the lousy fishing trips she'd gone on with me, far off in the Pacific "to those mosquitoey dumps that didn't even have seats on the toilets." Had she ever complained? Of course not. So why couldn't I give her the one spiritual trip she really wanted? "And besides, darling," she conned me further, "we'll be there for your birthday. The ashram is on a river. Maybe you could even fish. Please. It'll be an adventure…"

When a friend heard we were going, he warned: "Dangerous stuff, Carney." A couple he knew had gone to "one of those places." The wife had gotten so much religion she ran off with the guru and hasn't been heard from since.

Now I wasn't at all worried about Teddy doing that, but I have a bad habit of being too protective about her. Too possessive. Thus, my negative emotions snapped me shut like a knife. Here I was being dragged into something "foreign," probably regimented, and I wanted no part of it.

The ashram, south of Madras, India was called Shantivanam. Teddy insists still that it's a heavenly place, garden walks and thatch roof cottages. It undoubtedly is, but I missed something in the translation. The melody that came to my mind when we got there was: "It's Only a Shanty in Old Shantytown."

To me, the place looked like our tent camp on Guadalcanal that I'd tried to forget for forty years. Yes, there were palm trees here and no Jap snipers in them that I could see, but the hapless scatter of housing in the coconut grove ranged from thatch-roofed barracks to abandoned surplus shacks from the British Army during the Raj time. In the miasmic heat every possible kind of insect flew or crawled, and the smell from the chow-line made me want to fast for life.

No sooner had we logged in and been assigned our penitent hutch, we were called to assembly in a tent-like chamber known as a yert. Rhymes with "hurt" which was the reason we'd come.

Father Bede Griffiths, the guru of the ashram,

was already intoning: "The ego of western man is out of control."

Mine sure was. I felt like Alec Guinness buried alive in the tin house in <u>The Bridge on the River Kwai.</u>

"For God's sake, darling," I whispered to Teddy. "This is supposed to be my birthday, cooped up here listening to a lecture!"

"Just try it," she said savagely, "and stop talking."

In the yert, which was sighing in shimmering heat vapors, dozens of our fellow penitents were seated yoga style on the hard dirt floor. My bony butt groaned, and all the old horse falls that had crunched my spine began telegraphing sciatic screams down my over-length legs, which weren't designed to be jackknifed into the closed position.

Teddy and I were the only American sinners who had come this far to be cleansed. We were also, I noted, the only married couple, and worse, the only Lawrence Welk generation folks, stuffed in here beside young searchers from India, England, Europe and Asia. Most of them had arrived lugging backpacks filled with worn spiritual treatises. Their bodies were so supple and suffered they could knot themselves into instant yoga positions. They thrived on moaning the chants and having sacred oils ungented on their foreheads. They had inexhaustible patience, soaking up like sponges the torturous theological tracings of Eastern religions interweaving with Christianity.

Father Bede Griffiths, whom Teddy wanted so much to hear, was clearly a brilliant and holy man. His books were internationally known. People came from far and wide for his teachings. An English Benedictine monk educated at Oxford, he'd gone to India years before because he felt that if Christianity were to survive, it would have to reconnect with the parallel roots of Eastern religions. The West should learn from them and end the dualism between body and soul that was robbing us of our wholeness.

Probably it's the Irish in me, feeling that God intended life to be joyous, a lark, lived to its fullest. God, I think, wants me to love myself, take care of my flesh, not drive nails into it and then hate myself for being so weak.

In the steamy yert, I sat as if at a tennis game. The spiritual ball would ping from white-haired Father Bede across the net to the penitents. They'd stroke it and send it back, zinging with some new ideological top spin, some detail the

Upanishads had uncovered centuries before Christ. Father Bede was a helluva back court man. He returned everything.

I squirmed and pained and looked pleadingly at Teddy. But she had trapped me in the first row, no escape possible without clumping over the lotus folded bodies. After the first hour, she wouldn't even look at me. She was too busy writing down everything Bede said.

Along about three in the afternoon, when the temperature had cooled to 90, the endless spiritual tennis dribbled to match point. Eagerly Teddy joined the other straights and trooped off to the thatch chapel where incense burning and team chanting were already in progress.

I fled down to the riverside. It was water, all right, an expanse of trickling yellow mud about a half mile wide. Upstream, I could see whitish herds of sacred Brahman cows dumping and peeing in it. Closer, clumps of soggy Indian women were washing clothes and slapping them on hot rocks. Undoubtedly thousands of others were doing that or worse for the hundreds of miles the river flowed. Then, nearby, I spotted an Indian kid, seated in lotus position and dunking a bamboo pole.

"Fish?" I said.

"Yes," he was answering , but in the Dravidian tic of southern India was shaking his head as if he meant "no." I said, Show me some fish. A few moments later, he pulled in a minnow about three inches long. When I reached out to identify its species, he popped it into his mouth and ate it.

By then, my thermostat was on boil. Guadalcanal was the Alps compared to this inferno. I stripped off and plunged into the kid's fishing hole. Thunk! Ten inches of water for three inch fish. I felt like a mud wrestler, wallowing on TV. Swimming was impossible. All I could do was to lie on my back, cooling myself like a water buffalo, and taking pains lest a drop of the offal water from upstream touch my lips.

Scraping the mud off, I went back to our thatch barracks. It was now dusk. Some new form of chanting was going on in the candlelit chapel. To fend off the possible diaharreal effects of my swim, I rummaged out my pipe and a plastic jug of Scotch. Then, sembling I was a penitent going for meditation, I skulked back down by the riverside and began sinning again.

When I groped over to the mess hall, (Teddy's correction: "a beautiful building") I found it lit by weak, naked bulbs. The penitents were all there,

187

operating on a schedule of events I wasn't party to. I wriggled through them and creaked down beside Teddy. We were seated on a stone floor, not a cushion in sight, legs folded under us. Father Bede was intoning Grace in several languages. Well, I thought, if silence was over, at least now we might have some dinner conversation. Then on came an ancient Victrola with a monk in some obscure language spooling out a rich doze of new theology.

Our first meal at the ashram: Teddy's version: "Otis was sitting akimbo, his bony limbs trying to find rest on the cold cement floor. He was slouched over his tin plate pursing his lips and staring in utter disbelief at the foreign mounds, spiced far beyond his palate. He'd sigh, purse his lips again and again, and finally, like a child handling a dead worm, would bring some little wad up to his mouth. I had to clutch my sides and look away to keep from laughing. When I finally got him a spoon, he'd hold it like a biology student about to dissect his first frog. Even the porridge, which he normally tolerates, was repellent to him. After minutes of dejected examination, he'd just give up, unable to cope with the brownish lumps, and most of all, the lack of choices."

My version:

Barefoot Indians and nuns began passing among us carrying bowls of gruel, formed, ricey gruel that they slapped on out plates with a rusty ice cream scoop. Next came steamy bowls of brown liquid wriggling with unidentified objects resembling portions of worms. I glanced around for a knife and fork. Forget it! This was manually operated feeding, everybody bending over their tin plates and slurping the stuff into their mouths. Some were even smiling. How yummy!

I gulped. I wanted to throw up. Teddy jabbed me in the ribs. Don't be such a baby. Slowly, I tasted the gruel---and my lips went on fire. Heavy duty curry, had to be to keep the concoction from rotting in the heat. Next came soggy pancake-type objects, tasting like library paste. I was so busy with the food, I missed the final blessing.

Teddy went off to evening vespers, which went about eleven innings and took several hours. By then, I was getting separation anxiety. I hoped she wasn't back in the toilet room again. That afternoon, to be a devoted penitent, she'd joined some of the European hippie girls in swabbing out the latrine. They'd used straw pads which, God willing, were not the same ones we'd cleaned our plates with!

When she finally came into the darkness of our bower, I stabbed my penlight at her. She was in her nightie and smiling, as if: "Happy Birthday, darling."

Our beds were two singles, two boards per, just wide enough for a very starved down martyr. And exactly far enough apart so that I could reach over and touch Teddy's weak flesh---down, boy, not here! The walls of the cell were about five feet high, and above them dark airspace up to the thatch roof. An airspace that was becoming filled with the grunts, snores, sneezes and farts of our fellow penitents, processing dinner. Though in our separate cells we might as well have been face to face, none of our neighbors were married, of course, devout women bunking with women and men with men.

"For God's sake," I seethed to Teddy, crouching on hard stone beside her ear. "This is supposed to be fun? Our romantic vacation!"

"Oh, you are so spoiled, rotten spoiled!"

"Damn right I am!"

"I really want to do this, and if you can't take it, then please go someplace and leave me alone. It will be a relief not having to worry about you!"

"Don't you miss a minute of it," I said,

casting myself down on my hard, lonely boards. But not for long. Bells and chanting wrenched me up at 4:30 a.m. I bailed out just in time to avoid another breakfast, by some miracle locating a car that rocketed me to a plane, and finally to a beach hotel as far away as I could get. They had window screens here, lovely Eurasian girls swimming in the Indian Ocean, and a big double bed that yearned for its empty half.

When it was too hot to swim, I lay under a palm tree and scrawled angry notes about the excesses of punishing religion, which I felt was keeping these Eastern and Asian peoples in bondage. I'd seen it in the Hindu temples and Muslim shrines in Singapore. If their custom worked for them, that was their business, but to me there was a heartless futility in sacred cows being kept fat while humans starved and died in the streets. Did God really want us to accept and ignore such suffering just because sects of men had invoked it in his name?

To pick up my particular Cross meant to give of my time and money, didn't it? But how? Lay my hands on the sick, as Mother Theresa was doing? Or try to heal the brutalized, the walking wounded of our system by accepting and loving them, as they are. Or could I become an advocate to help change the system? If I had a calling, it was only to do what I believed God was telling me to do, and to be detached and not caring enough---to be stilled enough to hear. In groping for my own truth, perhaps my tiny voice was all I could give, and pray that God heard it, too.

With some reluctance, after three weeks, Teddy finally agreed to leave the saints in the ashram and come home to the sinner. As we drove away from Shantivanam, an Indian couple she'd befriended began clinging to our car. They were Biblically named Joseph and Mary. Teddy had already bought some pajamas from them for our granddaughters. But now their medical problems had become acute, Joseph trotting beside the car and imploring me with his X-rays and letters of doom from doctors.

I rented us the bridal suite in a small town Indian hotel, clean enough but the door handle kept coming off in my hand. We had to wait here to get out of India which you don't do readily and without pain. In the middle of the night, Teddy caught the pain. She was running a raging fever and doubled over in stomach complaints. At daybreak, I rushed her to a gloomy stone mausoleum that was the local hospital.

Because it was Sunday morning, only a small

staff was on hand. The stone corridors of the hospital were filled with suffering Indian men, women and children; mothers were solacing wailing babies, old people were hugging each other as if there were no tomorrow. Teddy was flushed with fever, lying on a wooden bench with me stroking her head in my lap and loving her very much.

A young Indian woman doctor rescued us. She was bright and English-trained. "Oh, yes," she sighed. "The ashram at Shantivanam. They are friends of ours, of course, and good people. But we have warned them many times: please do something about your well. It's so shallow you are drinking ground water, and God knows what that's filled with."

When people ask me: What did you learn from the Indian experience?

Only this: what a long way I still had to go, if ever, to reach Teddy's level of devotion. To learn what she knew in her heart and by heart. Just let go to wherever the spirit led her.

We never dreamed where it was about to lead both of us.

PARADISE ISLAND

In 1973, my father Roy died. I missed him so much. It was as if the captains and the kings had departed, and I was at a loss now to know how I'd make it on my own.

All the politics I'd written, all the angry novels had been only paper airplanes floating off to nowhere. All the anti-war words I'd spewed out hadn't done a thing to shield us from the Vietnam disaster. Teddy's younger brother Bill, who'd been raised on my Marine tales, quit school and joined the Corps himself. Spent two nasty tours in the front lines as a radioman, the one Charlie always shot first. He came home, like many, dismayed. Tom and John, our oldest two boys, just graduated from Yale and Stanford and plunging out into the hippie revolution, a divided nation.

In asking what had become of us, I couldn't help but remember the values of my father. No matter what island I was on, in whatever mail call in the rain, there was always a letter from him. Giving me hope, giving me love.

By early 1974, I wanted to take Teddy on a

slow boat to China, just the two of us again, trying to figure out where our world was anymore. So I wonder now if it wasn't love that led me back to the Pacific, in a search to try to get beyond war and mostly, hopefully, the war in me.

A 727 jet of Air Micronesia was our slow boat. Sometimes the young Vietnam vet pilots would let me sit up in the cockpits and body-english their screaming landings on tiny coral rocks. We didn't hit Guadalcanal, the Solomons or that South Seas part. It took us weeks, in fact, slogging back just to revisit Guam and Pelelieu.

I was not only drained by the heat which had never bothered me at 22, but more than this, the rust, junk and death still staining all the islands seemed so forgotten, so meaningless. Finally I just wanted to get the hell home and forget it. But Teddy said, No, we'd come this far, we had to take it through to the end, which was our last scheduled stop, Truk atoll.

It was not a memory that I wanted to re-live.

Far out in the Caroline Islands, Truk had been the main Japanese fortress in the Pacific. It was their Pearl Harbor from which their fleets and aircraft had been attacking us throughout the war. Truk's giant scatter of islands were so impregnable that all of us dreaded going anywhere near them.

Unfortunately, we didn't have a choice. After General Geiger had declared Guam secured, we flew him back to his headquarters on Guadalcanal. To keep him out of harm's way, we'd had to give Truk a wide berth, flying instead via the safe Marshall island of Eniwetok and then south to the Solomons.

It was a grueling 17 hour trip. We were all pretty jumpy and worn out. For two weeks during the Guam battle, we'd been living under the wing of our plane, being treated nightly to sniper fire, and in one case, to a Japanese soldier who must have stepped right over us, but mercifully left us alone. His target was a Corsair fighter parked next to us. He crawled in behind the armor seat and when the Marine pilot got into the cockpit for a dawn flight, the Japanese blew up the plane and himself with two grenades. The pilot wasn't even scratched. The Japanese hadn't figured on the armor seat.

We'd no sooner landed Geiger safely on Guadalcanal when he came up into the cockpit and told us that we'd have to turn around as soon as we were gassed up, and fly back to Guam that same night. But this night, which was August 13,

1944, we wouldn't have the luxury of taking the long way around. Instead, he was sending us directly through the lethal Truk airspace.

The urgency, we were later told, was to bring back to Geiger crates of plans for the Pelelieu operation, less than a month away. His staff officers had been working on them during the Guam operation.

To make the trip by this quickest route, we'd have to fly a thousand miles north from a U.S. held island, Emirau. The idea was to sneak past Truk the first night, and if we made it, turn around and tip-toe back the same route the next night. We'd have to do it alone, no escort. Fighters didn't have the range to accompany us. The Navy commander at Emirau had just had a patrol bomber shot down in the same vicinity. He tried to cancel our flight but Geiger countermanded him. Send them, the General said, and we went. Our only armament was two Thompson submachine guns.

To pull it off, we'd have to hit in the darkness a 60 mile slot between two atolls, Puluwat and Lamotrek, less than a hundred miles from the main Truk atoll. One had an enemy fighter strip, the other a seaplane base. Should we drift too close to either one, their radar would pick us up and they'd blow us out of the sky.

We were lucky the first night. The stars were out. Using celestial navigation, we strained our eyes for any speck of island below us, but saw only the blackness of the sea. We must have hit the slot. Landing in the dawn at Guam, we slept all day in a wrecked building. By dusk, somebody rousted us out. We went down to Orote strip and loaded aboard the crates of plans for Pelelieu that the staff officers were working on.

Then came a moment of truth. Standing beside our faithful, coral-caked R4D (the old DC-3 of the airlines), which at the blinding speed of 140 knots had so long carried us safely through all Geiger's battlegrounds---we stood and stared up at the sky. Rain was already stinging our faces. No problem, we'd had a year and a half so far of fighting angry Pacific weather. But nothing like the cyclonic wind that was hitting us now and tearing off our baseball caps. One of the blackest, lightning-flashed storms we'd ever seen was roaring down on Guam. A bitch, almost hurricane strength. We'd have to sock right into it to get home.

We'd barely roared up off of Orote strip before the rain began lacing us as if some giant were flinging buckets of gravel into our face.

Blinding waves of rain were so powerful that they hammered through the frayed rubber window seals and soaked us in the cockpit. The turbulence was violent. We'd pop down landing gear and flaps, cut throttle trying to slow the roller coaster, but massive thunderheads were flinging us two thousand feet a minute upward at 95 knots. We'd tremble there a moment, pick up flaps and gear, shove throttles to the firewall. No use. The next thunderhead would slam us roaring back down, two thousand feet a minute, engines screaming at 195 knots which was far more than the plane should stand.

We were wildly out of control. No visible sky above, no sea below. We had no stars to shoot, no drift sights, nothing to steer by. It was impossible to hit our slot between Puluwat and Lamotrek. It was strictly dead reckoning now, and if we reckoned wrong, dead we'd likely be.

When we neared the estimated position of Puluwat and Lamotrek, we shut off our radios. We literally tried to whisper past whatever was below us. When the radioman spotted running lights paralleling us, he shouted: "Jap!" It must have been. We think a Betty bomber, heavily armed and possibly looking for us in the wildness of the storm.

The only thing we could do was to plunge into massive, fisting thunderheads and lose ourselves. The Pacific at night is such an enormous blackness that when you're lost within it, you almost want to weep at the futility of ever hoping to survive such violence. And we had five hours of it still to go.

We'd zigged and zagged so much that finally we had no idea where the tiny speck of Emirau island lay. Our one hope by then was to pick up either the radio range or the homing beacon that had been recently installed on the island. But these were still primitive instruments, reaching only a hundred miles or so. The static of the storm was also garbling the signals. We tried the radio range and its signal never seemed to get louder. Then we switched to the homer with the same result. In the darkness of the cockpit we stared at each other. What the hell was going on? On the radio compass dial, the range and the homer were giving us positions sixty degrees apart. How could this be when the island was so small that the two transmission towers had to be less than a mile apart.

We had to choose. Which was the true signal?

For some reason, we chose the homer and began roaring down its dark path in the sky.

Several moments later, the radioman thrust into the cockpit. Good kid, he wouldn't give up. He was clenching a frequency book. Townsville, Australia, he cried, had the same frequency as the homer on Emirau. Could it be that in the violence of the storm, Townsville's stronger signal was hitting the ionosphere and bouncing back to us? If that were the case, at 8,000 feet, we were minutes away from slamming into the 12,000 foot Owen Stanley Range in New Guinea.

We made a screaming turn off of the homer and back onto the weaker range. The signal didn't grow or give any hope that we were closing on the island. It was procedure to use a new code book for every day, the radioman tapping out puzzles in Morse that the enemy couldn't break. But we were way past that now. Navy regs went out the window. In forbidden plain English, we begged Emirau tower that if they heard us, turn a searchlight up at the sky.

I don't know how long it took then, still banging around in rain and fisted by thunderheads. In gritted silence, staring at our faces in the cockpit windshield, one of us cried out. A distant flash of light in the dark clouds. We broke into a cheer, roaring down a few minutes later onto the rain-soaked Emirau runway. Our gas gauge needles were ticking on empty.

Well, we'd made it, beat the sky. And the rest of the trip would be a lark. We only had five hours left to Guadalcanal, but we'd be flying now down across the conquered islands, the Solomons Slot, an American lake. We gassed up and at about 2 a.m. took off again.

We hadn't even reached cruising altitude when the radioman rushed up to the cockpit. Our IFF---identification friend or foe signal--- had just burned out. Meaning that for the next five hours, we'd be showing up on radar as a Japanese bogey. On all the various islands we'd be passing, eager U.S. night fighters would be scrambling, howling up, homed into us by radar. Just lock on---boom!

We sent the radioman back to get on his key, and one by one rattle out to every squadron that we were friendly, leave us the hell alone, and pray. We fled through the long darkness with our shoulders hunched up, waiting for the flash that never came. Somebody had us by the hand. The first real light we saw were streaks of dawn, over the jungles of Guadalcanal. Somebody said, "That lovely sonofabitch," and we went on in to land.

So why was it, I wonder, that now, nearly 30 years later, I'd be in a Pacific rain squall again, down on the coral of that once-fearsome island, Truk. Though I was already soaked, I happened to run down the beach and take shelter under the palm fronds of a fisherman's shack. Beside me was the fisherman himself, a brown-skinned Trukese native in a breechclout. He was trying to light his limp home-made cigarette. Fortunately, I had the kind of Zippo we used in the war.

We stood there like wet puppies, grinning in a kind of smoker's pidgin English. On the wet skin of his back, I noticed ugly scars, great long welts. How come? I asked. "Japan time," he said. They had bayonetted him and forced him to work for them building airfields. He sucked at the cigarette and his coffee eyes studied me. "You know Japan time? You come here like other 'Merican guys, break oil tanks, plenty smoke, bomb going off?"

I said no, that was the big carrier strike in '44, but a few months later, I did fly near here for a couple of nights, through Puluwat and Lamotrek.

He howled. "Lamotrek!" He clasped my hand, then threw his arms around me. "I raised on Lamotrek! Home island. Maybe I there them nights! Look up in sky, see you!"

With the rain drumming the thatch roof, we

talked long of the wartime days until finally he gripped both of my hands. "Yah, we same, you know us here, we friends. Hey, 'Merican guy, I got place you gonna see. Beautiful. Best we got. Tomorrow, I take you in my fishing boat. What you think? We go Paradise Island!

Oh, come on, I thought. Was this a tourist scam or something he was making up?

But Paradise existed and we went to it the next day. Max, the fisherman, his boat boy David, Teddy, and me. At the last minute, while we were loading our gear into Max's boat, a shy young Japanese approached us. He did the requisite bows, and asked to be taken along on the trip.

Max scowled and said something in Japanese that must have been nasty. The young man flinched but still smiled. Max shrugged then, life is like that in the islands. Accept. So we had a passenger from Tokyo. Akio was his name, an earnest young employee of the Japanese Tourist Bureau. Down here to explore tourist facilities in the area.

As we roared across Truk lagoon, the largest in the world, I think Akio began to regret coming along. Max was running the tiller of his outboard with his bare foot, and even over the noise of his

Johnson 50 horse, he was barking angry Japanese at Akio. They were re-fighting their war now, obviously the abuses Max had suffered as a prisoner. Akio would turn away, his face so tight with humiliation that Teddy and I felt embarrassed to watch. But then, like an island storm, it swept on past. Max scrambled up to the bow and flung out his arm. "There, 'Merican guy! Paradise!"

It was spectacular, a fragment of island no more than a reef, white sand beaches shaded with palms. Inland, beyond a thicket of heavy mangroves, I could make out the seaward side, naked battlements of coral, pounded by the open Pacific and thundering misty spume hundreds of feet into the air. The roar was constant and awesome, a symphony of rainbows, seabirds arching in screaming parabolas and plunging into the shattering waves for prey.

Max slowed the boat and we glided over vermilion and ochre coral gardens. Schools of brightly colored fish drifted below us through forests of yellow lace. They didn't seem to sense our presence. They made no attempt to run away. When Teddy and I slid into the warm softness of the water and coasted through the coral gardens in the hiss of our snorkels, the fish were so tame they'd stream between our legs. Some would even gup their mouths on the strange taste of our tennis shoes.

"Bad sharks here?" I asked David, our boat boy who was paddling beside us. He was grinning, wearing a mar-mar headband of green leaves. "No bad." A moment later, a dark shadow appeared in my face mask. An eight foot shark, lazily studying us and drifting on past.

The scene was so fierce and primeval that I seemed to lose consciousness of time and my place within it. Here, I was part of the eternal struggle of the coral to replenish itself. I was the crash and suck and refueling of the waves, my energy somehow tied to all of it. The trembling reef beneath my feet was connected in its bedrock to the ancient burned-out volcanoes that had formed the atolls of Puluwat and Lamotrek. My nights of fear above those islands---how insignificant they'd been against nature's flaming battle through her eons of time. That was the real and only war, the nobility of her life force, pulsing in every particle of living matter, coding into them the ultimate meaning that life would prevail.

Behind me I heard a human cry, and reluctantly I turned away from the thundering reef. Akio was dog-paddling toward me, spluttering apologies. I'd loaned him my spin-fishing rod, and he'd lost my only lure. He was determined to send me a dozen lures from Japan.

I smiled and told him to forget it. We hadn't really come here to fish. But as we paddled on together into a hidden bay, I spotted something that wrenched me back to the past, and old wars gone down.

A silver metal fin was protruding from the shallow water. I gulped a deep breath and dove, then blew out a gasp of astonishment. Resting on the soft sand bottom was a Zero fighter, not a mark of rust on it or a scar. It appeared to have landed here moments before. I clung to the canopy of the open cockpit, fully expecting to see a skeleton within. But there was only emptiness and the red needle of the airspeed indicator ticking in tiny bubbles.

Akio clung to the tail section as I made repeated dives. In the sand I found a fragment of the Zero's wing flap, which seemed to be the only damage when the pilot crash-landed. As I carried the relic back to shore, my mind was spinning. Who was in that plane? Had he been some eager young kid, fighting our fleet in the carrier strike? Did he parachute out? Or could it have been possible that he, too, had been ordered to fly that night of August 14, sent up into the storm to chase an American bogey that had somehow slipped away between Puluwat and Lamotrek?

I sat in the warm sand and studied the fragment of the wing flap. Akio knelt beside me. I showed him splinters of wood, laminated between the Zero's outer skin. I was amazed that they'd used wood. Akio nodded. Yes, bamboo. That's all Japan had left by the end of the war.

His voice had tightened, his eyelids squeezed shut. In dignity, he was weeping. At first I pretended not to notice, but then he touched my arm gently and said, "It is Japan's fault, all this here. Fighting war. So much destruction, so much horror we caused. I knew nothing about it. I wasn't born then. But my father had to go. He fought..." He shook his head and tears ran down his cheeks. "What we did, I am so sorry..."

When I answered, my throat was tight. "It's nobody's fault," I said. "Put it behind us. It's done now."

Then, in a moment, the awkwardness was gone. From down the beach Max was shouting to us. He'd speared a giant clam and came sloshing in from the reef with a purpling, blobby object in his hand. By the time Akio and I reached him, he'd sliced the muscle from the clam and was drenching it in lime juice and soy sauce. We ate it raw, washing it down with Kirin beer, and then stretched out under the palm trees.

Teddy lay sunburned in the sand and looked as lithe as she had at 21. Even the sea tousle of my hair I could consider as resembling salt, not grey. Whatever our delusions, we felt youth and liberation, unfettered by wrist watches and baggage. Trukese, Japanese, American, we seemed joined into the life force, our strangeness to each other and our enmities fading away.

As if to heighten the unreality, we began hearing new sounds from out on the reef. Distant dots moved toward us across the coral flats until they became native canoes. Tapping their paddles against the wooden hulls, two boatloads of Trukese fishermen glided up to our beach. Max hailed them and they spilled out, the women waddling up in their bright mumus, several of them squatting shamelessly in the shallows to complete their toilets before joining us. Max told me that these were several families of fishermen, from babes at the breast to wizened elders with blue tattoos in the wrinkles of their cheeks. They lay with us in the shade of the mangroves, their brown limbs melting into the sand in instant relaxation.

Soon, with Max translating, they began telling us tales of the great ocean voyages of the Micronesian people. They spoke of the Magic Men who were trained generation after generation to guide the canoes across thousands of miles of open sea. Riding with them, too, were the Navigator Men who could track the stars with the naked eye, watch the direction of birds and the coloration of the water to give them their bearings.

Sea life, they called it, and to preserve their lives on their journeys was the Shark Man. Trained from childhood to sing a special mantra, he could slip into the water and confront a massive shark that was threatening the canoe. Because ocean waves swamped the boats, these Micronesians were often sitting in water with the shark's great fin only a few feet away. But armed only with his mantra chant, the Shark Man would approach the monster, gentle him until he could rub his belly. Then he'd slip a mar mar of palm leaves over the shark's head and he'd drift harmlessly away.

I glanced at Teddy. She was sitting bolt upright, half-frown, half rapture. Could we believe such a thing? No, certainly not back home in our normal lives. But Paradise Island, the sudden confronting of the past buried within us, the primeval spirit---was this not also home, the real one?

Then, like most moments of grace, too soon it was over. Without any predetermined signal, the Trukese left us, their laughter trailing down to their canoes; their footprints in the sand were slowly washed away by the creeping tide.

They disappeared toward the falling sun until they were tiny specks again, floating off to probe some other reef. We, too, departed then, our bodies sunburned, our limbs soft and nerveless from hours in the sea. As we rumbled across the enormity of Truk atoll, a night of yellowish stars closed over us. Sometime in the long trip home, Akio, perhaps thinking of his own wife, said to Teddy: "Ah, madam, please tell me: what flowers do you choose for your arrangements?"

I stared at him in the darkness. You, my enemy? You the demon I was taught to hate? Something in me died here, and was being reborn.

Then the enormity of stars closed over us. In the rising of the moon, the Southern Cross was still as bright as it was that night it navigated us through those islands. Teddy smiled at Akio and told him the flowers she likes in her arrangements. Together, with only the boat's silver wake to remind us of how far we'd come, we rumbled on again toward home.

*

Back again finally in real world, we not only carried the experience with us but were trying to sort out what it meant. How did we get to where we were now? What forces had influenced us?

Like every human being, Teddy and I had been raised with the values of our parents and our particular culture. Though she was South and I was North, our upbringings were quite similar. We came from reasonably affluent families, went to the "good" and "right" schools. We were bred to be ladies and gentlemen and someday, if possible, leaders in our society. Vote conservative Republican, love our country and love God.

But Teddy has always done her own thing. As a descendant of the John Smith family of Pocahontas fame in the Virginia Colony, she had no status or performance ethic to serve. When she became a convert to Catholicism so that we could be married in "my church," her Episcopal family groaned and her old nurse said, "Miss Frederika, that Mister Otis is not only a damn

Yankee but an Irish Catholic damn Yankee."

From childhood on, Teddy had always had a strong spiritual yearning. It wasn't particularly churchy, it was sometimes emotional, but always caring. A friend once told her: "You've found your way. It's devotion." As for me, a cradle Catholic, I squirmed through ritual. When Teddy began really digging into the works of the spiritual masters, she exposed me, often kicking and fighting, to concepts of the spirit that I hadn't wanted to think about or even knew existed.

Thomas Merton was one of her favorites. "The wars, cataclysms and plagues," he wrote, "that convulse human society are in reality the outward expression of a hidden spiritual battle. To be consciously and spiritually committed to the worldly power struggle in business, politics and war is to founder in darkness, confusion and sin."

Such words focused us on the meaning of life, and thus we began to question the materialistic preoccupations of so much in our society. This was hard going. Slowly we found ourselves at odds with many of the values of men and women whom we admired and were our best friends. They seemed to have their eyes on a different goal.

Once we'd moved out onto cattle ranches, Teddy began teaching catechism in a rural parochial school. Then she helped organize a food bank for migrant Hispanic field workers. The quiet of the land, the remoteness and healing cycles of nature all played a part in expanding our view of the meaning of life. What were we really put here for? As Emerson said, "You can have truth or repose. You cannot have both."

By then, at an occasional party with old friends, we not only didn't agree with their politics and values, but we felt we were almost spies, "passing" in a world that was not ours anymore.

When I read Jonathan Schell's <u>Fate of the Earth,</u> the enormity of the nuclear challenge and the problem of violence really hit home. Almost from that moment, I decided that what little I could do in writing would at least now be directed toward trying to shed light on some of these major issues. I became increasingly anti-war and read everything I could dig out. Howard Zinn's classic <u>Peoples History of the United States</u>, Noam Chomsky's many works, Gore Vidal's, Jonathan Kwitny's <u>Endless Enemies</u>, William Greider's <u>Who Will Tell the People</u>?

From these and many more, I began to sense a common need for citizen activism and change. Everything I wrote began to be influenced by a gradual awakening to a larger view of behavior, conduct and governance.

RISING TO A HIGHER CONSCIOUSNESS

Cora, Wyoming, 1995: It's been pretty much upstream that morning on the Green River. Hard as hell to row against the current in my tin john boat, but I'm teaching two friends how to fly fish. Their lines get wrapped around my neck, their flies impaled in the willows. I want to break 'em off, give 'em to the birds---they can buy more from Orvis. But no, dutiful teacher, I plow the boat into the bank, grab willows and hand over hand us uphill to snatch the little treasure.

After lunch, I lie down to take a nap. Forget it! I'm all nerves. Now what is going on here? I can't sleep. My heart is thumping like a trip hammer, my neck hurts. Say, this is not me. Doesn't go away. Two days later I'm in an emergency room.

Arrythmia, the doctor says. Not unusual. Even our leader George Bush possibly swooned from it and threw up on the premier of Japan. With medication, it can be controlled, if not it could lead to a stroke.

That's the good news? I'm furious. I hate

hospitals. I take a stress test. The Utah Jazz basketball players can run 12 minutes on the treadmill. Most old farts like me drop off at 2 or 3. I make it to 9. But I'm still hurting, my breath is short.

It doesn't go away. Teddy and I rush back to the lower altitude of the ranch we have then in California. Shoot quail again? I can't walk fifty feet to the first cattleguard on our road without getting out of breath and my palms sweating.

Because we'd been away for four months, Teddy was sorting through our second-class mail when randomly, she picked up something that had been tossed into the waste basket.

In a mound of unread periodicals, her eyes happened to strike the title of a book: "Power vs. Force." It was being reviewed in Brain-Mind Bulletin, a scientific journal. To Teddy the first paragraphs leapt off the page:

"Dr. David Hawkins has evolved what he calls The Map of Consciousness. The Hidden Determinants of Human Behavior. His 25 years of research have led

him to the radical principle that our consciousness instinctively knows truth from lies, and manifests this knowledge in our bodies.

"If he's right, we could be in much closer than

we think to comprehending everything from the failings of public policy to each individual's place in the universe."

Teddy was intrigued. By lunchtime, when she'd brought our hamburgers out onto the porch and sat down beside me, she'd practically memorized the review and began to quote it to me.

Using a science called kinesiology--- testing your muscle response to ideas you hold in your mind---Hawkins has calibrated emotions according to their electrical energy. He and his assistants have tested thousands of people with kinesiology in many countries. Whether they're male, female, rich, poor or from many different races, the results are uniform. When the body hears a lie, the muscles go weak. It rejects it.

The low-end emotions of what Hawkins calls "The Box," are all negative, death-enhancing energies. The entry point to life enhancing energies is the emotion of Courage.

If we live in these "top of the box" energies, we take back our power from "out there" and use it "in here" to heal ourselves.

I couldn't totally absorb what Teddy was telling me, but my body believed *something*. It seemed to *know* what Hawkins meant. As we sat on the porch, we replayed what had happened during the last months.

Shortly before my heart flashed its warning, I'd published a new novel, <u>Frontiers</u>. Its hero was an Irish immigrant, fighting all the American wars from the Sioux in 1876 to the Japanese in 1941. He literally crossed all the frontiers of recent American history, from the plains to the oceans to the world. I never dreamed in writing it that these hundreds of pages would hurl me across my own frontier of consciousness.

It was my 13th book, years in the writing, and more or less my tour de force. I had high hopes for it. Film studios were talking about it as a mini-series. My publisher was enthusiastic, but didn't have the money to promote it. When it hit the public, it came out not with a bang but a whimper. Sales were slow. In the mass of other well-promoted fiction, we didn't get reviews. Nobody knew the book existed. We died on the vine. Could it be that at my age I was too removed from the youth cult, the hype and necessary clamor that create success in today's market?

As the realization struck me, I was literally heart-broken, but couldn't admit it. Instead, I hammered out a critical essay on what was wrong with the United States. Though some of the points were valid enough, nobody wanted to publish the piece. Another failure. I became even more angry at the rejection I felt.

When you live in the low-end emotions, they always bunch up on you. You don't just act out Shame or Fear or Pride, you condition your heart to respond to negative programming.

To Hawkins, 85% of our physical ills are caused by our living in the low end emotions. "Subtle grades of depression kill more people than all other diseases combined. The body is a reflection of the spirit in its physical expression, and its problems are the dramatization of the struggles of the spirit which gives it life."

Think of your consciousness as a computer. It's a perfectly neutral mainframe. What runs it are the software programs, your emotions that you put into it.

So when I inserted the negative-energy floppy disks of Guilt, Fear and Pride, consciousness sent that message down my acupuncture meridians. Find a weakness that consciousness thinks I want my body to act out. Heart seemed a likely place. So I get the heart flutters, feel lousy and scared.

Sitting there on the porch, looking out at the big oak in our garden, I realized something big had just happened to me. The pieces in the kaleidoscope were beginning to take shape. Suddenly I felt better.

Teddy says I slapped the table and stood up. It was that abrupt. "I'm not having the heart problem anymore," I said. "It's over!" Courage tells you that you can face, cope and handle. I'd put a new software program into the computer and cancelled out the old one.

But the process was only beginning. To get higher into healing, I had to go to Neutrality. This means I would take no position. If my book makes it, fine, if it doesn't, that's okay, too. Something else will come along.

Then to Willingness. Here, I'm willing to fail and climb back up. Then to Acceptance. Surrender my will to the greater will. Whatever happens, I accept. Then to Reason: face it, I was in my seventies in a tough business, I've never been Hemingway, what did I expect anyway? Big deal. Then to love: "Essential for recovery," Hawkins says, "is compassion for one's self and for all of humankind. We become healers as we are healed." Charity begins at home. Now to Joy. Seeing the Oneness, having the serenity of it. From there to Peace. Bliss, no cares. And finally to Enlightenment, so far above us that it seems unreachable. But others have reached it. The constant trying is all that counts.

It was eight years ago when I got up from that porch table, so excited I didn't even finish my hamburger. "I'm getting the dogs and going out to hunt quail!"

"Now?" Teddy said.

"Now!"

From that day to the present, my heart has never missed a beat.

Why?

Could a stranger's words alone have healed me? Or was there something far more astounding here? Had I, for reasons I didn't yet understand, been suddenly lifted to a new level of consciousness?

If that was the case, David Hawkins says with a twinkle, "You got the message pretty damn quickly. It usually doesn't happen like that."

David is no off the wall guru. In the years since we first read his work, we've become friends; Teddy writes study guides for his books. At Columbia-Presbyterian hospital in New York, he'd had the largest psychiatric practice in the U.S. A new wing had to be built on the hospital to accommodate his world wide stream of patients. He also co-authored a paradigm-shattering book with Nobelist Linus Pauling, and was an advisor to Bill Wilson, founder of Alcoholics Anonymous.

Now, living on his isolated "Rattlebone Ranch" in Arizona, David ministers to abused Navajo girls, and in his spare time, of which he has very little, he teaches and writes. The genius of his <u>Power vs Force</u> is so subtle and electrifying, so foreign to us that we don't "get it" at first. How can it be otherwise? We've been raised to be competitive, controlling "winners." But he's talking about surrender to forces in our consciousness that we are unaware exist.

"Healing,' he says, "only occurs in the higher levels of consciousness. To rise up to them most often requires struggle, despair and only through a painful surrender. Out of defeat comes victory, out of failure success, out of humbling, true self esteem."

It's recognizing our flaws. We don't have the answers for everything. We make bad choices, we often do what we don't want to do. It's out of this admission, facing this truth, that our self-esteem rises.

"We may choose to no longer be enslaved by darkness."

This was exactly the process I went through:

despair over the book, defeat, and out of failure, not only surrender and humbling, but the victory of true self-esteem.

When we live in the low-end emotions, we give our <u>power</u> away, trying to control events "out there." Hence, our satisfaction is never here, now, this moment. It's always contingent on something that might happen tomorrow or next month. We live in wantingness. We are perpetually unfulfilled. Our energy goes negative; we suppress our immune systems. We sicken.

However, when we live in the high-end emotions of courage, neutrality, willingness, acceptance, reason, love, joy, and peace, our bodies know that we're living in havingness. We're fulfilled. We take back our <u>power</u> begin using it "in here," in ourselves. Our immune systems respond. This is our <u>power</u> that heals us.

Just when I seemed to have no solution for my heart problem, what had led Teddy to pick up one review of a book out of a stack of unread mail, and happen to hand that exact one to me?

What had caused me to give up control, finally let go and let God?

Could it have been that I tapped into the synchronicity of consciousness, my body rejecting the lie of the false self I was trying to live, and freeing me, healing me, when I finally chose to begin living my true self.

How could I do it again? What path would we have to take so that you and I could live in the higher emotions as much as possible, and pray that here we could be guided to change our lives, and even, hopefully, in our rising consciousness, to help in the healing of our nation.

So the search began. The quest for certainty, in a mystery that had none. Only "hints and guesses" as Eliot said, from here on in. Dark, light. Wantingness, Havingness. Sickness or wellness. War, peace? Which?

Finding and losing and finding again.

And finally, God willing, the choosing between.

PART THREE

FINDING THE WAY HOME

On an afternoon in November, 2002, I was banging my pickup down that same Military Road where President Grant had a fort established at the height of the Apache war in 1872. It's a rocky, sandy track that runs for 4 miles through our ranch in Arizona. Except for my bird dog Lily in the bed of the truck, I was alone in the splendid isolation of the past.

And frankly, I felt anxious.

Early the next morning, Teddy and I would be leaving for a long trip back to Chicago and New York. We'd been raised in these cities. We'd courted there, I'd worked in the lofty office buildings. But what of now? I wondered, bumping along the Military Road. What did we always find when we went back to civilization? More and more we'd be Rip van Winkle awakening. But This is home. Our center. We don't want to keep being pulled off of it.

An old cowboy once said to me, "When you're living in the West, son, and trying to run cows, let me tell you this: You gotta come to stay. It's a business for stickers."

They were stickers all right, and on this Military Road, the relics they've left for me are courage. That's what I wanted to rub off on myself.

On this particular afternoon, my battle is tracking down a sly old cow. She's peering at me through the mesquite, her big red steer calf sniffing me insolently, as if saying, Wise guy, you never caught me, did you? He wears no brand because we missed the pair of them on our last herding.

Normally on roundups, most of the cows trot on ahead of us and don't fight back. Because we rotate them through all the pastures so the feed can re-grow, they seem to know that they're always going to greener grass ahead. The exception is a recalcitrant pair like the two that are watching me. Trying to survive in the high desert, range cows often become wild. With their big horns tossing so they can spear coyotes or lions trying to steal their calves, they've learned that a human on a horse often means pain, either roping, castrating or branding. So they'll kick up their heels and head for the mountains, hoping to avoid civilization forever.

We call these loners "hiders," and they can be pretty damn clever at it, holing up in arroyos. From where I drive on the Military Road, I can see the entire sweep of the ranch, from the mountains down to the high desert. The whole place encompasses fifty square miles. We only own about 5,000 acres of it. The balance is Federal and State grazing leases. Rising up to the east are the 11,000 foot Pinaleno mountains, a superb lion-colored wilderness, Ponderosa pines on the heights, juniper and live oak carpeting the lower slopes. Like the fingers of a giant hand impressed into the granite cliffs, cottonwood-lined arroyos slash down into the expanse of the hundred and twenty mile long Sulphur Springs valley. The birds and the beasts are still here, much as they've always been.

Mountain lions kill our calves when they're short of their preferred food, white tail or mule deer fawns. Or, less frequently, they dine on a fresh-born antelope or elk fawn. Troops of coati mundis, like monkeys, hang from their tails in the trees and chatter at the excitement. For a range of its size, the Pinalenos also have the largest population of black bears in the U.S. These comical balls of fur can be pests. When they're thirsty, they bite holes in our plastic pipelines which bring water from high springs down to the cows. Or, when they're really cooking in summer, a wise bear or two will jump into our water troughs. To get a good, steady bath, they've learned to bite off the float that controls the inlet. Then, as if in a kiddie pool, they play in the gushing water until the spring has run itself dry.

Three kinds of quail live on the ranch: the Mearns, Scaled and the most common Gambel's. I don't hit many. These gray magnificent bullets are usually too fast for my aging eyes. Hovering above them in the heights are Golden and Bald Eagles. Ducks and geese use our tanks or reservoirs in fall and winter. And rooting happily in the mesquite lands are herds of porkers, the hairy-backed little desert javelinas. Cavalry officers who served at Ft. Grant mentioned the "salubrious climate," but more often, imitating their nimrod General Crook, they wrote glowingly about the great hunting here. At least the animals didn't shoot back like Apaches.

On current maps, the boundaries of our deeded land still read: "Military Reservation." Government surveying hasn't seemed to catch up with history. A hundred and one years ago,

Washington decided the Apaches were done for. The fort's surplus land was auctioned off to pioneer ranchers like the ones who had homesteaded our place. One family of them had come all the way over from England. After surviving the Apache war, they thought it safe to bring their aging mother over, too. That doughty lady helped them set up a stage station on a spring. We still find old crockery littered about. When she died and was buried in an unmarked grave, as was the pioneer custom, her children put her name on the map: "Mother's Canyon."

From here, the Military Road slices on an arrow-straight line into the present Ft. Grant. In the 1880's, a far-sighted Major named Anson Mills commanded the post. Taking advantage of the mountain springs, he had his soldiers dig a lake fed by the powerful Ft. Grant creek. Early photos show Mrs. Mills, her children and other officers families paddling around in dories, the women in their best bonnets and shading their kids with parasols. Major, later General Mills, was a Medal of Honor winning hero of the Sioux and Apache wars. He also invented the Mills grenade and the Mills cartridge belt. Both were used by U.S. troops in our forthcoming wars. From their profits, Mills retired a millionaire with his name on an office building in El Paso.

At the crest of the Pinalenos, Mills and other commandants had their soldiers build log cabins so that their wives and family could beat the desert heat and luxuriate amidst the cool pines. Adjoining their summer place, in a grove still labeled Hospital Flat, the Army took care of its wounded, sick or just plain malingering troopers. During Apache raids, everybody was rousted out and came skittering down to the safety of the fort.

It must have been good duty back then, at least for the officers. Despite their encomiums of praise for the post, none of them seemed to be bothered that the desertion rate for enlisted men was running at 40%. The GI phrase, "nervous in the service" had to wait until World War II to be coined but something like it must have been going on in the loneliness of Grant and the other far-flung Arizona posts.

Nearby Arizona homesteaders, observing the troops, would comment: "Them sojers was mostly punkin' rollers from them starvy farms back beyond the border, kids knowin' nothin', or they was bindlestiffs from the rails, or they'd open the city jails and make the thugs join up. Hell, that thirteen dollars a month they think was a fortune. Then they come out here to this godforsaken see further and see less country. Drove many a one loco, it did. Even officers went to the bottle. I seen some so drunk their lackeys had to heist 'em up into the saddle. More than one I knowed blew their brains out, just to get out. As for the punkin' rollers in the ranks, they had two ways. One was to sneak off, peddle their guvmint horse and trapdoor '74 Springfield rifle---them things was always in demand out here. Buy a ticket and git gone on the rails, heading east to home.

"Them was the smart ones, mebbe. The greedy ones, riding up some canyon one day think they see a gleam of color in a vein of rock. Godalmighty, there's their fortune, ain't it! Everybody else was goldbugging in the Territory right then. So one dark night they slip out with horse and rifle, going for El Dorado. A few months later, back they come. Oh, they're still mounted alright, but their cavalry horse is just walkin' sticks and hair. Strapped over his back is the punkin' roller, Apache minie ball in his head and his privates stuffed in his mouth. Army bluebellies never did understand them murderin' 'Paches. Herd 'em all onto the res, the Ginerals tell us. Then it will be peaceable around here.

232

Wal, you can take the boy out of the wild, I say, but you ain't never gonna take the wild out of them red devil boys."

From the Military Road, I can see a panorama of the old battlegrounds and the men who fought so bravely, and often stupidly, to conquer the land for us.

Out across the Sulphur Springs valley to the south lies the town of Willcox. When the Southern Pacific railroad reached here in 1881, Willcox rose up from a dusty street of tents and adobes and began to boom. Surrounding it were hundreds of thousands of acres of rich grama grasslands. With the Apache terror lessening, as everyone hoped, giant ranches, their headquarters fortified adobes, began to carve out empires for a hundred miles up and down the valley. Almost overnight, Willcox became the largest cattle shipping station in the U.S.

In addition, with a rail connection, it was now the main supply depot for Forts Grant, Bowie and Thomas. The business of the Army was fighting and feeding the Apaches at the same time. Up out of Willcox creaked jerk-line mule trains, hauling supplies to the San Carlos and Ft. Apache reservations.

The Apache War was a profitable cash cow

for civilian contractors in Arizona. "The Indian Ring" these tough traders were called. Perhaps out of gratitude, or in the hope that their bonanza would last forever, they named their new town for its current commanding general, Orlando Bolivar Willcox.

This grizzled veteran had been a Civil War hero, but by the time he'd been assigned to grueling frontier duty, he'd become a cranky, hard-headed leader. Given to fighting with his subordinates and barraging the War Department with dispatches that always placed him in the best light and weren't quite true, Willcox had an almost total contempt for his Apache enemies.

He proved this in 1881. When a relatively harmless Apache holy man, Nock-ay-det-Klinne, had begun dancing at a settlement called Cibecue on the Ft. Apache Reservation, Willcox decided that he must be arrested, and if he resisted, shot. To accomplish the mission, Willcox chose Colonel Eugene A. Carr, 6th U.S. Cavalry. Willcox had been jealous of Carr over some grievance in the Civil War and had been feuding with him ever since.

Simply, it was a poison pill for the well-respected Carr. Willcox sent him out 45 miles east of Ft. Apache with 5 officers, 79 enlisted men and 25 Apache scouts, enlisted in the Army. When they arrived at the holy man's camp at Cibecue, they found themselves surrounded by 500 well-armed Apaches, all refusing to stop their dancing and give up their holy man.

The end was predictable and tragic. Coolly, Colonel Carr spirited the holy man away, but when they reached the Cibecue creek bottom, the Apaches lit the fuse. In a violent shoot-out, they killed a Captain and several enlisted men. In desperation, the Apache scouts turned on the troopers and killed more. In the melee at close range, when the holy man tried to escape, a sergeant shot him but he didn't die. Ducking bullets all the while, the soldiers shot him again and also his wife who had scurried in trying to save him. Still not dead, another soldier chopped off his head with an axe. Then, under cover of darkness, the troopers made one of the most miraculous escapes in frontier history.

But it was too late by then. The rage of the Apaches caused many of them to flee the reservations and launch what was to be their final, bloody campaign.

In this military paper chase, Geronimo and an ancient leader named Juh outfoxed the cavalry one more time. A few miles northwest of the ranch is a brown hill named K-H Butte---no doubt an early cattle brand. Behind it rises a wide, rocky canyon lifting into the Pinalenos. The Apaches, fleeing the despised San Carlos Reservation, had already slaughtered a half dozen Mexican freighters and looted their wagons, delighting in ripping out women's finery, and draping pantaloons and corsets on mesquite trees. After shooting several cowboys who had unfortunately blundered into their path, the Apaches surprised four soldiers from nearby Ft. Grant. These hapless recruits who had never seen an Indian had been sent out to repair the telegraph line that ran from Grant to Ft. Thomas. Because the line was down, they had no way to know about the Apache outbreak to the north.

According to military records, shortly after the Apaches had killed and "horribly mutilated' the soldiers, one of the hostiles spied a dust cloud approaching from the north. In it were two columns of cavalry from Ft. Grant. General Willcox himself, whose rash actions had started the outbreak, was riding in an ambulance. His troops were escorting 47 Apache scouts, shackled as prisoners because they'd turned on the soldiers in the Cibecue fight.

Now, at K-H Butte, Willcox had a good

chance of "tasting ball himself," as the vets used to say. Prudently dispatching two troops to pursue the nearby hostiles, he took the better part of valor by rattling off several miles to the west to the safety of a fortified ranch.

At that moment, there were only 20 soldiers and 2 officers protecting the women and children at Ft. Grant. A brave young lieutenant, hoping to save his wife and baby daughter, volunteered to charge the Apaches. His Major was delighted to oblige, having just come down with a case of what was described as "effects of malaria." Fanning himself in the shade of a mesquite, he watched his troopers make a rush up the canyon. They had 80 cartridges apiece, and in a very short while, mainly shooting at white puffs in the rocks above, they were almost out of ammunition, and four of them wounded or dead. No Apache casualties were reported.

Cannily, Geronimo had suckered the troopers higher and higher up the impassible canyon. Just before darkness fell, the Apaches did something unusual. Rarely did they charge the Army head on, but this time down they came whooping and firing to within 10 feet of the soldiers' positions. The troopers, trying bravely to hold, finally fell back to get more ammo which was supposedly being delivered by mule train. It arrived an hour after the battle was over.

By the time the smoke cleared, the astounded troopers saw what had happened. The Apache close-in attack was a feint. In the excitement, Geronimo had sent his women, children and 150 head horse herd down another canyon the Army didn't know about. They even slit the throats of any light colored or buckskin ponies lest they give their escape away.

What the troopers saw next, ten miles to the west, were fires winking in the Galiuro mountains. It was the all clear signal. The squaws, children and precious horseflesh had made it to safety. When the enraged troopers roared up into the rocks where the hostiles had fired from, there was not a sign of life. The Apaches had given them the slip one more time.

Rejoined with Geronimo, they even dared make camp and have a good night's sleep. The morning after, on the road again, they did more raiding and stealing livestock. When they finally clattered down to the newly laid Southern Pacific, a few miles south of us, they had increased their herd to 500 head. The presence of wild Apaches driving this dust-clouded juggernaut of horses stopped the SP train dead in its tracks. The engineer was reaching for his rifle and the passengers staring out the windows in horror.

Where was the cavalry? Where the protectors?

Very far behind, as it turned out. Some historians suggest that the Army was not all that eager to close with the hostiles. Meanwhile, a bunch of drunks in Tombstone, "The Town that Wouldn't Die," left the dance hall girls and faro tables and saddled up, bound to wipe the Territory clean of the red devils. They swept out into the desert only to run into a torrential rain. Their horses were sinking in wet cienegas up to their hocks. By nightfall the "Tombstone Rangers" as they bravely called themselves, had either drained or lost their bottles. Hunkered down, soaked to the skin, they decided to let the Army handle it, and straggled like wet puppies back to town.

The Army didn't handle it---which, despite all the John Wayne movies---was more than often the case. Geronimo and his bunch slipped through the ring of forts, swept across the line into the ancient Apache hideout, the fierce Sierra Madre of Mexico.

There they stayed for the next five years, hunted like animals by 5,000 troops, which amounted to three-quarters of the U.S. Army. All this to catch a band of terrorists numbering 86 individuals, the majority women and children.

Where I drive now is a whitish stretch of sand, rock-studded and dipping into bumpy arroyos. You have to go slow or you bang your head on the top of the cab. I wonder about the greats traveling it as they did. In the curious way history has of melding one era into another, I'm literally following their tracks: President U.S. Grant, out to inspect the post named for him. General Sherman, chief of the Army, and feisty Phil Sheridan made this same ride. General Crook probably did it on his mule. He loved that animal more than any cavalry horse because a mule could get him into the most impassable country. And here he knew the Apaches were lurking, for it was their last redoubt.

Back then, for most of the officers, the Doughtery ambulance was the staff car of choice. It was probably only a little less hard than a carriage or a McLellan saddle. The center was cut from it so that your most vital parts dangled in thin air. Small wonder that Lincoln cashiered McLellan from command early in the Civil War. Maybe he just left McLellan's name on the saddle as a reminder of the anguish that timid general had given him.

Along the road now, I pass another memento of the old ones. It's a shelf of rocks, carefully morticed together with a few old bricks thrown in. No Mexican or cowboy had done this. It had to be soldiers, poor doggies out there to dress the road for the brass with a mule and scraper, and harden the road's edges against erosion in the summer monsoons.

But where it connects to me is through the men who traveled from Ft. Grant to my own war. Flying in the Marines, I was only in the Navy area of the Pacific, but 500 miles to the west of us were the Philippines, the Army zone. MacArthur's chief of staff there had been General Jonathan Wainwright. Poor "Skinny" Wainright was left holding the bag. In the disaster of Bataan, he had to surrender the Philippines for "Dugout Doug," as the Marines called MacArthur. Wainright spent the rest of the war in a Japanese prison, a long trip from old Ft. Grant where he was born.

Another army brat born at Grant was battleship Admiral Jesse Oldendorf.

In 1944, I watched Admiral Oldendorf's fleet pounding the island of Pelelieu so fiercely that the Navy brass assured us that we Marines could seize it at minimal cost. It would take only three days, they said. Three weeks later, with 9,121 Marine casualties, we were still there. So was an Army division. And fifteen years later, shortly before I'd returned to see the forgotten abbatoir of Pelelieu, a handful of Japanese soldiers had just come out of the coral caves, blinking in amazement that the war had finally ended.

Another Marine captain, an old friend and hero in the battles of Saipan and Iwo Jima, had been commanded by a Colonel C.C. Smith, Jr. Colonel Smith's father, as a freshly minted 2nd Lt. of Cavalry had done his first tour of duty at Grant. The commanding officer then in the '80's was Colonel William Shafter. This wheezing, 250 pound hulk was known as "Pecos Bill." He prided himself on his team of trotters, and one afternoon, dared young shavetail Smith to race him up the Military Road to the fort.

Lt. Smith, a superb horseman, was riding a thoroughbred. Off they went down the narrow road, lined with cottonwoods in that place. Shafter was holding his own until, rounding a bend, they screamed toward a Mexican driving a wooden wheeled cart filled with mesquite firewood. No room to pass. Shafter's fine team spooked, dumped the Colonel's carriage, and rocketed his huge bulk out into the rocks.

No record exists of his discussion thereafter with Lt. Smith. All we know is that Smith won a Congressional Medal at the Battle of Wounded Knee in 1890. Eight years later, fat Pecos Bill Shafter commanded U.S. troops conquering Cuba in the Spanish American War.

In the dusk now, heading toward home, I can see to the south two more relics of what this land used to be.

Sometimes, herding our cattle, we're helped in the gather by a wonderful crew of Mexican cowboys. It's called "neighboring" in the ranches of the West, and though dying in many areas where the riders now expect payment, we're fortunate to have the grand old custom still very much alive on our ranch. In fact, the seemingly endless mesquite flats we work, looking for our needles in a haystack---all this land here was once part of the historic Sierra Bonita Ranch.

In the dawn, when the Sierra Bonita's Mexican cowboys trailer their horses over to us, they're passing through the heartland of the great old range cattle business in Arizona.

In 1872, when Apache violence was reaching its peak, a dogged New Englander, Colonel Henry Hooker, rode into our Sulphur Springs valley with a herd of cattle. He was stunned by what he saw: an empire of gramma grass stretching to the horizons. Springs bubbled up, creeks flooded down from the mountains, and soggy cienegas or swamps grew rich bear grass and sacaton that reached to his stirrups. Unpatented, belonging to no one, the land was his for the taking, and he took it.

Hooker carved out the first Anglo ranch in Arizona. In the center of his 400,000 acres of the Sulphur Springs Valley, he built an adobe fortress. It's still in use, a quadrangle of 2 foot thick adobe walls with a precious well in the center so that his defenders could always have water when they withstood an Apache attack. The flat roof of the adobe is lined with a parapet of adobe, cut with rifle ports, a strong position for his shooters if it ever came to a last stand.

But Colonel Hooker was ahead of his time, and wise enough to do two things. He recruited 100 cowboys as his private army, including such quick triggers as Wyatt, Virgil and Warren Earp. Also, he used many drop-in mercenaries. He never seemed to mind that they rode under mostly assumed names. If they could help him protect his quality Hereford cattle that he was selling to the string of forts, and feeding the tame

Apaches on reservations, he asked no questions of Butch Cassidy, Harry Longbaugh, Johnny Ringo, Curly Bill Brocious.

He even extended his hospitality to Doc Holliday, the tubercular, psychotic dentist who, between gunfights, had a problem with the bottle and whatever drugs were in his medical bag. Hooker provided him a drying-out room at his Sierra Bonita fortress. It's intact in the old adobe with its four poster bed, period chiffonier and white lace curtains. And so is Hooker's dream.

Though the Sierra Bonita ranch is much reduced in size, his great-granddaughter still owns and operates it, 131 years after it was founded. This great lady, Mrs. Rinky Davis, has enough of the old West way in her that, though we trade labor free with her hands, she always at Christmas gives our cowboys a few beautifully wrapped toys for their kids.

There are no guns on the saddles anymore, except maybe a .22 to shoot a marauding, calf-killing coyote or wild dog.

The second wise thing Hooker did in his day was to feed the raiding Apaches rather than fight them. Instead, he always kept some bait steers somewhere out on his vast acreage. Apache raiders usually worked in small bands or family clans. Why not let them butcher a few steers and go on their way?

It must have worked out exactly as planned. Though Hooker always came up a few head short at shipping time, there was no bloodshed either. Only once did his generosity backfire. In the 1881 outbreak, after the Cibecue tragedy, Geronimo and his bunch came racing through the Sierra Bonita. Instead of slaughtering a few bait steers, they chose to slice out 100 of the Colonel's finest Morgan-bred ranch horses. Then, well mounted on the swiftest horseflesh in the Territory, the Apaches easily outran the army and reached safety in Mexico's Sierra Madre.

Hooker boiled, billed the government, and finally, years later, received a check for $15,000.

Still hanging on the dark, musty walls of the old Sierra Bonita fortress is a ten foot square red and black Apache blanket. It was made by one of Geronimo's wives, and sometime, probably after his surrender in 1886, he had given it to the old Colonel as, one wonders, a thank you?

To the east of the Sierra Bonita, I can see another historic piece of land that's now on our ranch. The old windmill on it is bent and jammed, many blades missing. Just a gray skeleton moaning softly in the dusk breeze. Its well has long ago gone dry. But there's still a spring that works and fills a dark black pool, like a grave. Perhaps it was the life-giving water that brought Caleb Martin to this land.

The 640 acres here was his future and he must have blessed it. He took up on the land in the early 1880's. Homestead Act. The government just gave it to him on the condition that he would improve it. All that is left are shards of what he must have put here. Twisted strips of rusted iron. A few adobe bricks, crudely morticed into what must have been a wall. A shed for his goats? A house?

Nobody knows anymore. Yet shortly after I'd bought this ranch and incorporated the Martin section into our ground, I happened to visit the Copper Queen Museum in nearby Bisbee, Arizona. There, in two panels of faded old photographs was the story of Caleb Martin's life.

Born a slave in South Carolina---Mrs. Martin was the same---they had emigrated West to what they hoped was a new freedom. Somewhere in that era, Caleb Martin had enlisted in the Army and joined the famous black frontier regiment, the 10th Cavalry. He could have served with them fighting Comanches in Texas under Pecos Bill Shafter.

Then, in the 1880's, Sgt. Caleb Martin was winding down his service at Ft. Grant, six miles away. He and his wife hardscrabbled the place, dug the well, improved springs. Atop a twin-peaked mountain just south of their homestead, they discovered something that's still there. A low-walled Apache fort that commanded the entire valley.

Old timers tell that Apaches were still crawling all over Martin's land when he settled it. Often, out riding for cows or hunting quail, I'll stumble on another memento. It's a plantation of agave cacti, giant bursts of spikes so old that their leaves are shriveled and brown, throttled in grey ropes of decayed fiber. Their proud stalks, some ten feet in length, are now fallen like forgotten spears. But walking through them, carefully because they can still spike your leg, you see the Apaches planted these in neat rows, all the better to tend and harvest them. This from a people that historians claim never had the skills to farm or grow much. What they were really doing here was very shrewd. Now that the bluebelly soldiers had come and were chasing them, why not divert their eyes by growing a cactus that could be baked into tiswin---the strongest of the "white mules?" Sell it for white man cash money up at the fort, and hope it would kick the heads off the troopers.

Caleb Martin's first act in taking up on his land was to run the Apaches off. It probably was dicey doing this, a single fellow, armed with only the clumsy service issue '74 trapdoor Springfield rifle. Though we have found an occasional 45-70 cartridge from one of these blunderbusses, none have showed up on Martin's land. The danger was, disgruntled Apaches had a habit of coming back some daybreak and slitting the evictor's throat. Apparently it never happened with the Sergeant. The interlopers just went away someplace and the booze business had to be picked up by the adobe saloons and whorehouses that crusted the boundaries of Ft. Grant.

Bonita, the town was called. Now its population amounts to several scattered ranch families, ours included, but back then it had two or three thousand people, white and Mexican whores, drummers, drifters, bull-whackers, everybody scrounging for their piece of the fat U.S. handouts.

The Martins raised a family on their homestead. Photos at the museum show milk cows, goats, and curiously many other black families. Originally there was a simple rock house near the well. A few rocks are still scattered around but certainly no rusted tin cans, curled up women's shoes or the usual detritus of settlement. But studying the photos more closely, you see more rock houses were up the canyons behind the homestead. These ruins are still there. At the time they'd been occupied by other black families, probably discharged troopers who were following Caleb Martin's example and trying to make a new life in freedom.

Martin also moonlighted as a waiter in a small hotel in Bonita, a mile or so from Ft. Grant's gate. According to military records, the officers had many dances here in a room that wasn't much bigger than a squash court. Also in attendance was the yet unknown artist, Frederic Remington. For weeks at a time, he was a guest at Colonel Hooker's Sierra Bonita. It was at Ft. Grant that Remington sketched or painted many of his epic scenes of the frontier Army. He portrayed black troopers in them. It's even said that Sergeant Caleb Martin was one of his models.

By then, in the rip-roaring whorehouse town of Bonita, another kind of history was being made. A young punk named William Bonney had been hanging around from somewhere. He did odd jobs and worked occasionally as a teamster. One day, in the Bonita store, which still exists, another teamster began shoving the skinny little Bonney around. The kid didn't cotton to it, drew his gun and shot the man dead.

Miles Wood, whose family still owns what's left of Bonita, was an immigrant from England. Almost by default, as a responsible, tough white man, he soon accreted the jobs of justice of the peace, hotel owner and sheriff. Because the murder site was only yards from his house, he ran over and clapped manacles onto William Bonney. Then he took him up the road to Ft. Grant where the Sergeant of the Guard threw him into the big rock guardhouse. (It still exists as a shop where the prisoners shape wood or metals into gifts.)

Bonney hadn't been in there for an hour before he decided he had to make a call of nature. When the soldier guards took him outside, he reached into his pocket for a fistful of salt and flung it into their eyes. Then he lit out for the Military Road, hoping to get from there into the mountains.

The guards shot at him and missed, but no matter, a cavalry troop was nearby and finally ran him down. History is confused on the next detail. Somehow Miles Wood remanded him up to the sheriff in the better fortified Globe jail. But again, relatives on the outside smuggled in tools, Bonney cut his restraints and hit the road.

Several days later, with more bravado than brains, here was Bonney back again in Miles Wood's hotel, sitting with another guy and ordering a nice hearty breakfast. He gave the order to the moonlighting waiter, Sergeant Caleb Martin. When Caleb went into the kitchen to fill the tray, Miles Wood, according to his great-great niece's writings, had already spotted the fugitive. He said, "Caleb, I'll take that tray."

Under it, he was holding a Colt .44. A moment or two later, instead of bacon and eggs, Bonney found himself staring into the black muzzle of his gun.

No one really knows whether it was bribery or simple sloppiness of frontier courts, but William Bonney went free again, and this time, not daring to press his luck around Ft. Grant, set himself up in New Mexico. He became a "regulator" or hired gun for cattle barons there, under the name of Billy the Kid. How many men he killed thereafter is a matter of legend, but there's no doubt about the first. It was the hapless teamster who had bullied him outside the Bonita store.

By that time, Bonita had a tiny schoolhouse

and Caleb Martin and his wife had small children. The only problem was, the local authorities had decided that their school was not for blacks, Mexicans or Indians. This would be white education only.

That didn't go down with Caleb Martin's wife. She went to see the Governor of Arizona and shamed him into intervening. The local board got such a strong reprimand that they finally opened the doors of learning for all races. A woman born a slave had dared to stand up for her new-found freedom.

The Martin's oldest son apparently went on to become one of the most noted black cowboys in the West. A few years ago, some of the Martin descendants came back from California to revisit the old homestead. They wanted to see where the Sergeant and Mrs. Martin were buried.

They were guided to a lonely arroyo not far from the old windmill. On its bank were two large smooth rocks. No inscriptions, no headstones. Such was all that remained of two pioneers who had left their mark here. From slavery through a Civil War and an Indian one, finally to the freedom of a worthy life and a well-earned peaceful repose.

That dusk, my last stop on the Military Road

was the shadowy grove of cottonwood and cedars that line a watercourse named Big Creek. A former owner, flying over the ranch, had noted strange irrigation ditches cut into the creekbed. To his amazement, from the artifacts around them, he realized that these had been dug by Indians to irrigate a large field down near Ft. Grant. Obviously these primitive dwellers had farmed here, probably maize, beans or even melons. Around the field we find metates, giant flat gray rocks where generations of Indian women had bored holes many inches deep, using *mano* pestles to grind mesquite beans into flour.

Tracking back from the irrigation ditches, the prior owner located the Indian town itself. With no more than a shovel and wheelbarrow, he excavated several houses to a depth of about six feet. What I see now, walking through them, are rock and adobe-walled rooms, interior windows and passageways to ceremonial kiva rooms. Stone metates still lie on the floors and pot sherds are scattered in profusion. On what was clearly an adobe stove, my fingers brush over tiny white skulls.

I thought at first they'd come from wild turkeys, but no, said my old friend, Dr. Bernard Fontana. Bunny, as he's called, is a much published author and a leading ethno-historian in the southwest. "There were no turkeys here then or now," he'd told me as we studied the ruin. "Those are skulls of parrots. The owners of these houses traded for them with Indians down in the Mexican coastal jungles."

Together we examined hundreds of broken pot sherds, some brilliantly painted, others of primitive construction where the red clay was roped into circles laid one upon the next and then fired. "See there." Bunny swept his arm across the creekside ground that's covered with mesquite trees. "Under every one of those that appear to grow out of a hump of earth, you're going to find a house." Sure enough, walking from tree to tree, we'd always find tiny red fragments of pottery edging up through the decaying foliage.

The town spreads over dozens of acres along both sides of the creek. Rocks, barely protruding from the earth, are lined in neat rows. "Probably foundations of kivas," Bunny said. "And that cluster of big smooth rocks, any idea what it is?"

"Beats me."

Bunny smiled. "A group of the women finding a nice smooth place to put down their butts and gossip."

"Do you have any idea how many people were here?"

"At least 500 from the looks of it. Maybe more. That's a big city in primitive terms."

At what time did it exist? From the sherds and the house construction, Bunny feels that the Hohokam culture lived here first. These "old ones" go back before Christ, the exact date unknown. But then they were gone. Some archeologists believe that they drifted north, above the Mogollon Rim and became the Hopi people. Nobody's certain.

The next Indians who built upon the ruins of the Hohokam settlement were the Salados, a mysterious people who, proven by carbon dating, had lived here between 800 and 1200 A.D. Then, unaccountably, they disappeared.

"But why, Bunny?"

He nodded toward the rocky course of Big Creek which had run several feet deep last summer but was bone dry now. "Water possibly. Drought like we're seeing these days, only years of it at that time. Actually, it could have been anything. Famine, a pestilence of some kind. We just don't know."

"What about war? It's wiped out other civilizations."

He shook his head. "No, not here, not then. The Spanish invaders hadn't even come to the New World by 1200 A.D. when the Salado disappeared. As for the Apaches, the only other potential enemies, they hadn't drifted down here from the north until the 1500's."

So the ruin stands alone, unknown and forgotten. But when I walk through it, kneel to pick up a sherd, touch a cleverly-tooled obsidian bird point, or rarely find bits of imported turquoise that graced some maiden's neck, I admit to feeling a wistful connection to these people who lived so bravely here in a harsh land, built a civilization so splendidly, and yet had to let it go, with nobody knowing where they'd gone, or why.

Would someone some day walk through our ruins, too, and ask the same question?

HOMELAND SECURITY

Tucson International Airport, November, 2002: The Military Road is long behind me. We're out of Then and into Now. Teddy and I are checking in for our round trip to Chicago-New York-Paris. Yes, the bags have been in our possession, no one else has touched them. No, we are not carrying any weapons. Yes, we take off our shoes and empty our pockets at the screening gate.

"This way, sir." A scowling security guard points his finger at me. He looks like the old World War I recruiting poster: an angry Uncle Sam in top hat and spangled with stars and stripes: "I Want You!"

Pulled out of line, step this way, please, the shoes come off again, I'm standing on two shoe marks on the floor. Now the black wand, searching my body crevices. Spread your legs, please. Check his background: U.S. military record, 4 years U.S. Marine Corps. Occupation now: writes, runs cows around. What does this old relic have to do with terror?

Maybe it's in his pants. So yes, I open belt and

zipper. The guard and a lady guard get an ogle at very little. At every airport on the long trip, I'm the one who gets jerked out of line and probed around the privates as a potential terrorist. I'm told I'm one of a quota. Someone selects a few passengers from every flight. Marked men and women. Shake them down and then pretend this process ensures our safety.

A couple of months after 9/11, before Mr. Ashcroft's iron grid has totally clanged down, Teddy and I go over to Texas to hunt quail with friends. I declare my .20 gauge shotgun and buy an expensive case for it. I do not carry any ammo. A pair of ordinary, harmless 54 year married old people, we wriggle through the federal weirs like salmon going upstream for their final spawn. We slick through Tucson, Dallas, Corpus Christi.

But now at the latter, coming home, the alarm bells go off on Teddy. She is taken into an anteroom and must remove from the back pocket of her blue jeans the tiny, two inch long knife she uses to peel her apples. They do allow her, however, to scurry out and stick it in her suitcase. As we finally get on the plane, she smiles at me and opens her purse.

In here is a six inch long real knife. It has

259

passed through every screener on the entire trip. Another forgotten fruit knife.

We have an awful fear that we will not have security. That we will not be protected. Were we always this way, always so afraid?

Cora, Wyoming, 1974: Gus is an old homesteader who lives on our ranch. I've bought his 160 acres. He's waiting to die here. He's Lithuanian, came to the country in the early 1900's, built his own cabin out of lodgepole on the banks of the Green River. He lives on the game he shoots and the fish he catches. This piece of sagebrush and his cabin are all he has, and it's frontier crude.

"Gus," I say, "won't you please come down and have supper with us one night?"

The night never comes. Sure, he's reclusive, having lived alone all these years, but beyond that, we don't understand why. Finally, I catch him one afternoon along the river and pin him down. "Gus, we've just butchered a steer. Have some good steaks. How about tonight? Why not just come down and share 'em with us?"

Gus has wild white hair and a bronzed cliff of a brow, shading his boresight blue eyes. "Why?" he grunts. "Yah, mister, I tell you why. Go down to that big house, sit at big table, you spoil me. I ain't gonna get spoilt by your place there."

A year later, he dies alone under a buck fence he's built. I have his cabin still and the echoes of his ghost.

He was us, then. He was what we once had. Before we became, yes, spoilt on our own excess, and then, with so much treasure to protect, to become estranged from courage. Clutching and possessing causes fear of loss. We allow ourselves to be herded. Follow orders and cling to the safety of the bunch.

One time, a young fellow from Chicago trailers out a horse for me to our ranch in Wyoming. He gets on the wrong dirt road, has to open four or five barbed wire gates. For centuries there hasn't been anybody here except the Indians and a cowboy or two. He crosses sweeps of sagebrush where herds of antelope pause before turning tail and bounding across the sage. Above this vast basin in the Big Open rise the spectacular, snow-capped Wind River Mountains, and below them, the Green River, winding through willow bottoms and grasslands as untouched and green still as the day they were born.

When he reaches our simple rock ranch

house, the poor kid gets out, ashen. He stares bleakly at the awful silence and gasps, "Mr. Carney, how do you stand the---" he gropes for the right word---"the...desolation of it?"

A young lady from New York, school chum of Teddy's, drives one hour from the Tucson airport to the old ranch we had. Sure, once you leave the tract houses, K Marts and 7-11's, there are quite a few miles of empty desert here, seas of mesquite where even roadrunners don't cross the road. She, too, gets out of her car, ashen. "My God," she whispers, "I had to pop two Valium just to get here."

On the first leg of our trip back to where we'd been raised, it's dusk when Teddy and I leave O'Hare. We're being driven by a hired man in my brother's car, so I don't have to worry about the traffic. I can just look. We're going north on the tollway to the suburbs along the lake. Sure, we have the usual traffic going our way, commuters from the city getting out into the "country." They work in the city and slowly chug their way home.

But now, a stream of lights is in my eyes. The southbound lane is crowded down to a bumper to bumper crawl. When I ask why all those people are going south, the driver says patiently, "Oh, that's just the normal reverse commute.

They work in the offices and plants up north, and live in the city."

Live? I wonder. For at least ten miles, we pass these reversers, locked in their herd. "Do they do it every night like this?" I ask. He smiles: "Also in the mornings."

Only worse. Several days later, going out to JFK International, flight at 7 p.m., the limo driver warns, We've got to leave by quarter to three, beat some of the outbounds that way. When all accesses are jammed, we wind through bleak little Long Island villages, stop and go for two sweaty palm hours, barely getting there in time for security check.

When we were still in the city, we spent evenings with young friends of our sons. They're all here to make it big in the Big Apple. And yet, how can they? These are creative men and women. They write songs or films or magazine pieces. But they're freelancers, always on the come, and on nobody's payroll in between. Meanwhile, for Being There in the Action, in one of the most expensive cities on earth, they're willing to pay $1,800 to $2,400 a month for shoebox apartments in unfashionable, inconvenient neighborhoods.

One creative hovel in an ancient building has

a décor of exposed steam and water pipes, intermittently leaking, and when the lights go out, the rats come in to scavenge. It's something out of Dickens' London in the 1800's, vile landlords and usurious Scrooges. And for a rustic Rip van Winkle like me, how dare he ask: does it have to be like this?

By the end of our trip back to Chicago and New York, I kept asking myself: Are these competitive creatures really what we are now, slaves to wages and material desire? As the Buddhists put it: "Christianity, particularly in America, has become spiritual capitalism."

When did that sea change take place? Did World War II do it to us? In the terrible trauma of it, was that when our true selves and the romance of our American Dream began to slip away?

All the way home on the trip, I found myself looking back at life in America as it used to be.

Chicago, IL, 1930: Start out with the fact that we're really little 8 year-old monsters. My best pal, scion of a meatpacking fortune, lives in a grand house on the North Side. A half dozen of us go there with him for his birthday party, crystal and lace on the table, young Irish waitresses serving us. After we pull apart the paper things that make a bang, and pop out a paper hat, in come my pal's parents, elegantly dressed for the theater. With them is their dear friend, the famous British actress Beatrice Lillie, then in Chicago appearing in a play. In their chauffeured Cadillac, they're taking her downtown to the theater.

But they leave behind a dividend. He is Beatrice Lillie's son, Sir Robert Peel, exactly our age but what a difference. His hair is beautifully slicked down and parted, he wears an Eton collar and a Bond Street tailored grey suit with short pants. We circle around him like mastiffs, sniffing his spiffiness. Shyly, he sits down at the table with us. Now we're all alone, nobody home but the servants.

The dining room has a high ceiling, embossed with angels in plaster and wreaths of flowers. With our knives, we pick up our butter pats and rocket them. Target number One—the ceiling. Some stick. Others begin to melt and drip yellow down onto the lace. Sir Robert Peel, our elegant guest, does not participate, sits there instead blinking in horror.

Target Two. Him. The pack of us pull him out of his chair, roll him kicking and screaming to the floor. We not only pants him, coat him and shirt him, we leave him sobbing on the parquet in only his undies and socks. When Beatrice Lillie and my pal's parents come home from the theater, they register shock and fury, but if there was any punishment beyond writing personal apology notes, which was gruesome enough, I don't remember it.

When we do grow up, a dozen years later, Sir Robert Peel, a lieutenant in his Majesty's Navy, goes down with his royal cruiser, in the debacle sea battle off of Singapore.

Now admittedly, on the Gold Coast of Chicago and on the elm-shade lanes of our insulated paradise, the suburb of Lake Forest, we were at the top of the heap. Rotten spoiled rich kids with our fabulous lead soldier and stamp collections, with servants feeding us and trainers honing our competitive skills in golf, tennis, polo and the manly arts of boxing and team sports, everything we did was on the tab, paid for by indulgent parents.

We thought it would never end. No reason for it to end.

We had glorious 4ths of July. Our parents would buy crates of fireworks for us and have afternoon parties on the lawns of the estates. We had ten foot tall red, white and blue paper balloons, funny Chinese writing on the instructions. Light a little wad of gas-soaked excelsior, the balloon would fill with hot air. Screaming, we'd run with it until it became airborne. Let it go to soar away out across the splendor of the suburb.

Then it was time to light off the works. They were still in three or four giant crates on the lawn. Sometimes we would be allowed to help unwrap them and set them up. Highballs in hand, our fathers would line up the various rockets and salutes and with their cigarettes touch off the fuses one by one. But as we crowded around the crates, one of the parents appeared to be quite tipsy. He was smoking a cigarette, too, and nobody ever knew just how it happened. Hot ash, hundreds of pounds of paper-wrapped powder.

In one giant roar, the crates blew up. We were running wildly away from the heat and explosions, my closest friend, a fat little guy, heaving and panting. Finally we both tripped and fell, hugging our faces to the grass. "Boy," he cried, "wasn't that great! Just to see it go, see it all go, all at once!"

Up until then, we were still reveling on our

side of paradise. In the great houses of Lake Forest lived many of the pioneer families. Their names were the trademarks of some of America's largest corporations. But as kids, we never recognized this. We had our minds on more important things, games and girls. Because, strangely, though some of the houses were tall and elegant, with expansive rooms and even ballrooms, they were maintained in a tight-lipped Presbyterian understatement. Perhaps the memory was still there of the deadly old labor riots, the Haymarket, Stockyards, the Pullman strike that the Army had to be called in to end.

The great growling herd of the working people didn't have the money, and we did. Would they someday rise up and take our things away?

When my Mother and father were newly-weds, they were invited to a dinner at the mansion of Mrs. J. Ogden Armour, the grande dame of Chicago society. After dinner, Mrs. Armour graciously patted the chair next to her. "Come dear," she said to Mother. "Sit beside me. I'm so anxious to hear about you."

Mother complied and Mrs. Armour smiled. "You're Irish Catholic, and oh, my, I'm sorry to say, I've never known any of them except my servants."

In those last days before World War II, the first car I ever had cost $800, new, and my tuition at Princeton, $700 a year. We had college boards, of course, and the usual screenings, but the bottom line was pretty much: in the tight-fisted last years of Depression, if your parents could scrape up $700 bucks, put on your freshman black dink hat and join the club. Now, I look at $28,000 each for my grandchildren and ask: Was it prosperity that did it, all the boom years, the flowering of the American Empire? Or was it the fact that when money blasted its way out through many levels of American society, in a burst of gratitude we embraced it as a new kind of God.

In our noble little groups at Harvard, Yale, and Princeton, there was an interlocking of friendships; we dated the same girls, went to the same summer resorts. We also competed furiously in our games, our Orange and Black versus their hated Blue or Crimson. Because if you were an athlete, you were marked as a winner, fast track up the corporation to the boardroom. And after the scores were counted---gentlemen are good winners or losers, we threw arms around each other, kissed our girls and got gloriously plastered in our secret enclaves. I remember pre-war parties at staid old Ivy where broken glasses littered the historic floors, many of the members so knee-walking drunk that some fell down the stairs and others passed out on the pool tables.

When I came back to finish at Princeton after the war, there were electric lights instead of candles at dinner and white scholarship boys served us. We were now here to make up for the worst years of our lives.

Of my 20 friends in our 1943 section of Ivy, one quarter never came back from Over There. Five dead heroes who wouldn't be around for our very new Here.

ESCAPE FROM THE HERD!

When you herd cattle into a squeeze chute or up into a truck, impatient truckers or lazy cowboys are wont to use a hotshot. It's like a long flashlight with batteries in it and two prongs on the end. Prod it into an animal's butt and he gets a sharp, hot message: get in there, you dumb bastard, go with the herd.

Though we don't like to use them on our ranches, not wanting to stress our animals, a prod is known as the quickest way to get action. And sometimes, I think, we Americans have been jabbed in our butts and our minds with prods we may not want to recognize, which have the same effect.

If we ever hope to live in our true selves, live our unique spirits, we have to learn how to resist being herded.

There are three steps in the process. First, listen carefully to the herd message---why the herder insists you have to do such and such thing. Why it's patriotic or "good for you" or for your family or nation.

Second, dig out the truth about what the herder is saying as a means of controlling you.

Get the story behind his story.

Third, listen to your spirit, your heart, and ask it whether the person he's ordering around is truly you. If it's not, put the spurs to your flanks and get the hell out.

Now, the way our society has evolved, there are a lot of prods and a lot of prodders out there.

Money can be a herding. So can Income tax. Work, too. Violence. Health obsession. Body worship. Religious paranoia. Sports. Tobacco, alcohol, drugs.

What helped me most in trying to resist being herded was to uncover the reasons why I, and perhaps most of us, are so vulnerable to it. Unfortunately, it seems to be a combination of our conditioning and our old reptile ego brain ganging up to work us over.

"Everyone's innate ego," says David Hawkins, "operates about the same as everyone else's. Unless modified by spiritual evolution, all ego false selves are self-serving, vain, misinformed and committed to endless gain, adulation and control.

"Because the ego self by its nature holds positions, it is vulnerable to guilt, shame, pride, anger, fear, jealousy, envy, etc.---an inescapable source of suffering. Above all, it fears the future and the specter of death. What the ego clings to most is its conviction of its separate existence. Surrendering this imperative to God requires great courage and faith."

We don't *want* to live miserably in the lower emotions. And the fact that we become so entrained by them is not really our fault. Because we're operating on a lower level of consciousness, we've never been aware of how wantingness has been programmed into us.

The process has begun very slowly when young, maybe four or five years old. We are just reaching the age of accountability. In the blissful, uncorrupted days of babyhood, we could pee in our pants at will, or slop around with food; everybody gave us the benefit of the doubt. But now this savage little animal has to be housebroken, conditioned into being an ordinary, decent, responsible man or woman. Our culture has insisted that there's no other way to go. It's a process of indoctrination that helps build an ego self.

"Like flocks of birds that follow an invisible pattern," Hawkins explains, "the behavioral patterns of whole segments of society accept the paradigm of reality that is within or near its field of consciousness."

It's natural that we want to be in the herd. We're drawn to it, and because everybody else seems to be there, we think it has to be safe.

I saw that herd mentality one day in California when I spoke to a local women's club. They asked me to talk about my new novel, <u>Frontiers.</u> But we never get to the book itself. Instead these women want to know what a writer's life is really like. To loosen them up, I begin by telling them some hopefully funny anecdotes, movie and TV experiences mostly. They listen politely enough, but nobody breaks up laughing. Then it occurs to me to mention my current struggle with one of my ego demons—the old fear of failure that triggered my heart problem when a network turned down a series on <u>Frontiers</u>. I had come across a line that had helped me out of my doldrums:

"Happiness is less a matter of getting what you want than wanting what you have."

It's as if I've flung a hand-grenade into the room. These women are wives of ranchers, farmers; they are secretaries, local business owners. Innately shy, yet now their eyes whip to me. A few clap, others cry out, "Yes! That's true!"

I'm stunned. Why in hell could the simple words "wanting what you have" evoke such an emotional response? When the speech is over, groups of them gather around me to talk about wanting what you have. One woman says, "When is enough enough?"

As Americans, we believe in getting. Happiness is getting what we want. To do so, we've been trained to compete, to control. These ordinary small-town women were no more avaricious than anyone else, in fact, probably less so because they lived outside the mainstream. Yet few of us can escape the influence of our culture. In myriad ways, desire has been hot-wired into us.

Millions of us suffer from actual or imagined physical ills. We're the most medicated people on earth, yet few of us heal. An estimated three-quarters of us mistrust our government. Less than half of us even vote. A strange feeling of unease persists. For many of us, our system doesn't seem to be working. Our traditional values are eroding. We don't quite know where we are or how we got there. More and more we feel depersonalized. We respond to the desecration of our lives in fear, doubt, rage and helplessness.

War, of course, is the cruelest herding we can endure.

New Caledonia, October, 1943: Our Marine Air Group has a thatch officer's club, and on this particular night it's howling with pent-up angers. The coconut log bar is jammed with young pilots pounding down rotgut Three Feathers whiskey and sweating it out in the tropical heat.

Over the bar hangs a nine foot long brassiere for a giantess. Under it, the banner: Remember Pearl Swanson! Well, sure, laugh at some broad we wish we had our arms around, but that was our patriotism. We were all risking our lives for it, weren't we?

Who's going to be next? Some of the boys that night were already mean drunk, quick tempered, edgy fights, rolling around punching each other, bleeding on the bamboo floor littered with shattered glass. And our fists were stuffed with money. Flight pay. No way to spend it on New Cal. So blow it on a game of craps, dice clicking on the floor. Who cares if you lose it. Might crater a plane tomorrow.

Walking through the stink of whiskey and piss and a fog of cigarette smoke, I happen to see my friend, Captain Bob, holed up in a corner, surrounded by about ten pilots, sweat blacking their khakis, their sunburned faces flushed with anger. "You miserable sonofabitch," one was shouting at Captain Bob, "if you say that again, I'll knock your fuckin' teeth down your throat!"

I edge in. "Say what?"

It comes back in a roar. "He claims that FDR, our President, he claims Roosevelt knew the Japs were going to attack us at Pearl Harbor. And he let it happen!"

Now they're pushing Bob around. He's older, a Marine pilot in World War I. I know him because he and I have just co-authored two articles for Air Transport Magazine, dramatizing how our air group is supporting the war in the South Pacific.

I like Bob. Sure, he's windy, red-faced, opinionated, but he's also amusing in small doses. Somebody shouts at him: "How do you know this? You some goddamn bird on Roosevelt's shoulder!"

Then, though they drown him out whenever he opens his mouth, he tries to make his case. He's worked as a reporter for a Manhattan daily. Then had his own paper in upstate New York. Covered Roosevelt for years. And knew that he was suckered in by Churchill, wanted to get the U.S. into the war to save England. The country wasn't buying it. Too isolationist.

The only way to do it was to provoke Japan into an overt act. Hit us where we hurt and then we'd rush into war. "A Navy officer, McCollum," roared Captain Bob, "Japanese expert, he laid it out in writing two years before Pearl Harbor. He wrote eight steps showing how we'd squeeze Japan into doing it…"

One pilot shoves Captain Bob against the wall. "And Admiral Kimmel and General Short, they just let it happen? You lyin' asshole!"

"They didn't know it was going to happen. We did because we and the Brits were breaking the Jap codes. But FDR never clued 'em in. He hung 'em out to dry. And what, two thousand plus swabbies lying now in the muck of Pearl…."

"You goddamn traitor! That's what you are. Say it!"

I don't see how the fight ends. Just slip away. Have to make the Guadalcanal run at midnight. All I know in my deepest gut is that what he said, that old windbag, can't possibly be true. God, if he's right, what in hell are we doing out here? All the stinking islands, the killing, the heartache of it. We can't have been sold out. Could we?

We were, though.

For decades, official Washington, the party line, denied the story. Mention it and you were written off as a wacko conspiracy theorist. But little by little, though much material was shredded, thanks to the Freedom of Information Act telltale records, correspondence, and cable transcripts began to appear in the works of reputable historians. Copies of teletype messages show that Washington was informed repeatedly about the position of the Japanese fleet, and knew without question that it was preparing to strike Hawaii. Admiral Kimmel and General Short were indeed hung out to dry. It cost them their careers and they spent the rest of their lives fighting to prove their innocence. Though I doubted Captain Bob's outrageous claims, the more time I spent in the Pacific, the more suspicious I became.

Many of the girls I knew in Hawaii were *haoles*, daughters of the Big 5 ruling families who'd lived in the islands even before annexation to the U.S. I was puzzled when they used to tell me that in the two weeks before Pearl Harbor, humble Japanese who'd been their houseboys or gardeners suddenly turned arrogant and hostile. "Why," said one grand dame, "they'd even elbow us off the sidewalks. Believe me, they knew something was going to happen."

They must have, but nobody understood why.

Shortly after the war, I happened to meet Admiral George Murray, a friend of my father's. He told me that about a week before December 7th, our three aircraft carriers were ordered out of Pearl Harbor. Murray was executive officer to Admiral Halsey on the Lexington. "We had sealed orders," he told me, "which we were only to open when we got beyond the 10 mile limit. When we did open them, the orders read: 'Fire on any unidentified aircraft. It will be Japanese.'"

One of the Pearl Harbor truth tellers is the noted historian John Toland. His biography of Hitler not only won the Pulitizer Prize but headed the New York Times bestseller list for months. Later, he did a book on our occupation of Japan, The Rising Sun. I had the pleasure of connecting with John after he'd written a generous quote for the cover of my novel, Frontiers.

Discussing World War II, he told me an amazing story. Shortly after his Rising Sun came out, friends of his in the Navy begged him to write the true story of Pearl Harbor. Researching it diligently, he did a book called Infamy. In it, he had copies of historic teletypes and other records that proved without doubt FDR and General Marshall's prior knowledge of the attack.

Washington was outraged. The Times wouldn't even review the book, despite Toland's impeccable record. Later, while studying his research notes, he happened to find a brief article that ran in the Times in early December, 1941. It noted that General Marshall, who'd been General Pershing's chief of staff in World War I, had given a dinner for a handful of his wartime contemporaries. The dinner took place several days before Pearl Harbor.

The story gave names of the listed guests. One of the officers was still alive. Toland met with him immediately and asked: "What did George Marshall tell you at that luncheon?"

The officer answered: "He said that in several days, we were going to be attacked at Pearl Harbor by the Japanese. We were not to worry about it. They were inept little toymakers wearing glasses and incapable of doing much damage. All it would amount to was a bloody nose. We'd get up off the floor and destroy their war machine within months."

So what they know, and use, to herd us into war, we never will know until years after the fact. By then, the dead are already dead.

In the conclusion of his book, Infamy, John Toland writes: "Despite shortcomings, Franklin

Delano Roosevelt was a remarkable leader. Following the maxim of world leaders, he was convinced that the ends justified the means and so truth was suppressed.

"The greater tragedy is that the war with Japan was one that need never have been fought."

Play taps for my friends who went down in the jungles. Maybe the ends were justified, but the means never let them come home again. One old Marine friend of mine said in disbelief, "But if we had to fight the Japs anyway, what difference did Pearl Harbor make?"

Only this, the lie of it and the carnage that followed. Because we did know where the Japanese fleet was, heading toward Hawaii, Roosevelt would have gotten his war to save England if we had stopped the enemy at sea with what strength we had. We might have lost a carrier or two, but we would have turned the surprise on them, hurt them badly as well and possibly even shortened the war. But Roosevelt elected not to tell us the truth and caused the needless sacrifice of thousands of brave men, trapped and breathing their last in the holds of sunken American battleships.

PRODS

THE MONEY PROD

Money, of course, is the basis for our foreign policy and our wars to seize new markets and enrich our corporations. But closer to home, money hits us where we live.

It's a pathetic enslavement, really, because our "spiritual capitalism" has taught us that unless you make money and have money, you're inferior. On a deep level, most Americans realize that their need to succeed financially is connected with today's malaise. But the denial mechanism blocks out what is too painful to see.

Cora, Wyoming, July, 1975: A friend calls and asks me to take his father-in-law, Roger, fishing. Well, it goes with the territory when a river runs through you. They also infer that I don't have anything better to do.

The next afternoon, Roger is with me in my tin boat. Grumpy old codger from New York, booze roses on his cheeks, he begins to lash the water on what to me is a postcard afternoon, lazing down the beautiful Green River. He's grunting about how lousy the fishing was where he'd been, a gyp joint dude ranch in Montana, cost a bloody fortune. I hadn't bothered to bring a rod. I'm there just to row him. Every time he snags a fly in the willows and snaps it off, he points his rod tip at me. Put on another fly.

We float several hours around serpentine bends and willow-shaded pools where I know there are trout, but he's so quick and agitated in his casts and retrieves, nothing hits. "I thought you had fish here," he grunts.

Then purpling cumulus clouds rise up above us. Rain shower maybe, change of barometric pressure. In the sluggish humidity, out come the mosquitoes. They swarm down on us. He's slapping, cussing, lighting one cigarette after another. "If you can just relax to them," I say, "they don't seem to bite you so much."

"Bullshit!" He flings down his rod. "We might as well quit."

I tell him we've still got a good stretch between here and the house. He grunts, his eyes sweeping our hay meadows, the slouching corrals, rusted machinery lying in weeds beside old homesteader log cabins. "This place," he snaps, "why, you couldn't possibly make a nickel out of it. They're all the same, ranches, damn losing propositions."

I stammer out the usual. Sure, ranching is tough, but we do manage to get a lifestyle out of it.

"Hell, you couldn't afford to be doing it if you didn't have outside income. That's the truth of it."

Tight-lipped, I resist the urge to tell him the ranch cost peanuts, and by God, I have earned some money. Fight back with my sense of worth, measured on the buck.

I turn away. "Start," I tell him. "A few brookies are rising on that shore."

Almost reluctantly, he begins to lash again. Catches pretty nice brooks. "That's three," he says. Then four, five. Counting numbers. Never looks at them, though. I unhook 'em and toss 'em into the bottom of the boat.

When we pull up to the bluff below our house and I beach the boat, he makes no move to get out. The river is amber, the dying sun flickering across his eyes. "My life," he murmurs. "Stocks and bonds. Rode the train into Wall Street thirty years. Made a ton. Did it all myself. And hated every goddamn minute of it!" He brushes at his eyes. "Ah, hell, let's go up to the house and get a drink."

He goes stumping up the bank, not even remembering to take his fish.

Tucson, Arizona, 1972: My dear father Roy

and I have just had luncheon with a contemporary of mine I want him to meet. It's a pleasant lunch, my friend insisting on picking up the check. After it, I drive Roy away and he turns to me in the car. "That fellow," he says, "what did you say he does?"

"Well, he's kind of between jobs right now. Just came back from the Peace Corps in Latin America."

Roy is quite deaf. He turns to me, frowning. "Came back what?"

"Peace Corps!" I say loudly.

Roy gets it then. He sniffs, "Why, there's no money in that, is there?"

THE VIOLENCE PROD

It always amuses me when I hear movie and TV gurus defending their use of violence in their films. They insist that their bloody or sexually explicit scenes don't translate out to the audience. Everybody knows it's just myth, right? On-screen violence doesn't effect us. But then why, I ask, do advertisers and film companies spend billions on commercials to hawk their wares if people don't respond to what they see on the screen?

Los Angeles, 1960: I'm writing and producing for Jack Webb, Sergeant Friday. I love Jack and admire him for always trying to tell the truth. "Just the facts, ma'am." We don't do violence on <u>Dragnet</u> because Captain Jim Hamilton, Los Angeles Police Department is our technical adviser. He sits in my office every afternoon with his snub-nosed .38 on his belt, and grinning he says, "I'll tell you about this cuke we had and the smarmy fiendish way he put his woman on ice. But you don't put that in the script, see, because if you did, I guarantee you that within a couple of weeks, there'll be ten nutcases someplace out in the country who will try to imitate exactly that way to murder their women."

Chesterfield sponsors <u>Dragnet</u>. Jack smokes packs of the product daily. One day, in comes their advertising manager, serious meeting, we've got to boost the ratings. "I'm telling you, Jack," he warns, "we need violence, we need it to bleed. Write your scripts so that just before every commercial, you hook the audience on a really violent shot. Stun the viewers. That'll hold 'em through the sales pitch, and then, sure, you can go back into normal story."

Jack doesn't do it. Dragnet eventually runs out. Too boring against the gun-blasting squealing tires competition that's now getting the ratings.

Beverly Hills, CA, 1961. I'm playing bumper pool with the president of the network that runs <u>Dragnet</u> and other shows of Jack's Mark VII Productions. My mistake, I beat him in game one. While we're chalking up for game two, I ask him, as deferentially as possible, "With all the shoot-'em-up crap that's out there now on TV, with all the really constructive programming that could be done, wouldn't you want to be known as the president of the one network that tried to uplift its audience?"

He puts down his chalk cube and his blue eyes are the same color and piercing. "I want to be known as the president of the network that makes the most money."

ADVERTISING PRODS

Sure, advertising has been with us since colonial days, penny newspapers printing prim black notices about things we could buy. Later, the Sears Roebuck and Montgomery Ward catalogues furnished the homesteads of America. Advertising herded us modestly then. But only a short 70 years ago radio's dramatic entertainments crashed over us like a tidal wave.

When I was a kid back in the '30's, I'd sneak my radio on at night when I was supposed to be doing my homework. Glue myself in fascination to The Shadow or the Lone Ranger. Even the commercials were neat and had little songs in some of them. When my father Roy would catch me, he'd whack me on the head and rip the radio away. "Do what you're supposed to be doing, not this drivel! Don't put it into your head!"

Almost overnight, advertising erupted into a commercial Goliath, a new god promising that we could satisfy the longings of our true selves by filling our emptiness with the purchase of things. Still in her 20's, one of my mother's sisters was a highly paid copywriter at the pioneer Lord and Thomas advertising agency. Though Mother never said it in so many words, I suspect she hoped that because I was already writing silly little stuff, I could do it for an agency some day. Little did she know I'd try it, and suffer at it.

The goods-myth---that happiness is getting what we want---was marketed by 100 supranational corporations who buy a hundred billion yearly of U.S. advertising. When the shattering visual impact of TV hit the living rooms, the invasion of our brains was devastating.

Electronic scientists have long known that though black and white photography is only partly hypnotic, the dancing pictures and *colors* of the cathode ray tube manage to shut off the left brain, which we use to make our critical judgments.

The brain's right hemisphere is the happy little kid in us who likes to have stories told to him and doesn't have to bother with sequential things. In the right-brain, *there is no power to analyze*. Without a developing left brain to say no, the right brain believes mostly anything.

In the first Gulf War, for example, the Superbowl and the war were aired at the same time. We were fighting (playing) both wars on the same day. Which was real? Then came the commercials, gleaming products we had to buy. The goods lust was bar-coded into us day and night, morphing us into pliant consumers, getting and spending in the Global Mall.

SPORTS PRODS

I love games. I've been raised on them. I've even been proficient at a few. But now, I fear, games have become just another way of objectifying our enemy and keeping score. Even the two nature sports that I love, hunting and fishing, have for many of us been monetized. The poor guy has brought the office right out into the trout stream or the duck marsh. Nature isn't worth revering. It's simply a place where the numbers live.

Up at a duck club in the California desert where I used to hunt, we had one particularly rapacious kill-counter. Whenever the canvasbacks would stream over our boats, we'd all blast out a barrage. Birds would fall. Nobody knew who hit what, but invariably, he'd be shouting: "My bird! My bird!" Off he'd paddle to grab the thing before somebody else could snatch his number from him. Particularly ludicrous because after the hunt we always divided the birds equally between all of us. The meat didn't matter. He was shooting ego.

I hunt for the joy of watching my dogs work and for the blessing of being out in nature, preferably alone. It's a vertical meditation, I think---until the money-shooters crowd in. How many they got and I didn't. I often feel a tinge of remorse at a bird that falls, whether from my gun or anyone else's. I love these noble creatures. Love them enough so that like the Native Americans, I want to beg the All to forgive me for removing one from the Whole. When I hear tales of my hunting friends, paying small fortunes to slaughter hundreds, even thousands of driven grouse, pheasant or partridge in the old hunting fields of Europe, I'm sickened at the pride with which they count their numbers.

Even in bird-watching, or "birding," the competitive urge surfaces. What could be more lovely and spiritual than a walk in the fields, glassing the tufted tit willow or the lesser scaup? But then when the peaceful seekers get back into the tour bus, are they overjoyed by their blessed moment in nature? Some surely are, but unfortunately, more and more now seem to have come down with the number sickness. On their little scorecards, they're checking off the species they've spotted that you didn't. I got six white-breasted nut hatches to your measly one common house wren and one shitepoke.

In the way we were raised, competition says you win, I lose, or vice versa. Your ego self insists that you have to beat somebody, some object. Now, what does this do to your true self?

Unless you can insulate yourself with incredible detachment, competition plunges you down into desire, anger and pride. Worse, whenever you fail to be a skilled enough competitor, you tighten up in fear. You just weren't good enough or tough enough to step into the circle with the winners. When applying for a job at a major corporation, the personnel screeners like you best if you have in your resume excellence in some sport. They're looking for someone with the competitive killer-instinct, and at the same time a loyal team player. I know of many people who have landed good jobs just because they were good athletes.

In the entertainment business in California, tennis, in my time, was the make-break game. If you hung around the courts and happened to have a helluva forehand, somebody might drop a picture into your lap. I was once playing doubles against a famous movie star. He and the court loungers were betting a thousand dollars a game.

Back then, I could usually hit a strong serve. In the midst of the game I whacked one, an ace that half-way knocked the racquet out of Star's hand. To my amazement, he roared: "Serve again! I wasn't ready!" Not ready? It was something like forty-five, in my side's favor. I'd served to him several times in the last moments. You don't play not ready in the middle of a game, but he was allowed to. Star, with a thousand bucks on it. When I served again, I was so damn mad I double-faulted. I guess he got the score he wanted.

We tend to forget that before the United

States industrialized and a majority of people still lived on the land, they played mostly land-oriented games. They walked, trapped, hunted and fished. They raced on foot or with horses, had a few turkey shoots and dances. They rarely even went to the seashore for recreation. It hadn't yet become fashionable.

But then, during the Civil War, when men were caged into prisons, one of them, Abner Doubleday, worked out a game with sticks, balls and running that became baseball. And soon, when restless, angry immigrants became caged as workers in the city factories, they couldn't very well punch their boss in the face. So they had to develop a new outlet for their anger. They could run balls, kick balls and smash into each other. Football was born. When there weren't enough city parks so that all the workers could play it, they picked helmeted gladiators to do it for them. Now they had the vicarious thrill of watching others play. Teams quickly developed, neighborhood against neighborhood, city against city. The gladiators got bigger and fiercer and more violent. They became millionaires, too, and thus the N leagues were born: NFL, NL, NBA, NHL.

A young cowboy in Wyoming is so addicted

to his Dallas Cowboys that he and his kids not only wear all their accoutrements, but when the Cowboys lose on a given Sunday, the father plunges into black depression and can barely say a civil word to anybody for several days.

For the true self, the positive emotion of detachment allows one to rise out of the driving, competitive ego of the false self. It's a shrug of the shoulders. Win-lose, who cares? That desperate competitor isn't me. Go back to the fun of games and leave all the self-proving out of them.

IN-GROUP PRODS

The other ill wind of competition that flickers the spirit is the herding into tribalism. When you position yourself in a group, you're extenuate difference, and alienating others, as religions do. We Catholics – Baptists – Fundamentalists - Jews have the true faith.

My father used to call it "pray, obey and pay"---religion can be the drawing of a pious circle around yourself and the "saved ones," and putting all the Others, "the sinners," outside.

"The 'gods' of hate, punishment, indifference, vengeance," says David Hawkins, "have prevailed to one degree or another for 5000 years, culminating in the 20th century slaughter of 100 million people killed in wars. Religion became society's worst oppressor and perpetrator of injustice and cruelty. To misidentify the 'gods of Hell' with the God of Heaven is such a massive error that the consequences to humanity are incomprehensible."

BUILDING OUR CAIRN OF ROCKS

The People's New America

This new world that you and I are hurtling toward---and more and more of us are destined to live in it---what will it look like?

Out on the Military Road again, wandering through the arroyos, the mesquite and the sherds of dreams gone down, I see our new America in the shape of a simple pile of gray, weather-beaten rocks.

They make a cairn. It's about eighteen inches tall. If it were red, you could even take it for a traffic cone on one of our highways. Yet this cairn, almost hidden now in the long yellow grass, has stood here for probably a thousand years.

One time when I was searching for it, I had a city teenager with me. The longer we prowled around and found nothing, the more worried he became. Finally he blurted: "Mr. Carney, we're lost, aren't we?"

I had to smile, and put him on a bit. "Could be. Why don't you tell me how you'd get us out of here?"

Gravely, he swung his eyes across all the points of the compass, the empty desert. Finally he sighed, "Well, at home, when we're on the freeway, we just keep going till the next off-ramp, then we start back-tracking."

So maybe that's what I'm doing today, taking the last off-ramp from being lost in Then, and back-tracking to be found in Now.

Because this isn't just any old day. It's that dreaded tax day. Race down our washboard ranch road with my tax return in hand, beat the postman to the oil drum that's our mail box. Hallelujah! Made it in time. He'll rush it to the Willcox post office where they'll bang stamp it April 15, 2003. My patriotic duty done, I have pumped my few drops of blood into the throbbing veins of our warfare state.

So right now, this isn't any new world. It's just our old dreary one. Oh, sure, maybe eventually when the system totally breaks down we'll have to fix a few things. All you can do is tweak it and make minor adjustments. Isn't that where we're heading?

Not hardly, as the cowboys say. That cairn

outlasted us all, didn't it? And that cairn is the new America I see.

The primitive aboriginals who built it had planted a seed in it. A tiny green shoot that would someday grow into a prized agave cactus. The cairn rocks would hold the precious life-giving summer rains, the darkness within and the damp earth would nurture the tough fibers that could be used for clothing and ropes, and the final fruit of the cactus would feed the little ones and all of The People. Baked in earthen pits, it would drain out powerful spirits, a sacrificial *tiswin* that could give not only exuberance and transcendence, but in the smoky *kivas* was offered to the gods as gratitude for their gift and their preservation of life.

The seed in this particular cairn must have died, otherwise the tough growing cactus would have knocked down the rocks. But just as surely, for every dead one, another seed survived. To me, the tiny plant in that cairn is the spirit, the true self of every one of us.

The hard heavy rocks that surround it were placed there so that the wild animals of the world---lions, bears, rooting javelinas---couldn't unearth the spirit seed and devour it. It's out of our cairn, the preservation of our spirit, our worship of its divinity, that our new America will evolve.

Right here, on this April tax day on the Military Road, I believe we are seeing the confluence of great streams of change. In this dawn's early light, when the streams join and roar down through all of us, they will sweep away the old and create the new America. This nation will at last belong not only to all of our people but, like the inspiration of our first American Revolution, our second American Revolution will become a model.

New American Dream? Yes, dream it! We must, because if we fail to---as history reminds us, all civilizations eventually expire--- so too must our beloved nation die.

Humankind has always felt impossibility when confronted with the insurmountable. Yet still, there have always been a few of the courageous, rising in consciousness to the true selves of their spirit. Those few, inevitably, made incredible breakthroughs that finally led the majority into brave new worlds.

What are our new levels?

"The turn toward inward development," wrote novelist Alexander Solzhenitsyn, "the triumph of inwardness (being), over outwardness (doing), will be a great turning point in the history of mankind, comparable to the transition from the Middle Ages to the Renaissance. There will be a complete change, not only in the direction of our interests and activities, but in the very nature of human beings, a change from spiritual dispersion to spiritual concentration. This ascension will be similar to climbing onto the next anthropological stage. No one on earth has any way left but upward."

Upward is where our spirit lives. It is there that we must go, and indeed we are headed exactly there at this very moment.

The mystic Ingo Swann who predicted the end of the Berlin Wall 18 months before it happened, is world-renowned for his ability to tap into consciousness. He writes: "1998 will be the year in which the future becomes irrevocably detached from the past. The completeness of the failure of most 20th century systems, mindsets and affiliated institutions will be clearly visible by then. Twentieth century system failures will result in a great sense of betrayal and great, unifying anger. It is out of this great anger that the centralizing, re-empowering highest values of the third millenium will arise. These values will not remotely resemble those of the 20th century."

Will it happen here? Can we make ourselves into new people, leaping to the courage of our spirit, so that we may face, cope and handle the challenge of our future?

According to Dr. Robert Mueller, one of the founders of the United Nations, its former assistant Secretary General and now Chancellor emeritus of the University of Peace in Costa Rica: "Never before in the history of the world has there been a global, visible, public, viable, open dialogue and conversation about the very legitimacy of war.

"We, the world community, are WAGING PEACE. It will be difficult, hard work and we must not let up. There are two superpowers: the United States and the merging, surging voice of the people of the world."

The second power that the people have never had before is the wonder of the Internet. Those millions of protesters out in the streets demonstrating against the Iraq war rallied, were joined, through their computer screens. In the U.S. and out across Europe and Asia, hundreds of web sites have sprung up, like minds, mobilized hearts all joining as one in a new vision for peace.

"Smart-Mobbing the War," writes the New

<u>York Times</u>. "Eli Pariser and other young antiwar organizers are the first to be using wired technologies as weapons."

Pariser, a 22 year old living in a shoebox room in New York has somehow managed to pull together a worldwide network of activists, until miraculously they were creating petitions 3000 pages long, dumping them on the desks of George W. Bush, Tony Blair, Kofi Annan of the UN. Half a million signatures protesting the Iraq war. And Pariser did it *alone*. Later he joined forces with a small group in California, *Moveon.org* and then both merged with another network, *Win Without War.*

Out of such efforts, three-quarters of a million phone calls and faxes literally flooded the U.S. Congress---all this from an organization with 1.5 million members and by now swollen to *four* employees. In $20 to $50 nationwide contributions, almost overnight, it raised three quarter of a million dollars to support a senate candidate who opposed the war. This is not bureaucratic, structured resistance. It leaps over the dimpled chads, the elections stolen from black voters. It threatens the two corporate controlled parties and their chokehold on the antiquities of the Electoral College and federal courts.

As the <u>Times</u> writes: "Dot-org politics represents the latest manifestation of a recurrent American faith that there is something inherently good in the *vox populi*. Democracy is at its purest and best when the largest numbers of voices are heard, and every institution that comes between the people and their government---the press, the political pros, the fundraisers---taints the process. 'We'll do it the grass roots way,' says Eli Pariser."

But even with all the flood of *dot.org* protests, with hundreds of thousands marching in our streets, even with mail to Congress running 100-1 against going to war in Iraq---what happened? We were ignored. Shut out of the fateful decision to go to war.

When the patriots of our first Revolution structured their "democracy," congressional districts were geographically laid out by how many miles a candidate could ride a horse in one day. Each elected person represented about 6,000 people. The citizen permitted to vote had a good chance of knowing his representative. Because it was a more or less personal polity, he could keep an eye on the fellow he'd sent to Washington. One might be a neighboring farmer, another an artisan, an innkeeper or small ship-owner.

But now, with our exploding population, each of our congresspersons has 600,000 citizens to represent, the number varying with the size of his district or state. Connect to that man or woman? Impossible. They must get re-elected as often as possible, and only the money can do that.

In the state of Wyoming where I've been a resident for 40 years, we're tiny, less than 400,000 people. Thus we have two senators and one congressperson. She's a woman at present, and like our two senators, with the right patriotic credentials. Yet when I write them protesting the war, I often don't hear back, or months later, get a boilerplate party line answer.

In speeches around the country, hawking my last book, <u>Wars R'Us: Taking Action for Peace,</u> again and again people in the audience have protested my suggestion that they write or call or try to influence their elected representatives. Exercise their responsibility as citizens. Too often, they just sigh, or sometimes angrily shout back that they've been deluging their representatives to protest the war, and they never hear a word back.

How to rectify the system? Take the money out of politics. All of it, every cent. Such money is a bribe for future favors. Other democracies such as Australia have legislated against this and finance elections only out of public funds. The power at the top has to be reduced, diluted and the decision-making returned to the majority, the people.

Radio and TV networks are, like all corporations, chartered by the state. They are using a public good, the airwaves. If in the opinion of state governments those corporations are no longer serving the pubic good, their charters can be revoked and sometimes were in the early days of the nation.

In the new America, because of the sheer angry volume of citizen protest, this rule will be enforced for *all* corporations, media and otherwise. What do they do for us here at home? That has to be the bottom line for the citizen. Corporations have given us incredible benefits and built the world's leading economy. Yet still, in many cases, certain regions of our land have become no more than their plantation colonies, the raw materials and labor ours and the profits theirs, shipped to distant corporate headquarters. Drive through the tank towns and you'll see far too many homegrown enterprises unable to compete with bigness, boarded and shut down, waiting for buyers.

Also, in the new view of America, there will be free air time for candidates. There will be an end to the antediluvian voting system. Each citizen has a social security number. Using that number as the key, the miracle of the internet or even the phone line can allow instant voting for every citizen who punches in his number. And they will be voting, referendum style, on decisions affecting their national destiny, war being the most vital.

Do away with the Electoral College relic.

Replace the income tax with a sales tax or flat tax so simple it can be done on a postcard and remove the billions of corporate deductions.

Bring the troops home from all Empire bases. Use our military might to repair and improve our infrastructure at home. And if we seek to end the enmity that has risen against us in the world, instead of spending billions a day on our weapons of terrorism and death, pay our own peaceful corporations to produce the food, goods, shelter and services for the pitiful and the starving in foreign lands. Let solace and peace be our American gift to humanity.

It's tragic and shocking that over 3,000 Americans were killed in the World Trade

Center. "Collateral damage," so needlessly caused by a diabolic response to what the foreign policy of our corporate warfare state, done in our name, that has waged war on humanity for a half century.

So what does the world want from us? According to UN statistics, it would cost about $40 billion to provide clean water, adequate diets, sanitation services and basic education to every person on earth. As of now, our warfare state defense budget is over $400 billion.

By diverting defense spending for <u>6 weeks</u> and putting that money into humanitarian programs, the U.S. <u>alone</u> could prevent the deaths of 29 million people every year. Eighty thousand lives could be saved every day!

God willing, our rising consciousness, our oneness with the world and the compassion in our hearts will someday make us face such ghastly truths. Make us realize that our opportunity now, our true American Dream, is to begin to serve all of mankind, not just ourselves.

Certain far-sighted thinkers have already given us glimpses of how a new, and true, democracy might finally evolve. Following the lead of Einstein, they're projecting the future from a higher level of consciousness. Americans can and will change their nation one person at a time.

Targeting our sheer bigness as the problem, Republican strategist and author Kevin Phillips sees *devolution* as our future. Breaking the Union into smaller, more manageable units. He'd accomplish it by moving much of the government away from Washington, putting various departments permanently in other states and rotating the capital from city to city. Recognizing the power of the *dot.com* voice of the people, he would also amend the Constitution, "setting up a mechanism for holding nationwide referendums to permit the citizenry to supplant Congress and the President in making certain categories of national decisions." Declarations of war being the most critical one.

Gore Vidal takes Phillips a step further. In his Dreaming War, he writes: "What do we do about income tax? As the people at large get nothing much back from the money they give the government---why not just eliminate the federal income tax? How? Eliminate Washington, D.C. Allow the states and municipalities to keep what revenue they raise."

He suggests dividing the country into several reasonably homogenous sections. Each region would tax its citizens and then provide the services those citizens want, particularly education and health. "Washington would then become a ceremonial capital with certain functions. We shall always need some sort of modest defense system, a common currency, and a Supreme Court to adjudicate between the regions as well as to maintain the Bill of Rights--- a novelty for the present Court."

To pay for what's left of Washington, each region will make its own treaty with the central government and send what it feels should be spent on painting the White House and our common defense which will, for lack of money "cease to be what it is now---all out offense on everyone on earth. The end result will be no money to waste either on pork or those imperial pretensions that have left us 4.7 trillion in debt. Wasteful, venal, tyrannous Washington will be no more than a federal theme park administered by Disneyland's Michael Eisner."

People want to be rid of arbitrary capitals and faraway rulers. E.g. George III's England. So let the people go. It will be a "coming together," Vidal concludes, "of small polities in order to have better trade, defense, culture. So we are back, if by chance, to our original Articles of

Confederation, a group of loosely confederated states rather than a *United* States, which has proved to be every bit as unwieldy and ultimately tyrannous as Jefferson warned. After all, to make so Many into One you must use force, and this is a bad thing, as we experienced in the Civil War. So let us make new arrangements to conform with new realities."

Off the wall, you might say? Sure, it might look that way. But changes are out there, more and more every day in the minds of gifted men and women. There are five major regions in the U.S.: the East, South, Midwest, Rocky Mountains, and West. The five tribes of America, as they've been called. And in truth, that's what we really are. Peoples joined together by land, culture and distinct lifestyle.

Is it so preposterous to believe that each region could become an autonomous Republic--- the Republics of America---each with its own president and governing body? Its rulers would be not a professional political elite but a government of ordinary citizens, presumably unbribed because some portion of them would be elected by the same lot system we use in selecting juries. If we're able to decree life or death for our fellow citizens, can't a small proportion of us be considered competent enough to help in deciding the life or death of our Republic?

The leadership pool would include physicians and health workers of all kinds, small artisans, store keepers, computer experts, farmers, inventors, mechanics who knew how to make things run, ecologists, shamans who belonged to no bureaucratized orders of the spirit. Not only men and women but even bright, evolved teenage youth should have an equal chance to serve the common good of the region.

What about the land and the lifestyle in each Republic?

Under the failed Federal system, the former United States had its greatest growth and success in its first hundred and fifty years. During that time, the Federal government amounted to only 5% of the total worth of the nation. But in the 20th and beginning of the 21st century, that same government had ballooned into being 40% of the nation's worth.

In addition, that government had accreted to itself 50% of the total land area of the United States. Theoretically, that land belonged to the people, but they had no say in how it was managed. They couldn't live on it. Special interest groups were allowed to despoil the land and profit from it, but the average citizen received little from it except precious open space and occasional restorative but controlled use of its natural wonders.

But if each region had such lands in it, and they do, why not return those lands to the true use of the people, not just for distant bureaucracies in Washington or remote exploitive corporations? Give the land back to the regions' people and let them and their governments decide how best to protect and use it.

Riches of the land would stay in the region where they were found. Much beauty would be preserved, but in other less desirable acreage, new communities would spring up. Establishment of them would create more local employment, a bigger piece of the dream land for ordinary people to own.

Visionaries like Alvin Toffler have long predicted that the electronic revolution of computers, internet and rapid delivery systems will serve to spread out the workplace of America. People could do much of their work at home and go to pleasanter places to live. This is already happening with newcomers setting up their own shops all over the West, and surely in other regions as well.

In the failed Federal system, cities had grown into sprawling, unworkable behemoths, breeding overcrowding, ugliness, poverty and crime. Chain stores have all but wiped out local shopkeepers. But new smaller communities would encourage local enterprise.

According to ancient Greek wisdom in the scale of proportion, the Republics might well deem that their largest new city could contain no more than 30,000 inhabitants, that size being in old records the most harmonious with free, congenial living. What would happen to the present megalopolises with their vast capital investment is not yet clear, though it's almost certain that planners of the new are already contemplating urban devolution and re-ordering as well.

In The Republics of America, the citizens of each would decide on their own wars or peace. It would also be their choice whether they would participate in any Republics of America international war. For example, suppose East Republic, with its strong international ties and financial centers wanted to protect the markets of its banks and oil companies by launching attacks on nations in the Middle East. But the other four

314

Republics had no such dreams of Empire. They had no need to seize anything that lay beyond their borders. They could refuse to participate in this war.

The same would apply to other "federal wars." Each Republic could choose whether to war on drugs or to take the more practical approach: legalize drugs in their region and make growers and dealers pay taxes like any other business. By levying their own taxes and chartering their resident corporations or local ones, they would be democratically choosing what they considered their own common good rather than paying, fighting, and dying for a remote, exploitive "federal" one.

Far out? Of course it is. But as some sage said centuries ago, if we don't dream, we die. And the dreams are far beyond anything you or I can envision now. We'll try some, we'll fail, we'll replace them with new, but eventually we'll move on to the best good for the most.

In the liberation to our creativity, in its inspiring hope, our cairn of rocks will have nurtured our shoot of spirit, protected it from the wild beasts of the world. More and more of us will be fighting our hardest battle to be nobody but ourselves. Accepting our failings---of course we'll still have them---they're our inevitable human lapses into falseness. But now, when the U.S. becomes truly ours and when we shoot ourselves often enough in this smaller, more manageable foot, we'll know at least who pulled the trigger. Perhaps even someday, we'll be evolved enough to begin putting that pistol down, and learning to live with each other, and with the world, in the dawn's early light of peace.

OFF THE TRACKS ONE LAST TIME

Talk about getting humbled! I write all these hopeful words trying to tell people how to rise up out of their ego selves and then, what do you know, here's mine all mine hurtling me down the tracks to a major train wreck.

Pray God, our last, but I wouldn't want to bet on it.

Teddy and I had a beautiful ranch in California. We'd built it, rejoiced in it, settled in for nearly twenty years, figuring to live there forever.

But we were both in our 70's now and beginning to hear the ticking of the meter in the taxi. Had the time finally come to get off the range and hang up our spurs?

Ever since we'd begun our ranch adventures, we'd always been more or less land poor. It goes with the territory. What we had of worldly blessings was mostly tied up in dirt, cows, and battered pickup trucks. On the other hand, at our ages we wanted to do what we could for our three sons, their wives and our six grandchildren.

Perhaps it was like my grandfather, Will with

his Irish clan sticking together, taking care of its own. To carry on the tradition, we gave both ranches to the kids. They'd grown up on our old home place in Wyoming and because we still loved it, everybody wanted to keep it. But by selling the California ranch, the boys and their families would get some cash they could well use for their educations, careers and futures.

So our splendid 11,000 deeded acres in golden California went on the market. And stayed on for seven years all told. It was on again, off again. Every so often we'd clutch up, call our dear agent and tell her we'd changed our minds. Then later we'd weaken and put it back on the market. How could people resist such a unique, incredible place? Very easily, as it turned out. As a friend said, "Nobody really needs a ranch." Too isolated, they told us. Too far from Walmart or the lush golf courses in Pebble Beach. Too big a chunk of chamiso and canyons and cows, "money losing proposition" that no smart city money man would touch with a pole.

And so the lookers trooped in. We had every kind of big talker, phony and tire kicker on the West Coast bouncing around our beloved hills, scaring my quail and pigs and elk. Promises, promises. Don't call us, we'll call you. The phone never rang.

For all my writing career, I'd never been a spectacular earner. Unless you're more gifted than me or just plain lucky, it's hard to beat a dollar out of a book. (Or out of a cow!) As for movies and TV, like a veteran producer told me: when you're well into your 70's, you ask yourself: "What the hell am I doing in a kid's business?" At 27 you're a king, at 37, well, maybe, what did his last picture gross? And at all the 7's thereafter, with a few legendary exceptions that "have legs" as they say, you're into a slow fade out to obscurity.

Precious land, though, wouldn't somebody want *that*?

But then in the dusk, Teddy and I would ride together through the golden hills. Every canyon, every thicket of chamiso held the memory of a horse that had bucked us off, a cow we'd tried to save or a bummed elk fawn we'd rescued. Or it would be just a quiet bed in the pines where she and I had camped, holding each other and marveling at the eternal peace of the stars.

Put a dollar value on that? Give it all up?

But Twain's "grotesque self-deceptions" made me convince myself that selling the ranch had to be good for the kids, and us, too. We weren't eternal. We had to go someday. Who needs the hassle of fighting drought and perennially low calf prices?

Finally, down the road came some young fellows who wanted it. Few ranchers buy ranches anymore. Can't afford them. But these were computer whiz kids from San Jose, who invented software. Furthermore, they were nice guys. Loved to hunt and this was hunt heaven.

They were wary, of course, never in their sleek laboratories having to deal with buying a ranch. Question after question. If the hunting was so damn good, why wasn't the public in here poaching all the time, like they did all over California?

"Absolutely no poaching," I assured them and it was the truth. "This is a totally protected block of deeded land at the end of the road. No way for anybody to get in here!"

We cruised on for a half hour or so, down a perilous HoChiMinh trail and into my favorite hunting canyon. I was pointing out the beauties of it, magnificent isolation, a big bubbling spring and ancient live oaks.

Patiently, one of the whiz kids tapped my shoulder. "Mr. Carney, what is that plane doing in here?"

Plane! I whirled in my truck seat. There, a quarter of a mile away, parked next to my fabulous spring was a yellow Super Cub. People, too, camos, rifles, shotguns, blasting away my cherished covey of quail, pinging at a distant wild hog. I roared the truck after them, collared every damn one. Excuses, excuses. Said they just were lost, thought it belonged to somebody they knew. When they finally slunk away and got airborne, I knew my jig was up with the whiz kids.

I wondered if it was an act of God. Once before, in the anguished years of trying to sell--- should we or shouldn't we?---I had prayed in this same canyon beside this same spring for God to give me a sign. Tell me whether He wanted us to stay or go. A moment later, I'd looked down under a juniper tree. For years, I'd hunted around it. Yet here, today, glistening in the sun was a superb red and white arrowhead. Not the usual tiny one. This was no bird point or small game head. It was five inches long, three inches wide. This head was for a big animal, perhaps a grizzly or some creature even more primitive. A treasure that said, Stay.

That night, I took the place off the market. It wasn't a month later when the old black magic got me again. Our agent called and told me the whiz kids were coming down the road for a second look. Motivated. As they say in the bad war movies, "This is it."

It was. Plane or no plane, the computer boys bought the farm. So did I, caving in rather ingloriously during the final nitty-gritties and shaved the price I'd dreamed of getting for the kids. But it was done. Three months later, Teddy had packed our lares and penates, all the memories dried up in the tears, and we were history there.

Our friends and family were telling us that they couldn't understand why we were doing this, but like the warrior or the lover who are entrained into their particular emotions of the moment, facts and reason are the first casualties of the inner war. When I drove out the ranch road for the last time, I never looked back.

And now what?

We were utterly miserably lost. God help us, where was home? We had sold our house, our lifestyle, our center. Oh sure, we still had our Wyoming ranch where we'd fled to out of the city years before. But long ago we'd learned that we couldn't take the fierce Wyoming winters, five months of snow banked three feet up on our house windows and fifteen feet in the higher part of the ranch. It just didn't work for cattle or for living. It was a summer place only, and we'd always had a winter one.

In a frenzy to find our next nest, I went through all kinds of romantic fantasies. Suppose we go back to my beloved Pacific? Shoot some waves, maybe the Big Island of Hawaii. No, wait. How about Tahiti? Beachcomb. All too expensive. Okay, try the Cook Islands, better still. Further away. No, Tonga would do it better. There it was! Unspoiled. We had many Tongan friends and a native priest we loved and had traveled the islands with on his parish skiff. Build a little thatch roofed beach *fale* for peanuts…

Fale indeed, spelled folly. Teddy, thank God, was too wise for any of it. She's an adventurer to be sure, but "those damn islands" she'd say are just too far away from our kids and grandchildren. Well, what else was warm in the winter?

The American South! You could at least get there from Wyoming, a major production to get anywhere from. And furthermore, some of our dearest friends, having heard we'd kicked our boots and saddles on the frontier, were now longing to get us "back East" where the real people lived. We'd be starting again where we left off when I was on <u>Cinerama</u>.

"South Carolina," cried one of my friends, "is the ideal place for you, Carney!" I could fish and hunt quail on one of those old plantations. Teddy was southern. She'd be going home again, and for me South Carolina was the home of my Civil War heroine Gwendolyn Guerin, before I got into my Teddy novel.

So into the South we plunged, landing in one of the most storied old rice plantations on the continent. An island all its own, broken up into estates, rich in beauty and wildlife, a mere hop and skip to our family members in New York or old pals sunning their days away in Florida.

Our sons warned us: "Now Fred and Big O, don't get too impulsive down there, don't do anything rash." Like we had always warned each of them. But we were the adults, they were the kids. Then, on a romantic tree-lined lane, our last afternoon of looking, a dream house! Signed, sealed and delivered, we had gated ourselves right back into the herd we'd been fleeing from all these years.

Our paradise island was a gated community, guards round the clock to keep the riffraff out. And the nicest people in the world there on the inside looking out. In true southern hospitality, though they were mostly all displaced Yankees, they did their very best to make us feel at home.

They tried and we tried, and it just wasn't us.

Our ego selves had plunked us down here. Mine mostly. Teddy knew better, but then, loyal soldier, she rooted in, did major remodeling and screwed in all of her cuphooks. Teddy's innate frugality surfaced. Across the golf course from us---yes, we were on the sacred grounds of a game I'm not competent to play---she had noticed a new mansion that was being erected.

They were tossing all kinds of good lumber into their dumpster. Teddy scurried over there and went dumpster diving. Just as was tossing several bright new boards over the side, two members, a spiffy man and his wife, were speed walking past. Teddy gave a little smile and wave. As they marched by she climbed out of the dumpster. Then suddenly, the member lady whirled and turned back: "My God," she cried, "aren't you Teddy Fly from Foxcroft!"

We were back to the old school tie.

The more gated we tried to become, the more it grated on our souls. We had four dogs in our ranch family – big bounding bird and cattle dogs, along with an orphaned, going deaf mutt named Bingo.

The plantation had hundreds of deer on land designated for hunting. But due to an overpopulation of deer, some of the woods in the residential areas were allowed to be used briefly at the end of the season. Notice of this was posted in the mail room.

At one of the community barbeques I overheard a fellow telling a friend: "Why, here I was all set up in my stand, had a deer in my sights. Along comes this dame on a bike with *four* dogs! She was screaming, 'Bingo! Bingo!' Over and over again. The deer vanished, cost me a fine buck!"

"Did you shoot her?" his listener asked.

"Damn well should have."

Sure, I could hunt there. They had bob white quail that were all pen raised. Fat little guys that a friend of mine called "Kick up birds." Averse to flying. I could also play at golf. But like any course in the world, you had to pay for your rounds. It was actually quite a bargain, but still paying to walk on the grass made me sad. So what I'd do---our house adjoined a fairway---I'd scan the horizon for any real golfers approaching. If the coast was clear, I'd scurry out with a 2 wood and a 7 iron, start smacking my balls, pretending I was in the game. Then I'd glance over my shoulder and freeze. A foursome was teeing off within sight of this gangly Ichabod Crane whacking around illegally. So I'd scoop up my tools and plunge into the forest, hiding in the steamy glade until the straights had passed.

I was such a lousy golfer, my drives screaming out to all points of the compass, often I'd find my lost balls from yesterday sparkling in the forest's dead leaves.

Despite our eccentricities, we began being invited to dinner parties. At one of them, lo and behold, here surfaced a woman I'd known from boyhood days in Lake Forest. We chatted pleasantly until finally she frowned. "But Otis," she said in some concern, "what in the world are you ever going to DO here?"

Oh my God, I thought, what in the world AM I DOING HERE?

The next morning, I awakened with a high fever. Hospital time. Five days there, feeling really punk, guys in white coats jabbing and sucking blood and nobody with a clue what was causing my winter of discontent. All the gilt edged tests came up with nothing. I seem to have been hurtled back to that day on the Green River years before when my heart had started the trip-hammering.

Strange that I couldn't make my leap to courage this time. That's what the ego self does to you, I guess. Keeps you down there paining, ducking your wrong decisions until finally you just say, The hell with you.

The way I got out of the hospital was to point to a little sore on my leg and say, "Do you know something, Doc? With all these ticks here, couldn't this be one that bit me and made me sick?" I'd had a dose of the real thing years ago in South Africa so why not try it here? The young doctors nodded gravely, said fine, that's probably it and gave me some medicine which I threw away. By then, I knew where the tick was all right. In my emotions: living in the wantingness of the "bottom of the box."

Back at home, I sat with Teddy on the swing on our lovely porch, gazing across the giant trees and fizzing sprinklers on the golf course. "We're out of here, darling," I said.

She cried. "We haven't even finished remodeling!"

She walked around the house, re-living all the work she'd put in. Settling us down finally. When she came back out to me on the porch, she just nodded, tears in her eyes. "I know it, too. It's not us. Can't ever be. We've got to go."

And so that night, we decided to get another ranch, go back to all the headaches and turf of our own that we missed now so much.

You don't just buy a ranch like you would an open house at some condo. Good ones are almost impossible to find. And then, too, the money. In the California sale, we'd given practically everything to the kids and their families. I kept calling all the ranch brokers I knew. We wanted small, wanted cheap. Loved the desert where we'd once ranched. Arizona maybe, even New Mexico. But we were out priced there. Land too high. A light flashed. *Old Mexico!*

Hadn't Teddy and I loved it down there? Bought cattle, hunted, fished. I'd written novels about it. What an incredible country it is. The people with so much heart, so *simpatico*. I was bubbling over with memories of the great times we'd had.

And doing my best to forget one of them.

My first foray south to *manana* land was right after the war. My brother Bill and I were on terminal leave. Using our father Roy's red Nash, we drove thousands of miles of bad road from Chicago and ended up in Acapulco.

Unmarried then and back to my old girl game

in exotic places, I met pretty little Lupe, an Indian *photographia* at a night club. When she finished work at 2 a.m. I took her out for a date. The moon was up. We parked in a fringe of jungle by the beach. And the flash I saw was no moon. A long pig-sticker knife, a dark-shirted Mexican guy running at me. I lashed up the car window just in time to catch the blow on glass. Roared out of there only to hit a spot in the road where about a yard of concrete was missing. Pre-seat belt era, poor Lupe almost rocketed through the top of the Nash. She was sobbing, saying she didn't know the *cabron* and I sure didn't want to know, because I suspect it was her *novio* or her hubby and they'd set it up between them to snatch the Yanqui dollar or even the damn fool's scalp.

But despite that bad trip, I was beyond reason in my new flight of fancy. The beauty of the scheme, I convinced myself, was that you could buy twice the ranch in Mexico for half the money you'd ever spend in the States.

So off we went, south of the border. Fortunately, years before I'd sold our earlier Arizona ranch to a Mexican *latifundio* from a noted family in Sonora. He'd come out nicely on that deal. Alfredo, when I did call him, was his bubbly enthusiastic self. Why of course, amigo Otis, he owned hundreds of thousands of acres of Sonoran ranches. We could be very close to the border, just run up to Tucson when we wanted to see our gringo friends.

With Alfredo at the wheel and his *pistolero* beside him, down we rattled on washboard dirt for what seemed about the distance to Acapulco again.

High on a windy hill with vultures circling for a handout, Alfredo proudly presented us with a sagging adobe. The ranch was an enormity of nothingness desert and what cows that had survived were bony enough to be used as hatracks. Try not to humiliate Alfredo. Well, he would show us other places he owned.

We never got to the next one. Far out in the utter loneliness of Sonora, up wheels a Mexican Army humvee. In it were about fifteen of the meanest looking trigger happy Mexican soldiers I'd ever seen. They were all kids, Indian types, recruited from way down south in Mexico. The idea was to get them far away from home, so they wouldn't desert or start a revolution. Meanwhile, send the northern Mexico boys to the southern hinterlands for the same reason.

Scowling, they clustered around Alfredo's

shiny SUV. I should point out here that Alfredo, though mayor or *alcalde* of a large town in Sonora, had for a side-line the drug business, hence the beefy *pistolero* riding shotgun with us. The itchy troopers growled, Alfredo kept shrugging and tried to ignore these little hornets. I glanced at Teddy in the back seat.

Out here on this road to eternity, I am going to entrust my innocent lady to the Mexican Army? Well, it was cheap down here for a reason and purely insane. *Adios*, Alfredo *compadre*. Hope the marijuana business holds up.

Yet still, in my search for a bargain, I was determined to give Mexico one more shot. A friend told me about a beautiful place, highly civilized, hardly an hour below the border at Nogales and freeway all the way. Motivated seller! Down we went; the owner met us in a beautiful grassy bottom where a river ran. The storied Santa Cruz, at that time in August running about a foot of water. "*Pero, senor*, wait for the rains. Monsoon. Paradise then, *vacas muy gordas*".

Fat of the land. I'd used the same selling spiel myself. A nice little white-washed adobe, red tile roof. Big enough for a Mexican cowboy surely, but where would Teddy and I live?

"Ah, senor," the owner flung out his arm.

"Otra hacienda grande, beeg house, otro lado del ferrocaril."

Railroad, I gulped? The tracks run through here? Well, only the main north south line of the Mexican National Railway. *"Pero muy poco trenes, senor."*

Very few trains? That was a little better. Maybe. The owner in his polished boots and white vaquero hat strolled with Teddy and me through the tall, swaying grass, up a slight hill, and onto the roadbed. Just a single track. Not much of a railroad. We could live with that.

I was staring down the canyon where the tracks almost disappeared. *"Que es esto?"* I asked. "That shiny stuff?"

The owner lifted his palms in his Mexican way. "Only some train cars, senor."

Cars? We ran down the canyon. And then we found it. A train wreck! Six hopper cars from the Mexican *ferrocarril* had jumped the track here and lay on their sides crunched and shattered. When did it happen? Well, some time ago, *senor.* You mean days, a week or so? *Meses.* Months? *Si.* For God's sake, you're trying to sell us a ranch with a train wreck on it? Are they ever going to pick up this stuff!

A shrug and a smile, the ultimate charm of

Mexico. *Quizas.* Maybe and *quien sabe, siempre.* Always, who knows? We decided to get the hell out of here and back home. The crestfallen owner was still trotting beside us, assuring us that the railroad would give us the cars and we could, say, cut them up into feed troughs or even little houses, *casitas.*

As St. Paul said about himself, "Why do I always do what I don't want to do?"

It wasn't a month later when we stumbled onto more *casitas* than we needed, all in shoddy repair, and in safe, sane old Arizona, a bigger ranch that we could afford in our wildest dreams. But maybe that's what the true self is. Wild. Dare to roll the dice, give it your best shot, and let God take care of the rest.

He did, and dream on we did. We finally sold our half-finished home in South Carolina. Our youngest son, Peter, who had ranched with us in the past was planning to marry a young woman from Australia, Jane Hawkins, who was raised on a cattle and sheep station. All the pieces began to fall together. They would buy the cattle and we would have the land.

So home on the range again, our hearts sing. Maybe it's even that ego and spirit have finally put it all together. Made a peace treaty, accepting our folly of traveling so far to get back to what we were all along, and to what, still, we can and must only be.

Just ourselves.

GHOST HORSEMEN ON THE MILITARY ROAD

It's the dawn's early light out here. A whole new day on this rocky track from Then to Now. The sun is just peeping over the Pinaleno mountains of the Apaches. The first golden rays are streaming down through the tall ponderosas and the granite cliffs with their dark eye holes of lion caves.

Lily's sniffing around for quail. It ought to be a good time for them, out scarfing up fresh soft seeds, gobbling the tiny green shoots that turn on their reproductive organs. They whistle nesting calls. The time is here to breed. Create new life.

But I'm not really hunting now. Just watching the dawn, and thanking God for the blessed life I've been given.

The Good Lord has let down rain a couple of days ago. Tiny shoots of filaree, the European plant brought here in the bellies of Spanish horses, their wet fern-like fingers are spreading across the damp, reddish earth. What rich soil it is, and the filaree is the strongest feed for cows. Maybe this is the year we'll finally break the drought, sell greasy fat calves and hurl the monetary monkey off of our backs.

But it's the earth that interests me now. Why does it have that particular ochre color that is found only in this locale? Often I've carried it on my tires miles from the ranch, stop at some gas station and the kid filling the tank will grin, "Hey, mister, that mud on your outfit, have you been around Ft. Grant lately?"

So sure, it marks us. Spilling down from the Pinalenos, this strange layer of reddishness stains the old cavalry post and slops across the Military Road that cuts through our ranch. I often wonder: could the stain be blood from the centuries of warfare here? Indian, Spanish, homesteaders, cavalrymen? Maybe even an orange suited druggie now, wounded while trying to escape. Or could it be the melted sherds from pots of Hohokam and Salado people, civilizations gone, and we don't know how or why.

You've taken a long trip with me, and I thank you for that. And truly, in the end, I feel badly that in my outpouring of words, I can't really be of any help at all to you. It's your patriot's choice or mine to live either in fear and war or courage and peace; I have no instant cure to pass on.

Getting to the spirit of our true selves is a do-it-yourself kit where, if you're like me, you can be so fumble-fingered as to lose the instructions when throwing out the box.

Accept. I could never be an intellectual. Didn't have the equipment for it, and much less the desire to work like hell so I could put on the Phi Beta key. Nor the burning desire to be Somebody, a Star, get on the talk shows and postulate my puffing ego. I'm as bored by business as I'm inept at it. No guts to drive the hard bargain and win. Love dogs and horses and my blessed wife. Love the land and the hard hands of men and women who gave it their lives.

Sum it up at the end, what? Small, insignificant and weak.

I get greedy, restless, jealous, stupid, thoughtless. I hate fist fights. I've been scared in the air on planes, averse to pain, lust for pleasure and leisure. Rotten spoiled, want to have it my way, the rest of the world can hit the highway. Had enough? Give up?

Because you know something? It's all just okay, being the me that God made me. The Rabbi Goldberg who couldn't be Abraham. And wasn't wanted as that. Only the true him.

Fail enough, lose enough, surrender enough--- you wake up to a new kind of courage, knowing at last that here you've found the life you always thought you'd lost in the living.

And that finding is not in words, never in the endless scheming of the brain. It's not intellectual. It's experiential. A felt thing that can maybe only dawn on you in the blessed silence between thoughts. My friend, the Franciscan priest and prophet Richard Rohr calls it, as do many Christians and Buddhists, "centering prayer."

This is the one trick that has helped me immeasurably, so much so that I'll try to pass it on to you. "Centering" is not really a prayer at all. It's getting into the divine silence where you can just possibly hear the voice of your true self.

You let your consciousness in, you join it. I do it by sitting still and silent in my closed off place. Twenty minutes every morning as soon as I wake up, when my dim brain is still drugged by sleep. You sit there and that cranky brain keeps flinging thought after thought at you. Your ego thinks it will die if you don't let it talk. Be Somebody.

So what you do is just smile in your silence and let the ego brain thoughts slide away down the river of nothingness. You're not grading yourself. You and God are not scoring anything. Some days the ego voice is hard to kill off. You can't blow away   the whole dreary fleet of thoughts. Doesn't matter. Let 'em come and go. And finally---only blessed sometimes---what do you know? Your ego brain sits in the corner and sulks. You are finally one person melded into one heart, alone with the silence of your true you.

When the alarm bell goes off at 20 minutes, I often don't even know where I am. But the restoration of it, the transcendence, stays with me. Thoughts and words begin to become clearer. Real life that you come back to is often more comical and surely more meaningful than you ever dreamed it could be. "To care and not to care," as T.S. Eliot says. Throw your heart into it, do your best, and then not care about any reward. "Ours is only the trying."

Can we save our beloved nation?

I don't know. But except for rising in consciousness and living in our true selves as much as possible, I don't know any other way.

We have all the force in the world, and that force has continued only to make it a horribly bloody place. Isn't it time for the courage of peace? Finding it, God willing, changing our nation one person at a time.

Says Richard Rohr, "Just as the Taliban can corrupt Mohammed, so have we been able to corrupt and use Jesus for our own cultural needs. How then do we become light and hope against such archetypal and irrational forms of evil? First, we must deny terrorists their victory by refusing to mirror them and do the same thing in reactionary and disguised form. This is the only true moral victory. We must not transmit and continue our human pain but must somehow transform it into a new kind of humanity, a new mind, a different society.

"We must find a new consciousness. We must make sure that our light is not just disguised forms of vengeance, fear, political expediency or knee-jerk political reaction. And by that I mean both knee-jerk pacifism as much as knee-jerk patriotism. Neither of them are 'from God.'

'Jesus' plan for social transformation is to free people from the system and thus unlock it inevitably from the inside. I believe it is just such people who have always kept humanity and institutions from a history of total violence. They are indeed the light of the world without even knowing it.

"As God said to Abraham, 'For the sake of ten just people, I will spare the whole city.' All it takes is for a small minority to stop believing the lie and the lie will die. All it takes is for a committed minority to believe in Love, and Love will use them as a channel into the whole world."

In the spirit life of the true self, that love to me is a simplicity costing not less than everything. I'm not very good at it. I can't get my head around it, get past the word and begin really *living* love.

A poacher will bust in on us at the ranch. I'll catch him with an illegal four wheeler, rifles, beer can litter and a white tail deer he's just shot within eyesight of our NO HUNTING NO TRESPASSING SIGN. So caught, he lies, says he didn't know where he was. Cusses me out. Threatens. Where is love when I really need it? I'm shaking all over in fury.

Take a deep breath and claw past my ego and back up top into the positive emotions where I really do want to live.

And this dawn on the Military Road, those, I think, are the ghosts I'm pursuing.

Like Ambrose Bierce's Horseman in the Sky, there are four of them I've been trying to ride for so long, leaving the herd and getting bucked off more times than I can count.

So the four ghost horses I try so clumsily to ride are, in the end, each of them a letting go to what is. A victory of surrender.

Humility, letting go of the ego of the false

342

self.

Compassion, letting go of the "I know" and "I am right," and embracing the other with his or her knowledge and beliefs. Seeing and caring for another human being. No longer an Us or Them. It's all us, now. All of creation is in us.

Gratitude, for this sacred moment we're allowed to live. In the joy of eternity, to be humbled enough only to say thanks.

Trust. If there is a God, if there is some Life Force who gave us all we have, isn't it possible that He is our divinity, lived only in the miracle of our true selves? He embraces the falseness, too, of what we, in our feet of clay, must be.

In trust we join the best and the worst of who we really are. Humble, we are guided by Him to our authentic self, who is sacred, one with all.

The trip has just begun. The ghost horses went that-a-way. Pray that together you and I can follow them home.